Gal

Murder of Ravens

Mouse Trail Ends

Rattlesnake Brother

Chattering Blue Jay

Fox Goes Hunting

Turkey's Fiery Demise

Stolen Butterfly

Churlish Badger

A Gabriel Hawke Novel
Book 8

Paty Jager

Windtree Press
Hillsboro, OR

CHURLISH BADGER

Contact Information: info@windtreepress.com

Windtree Press
Hillsboro, Oregon
http://windtreepress.com

Cover Art by Christina Keerins
CoveredbyCLKeerins

PUBLISHING HISTORY
Published in the United States of America

ISBN 978-1-952447-97-6

Author Comments

While this book and coming books in the series are set in Wallowa County, Oregon, I have changed the town names to old forgotten towns that were in the county at one time. I also took the liberty of changing the towns up and populating the county with my own characters, none of which are in any way a representation of anyone who is or has ever lived in Wallowa County. Other than the towns, I have tried to use the real names of all the geographical locations.

Chapter One

Hawke rode his gelding, Jack, and led his mule named Horse out of the pine trees. Dog trotted ahead of them into the clearing at the Freezeout Trailhead. Hawke's favorite thing about his job was spending time in the wilderness with his animals. Checking mountain goat hunters in the Hat Point hunt area in NE Oregon was a perfect work week.

The September weather had been warm during the days with a welcome coolness in the air in the evenings. This was the best time of the year to do trail and off-trail riding in the wilderness.

He studied the pickups and horse trailers that were parked in the clearing. Many hadn't been here when he'd ventured out four days ago. Riding by each vehicle, Hawke checked for recreational passes in the windows. As a State Trooper with the Fish and Wildlife Division, he couldn't do anything about the vehicles without a pass. He just liked to see who did and didn't follow the rules. If they didn't purchase a parking pass, they most likely wouldn't follow hunting regulations either.

At the end of the clearing, farthest from the trailhead and close to the outhouse, he noticed a pickup that had been there when he'd arrived early Thursday morning. There wasn't a camp or the sense of anyone having been near the vehicle lately. Most of the vehicles at this trailhead were pickups hooked up to horse trailers. It was an area best covered on horseback. He'd stick around until dark and see if anyone returned. Few people backpacked in and hunted. A hunter would have to pack out the animal they shot. Carrying camp gear and a hundred-and-seventy-pound mountain goat would take someone a lot stronger, and younger, than him.

Hawke dismounted by his truck and trailer. Dog sniffed the tires, peeing on them to reclaim his truck.

Once Jack and Horse were untacked and eating hay by the side of the trailer, Hawke wandered over to the vehicle that had captured his attention. He studied what was in the bed and what he could see inside the cab. There wasn't a single thing that said this person was camping or hunting. He jotted the license plate down in his logbook and walked over to his vehicle.

Settled in the driver's seat, he turned on the radio and called in. "This is Hawke, dispatch do you copy?"

"Copy, Hawke. This is dispatch."

"Please run Oregon plate, two-three-two, zebra, union, king. I'm at Freezeout without computer access."

"Copy."

He opened a bottle of water, poured some in a bowl for Dog, and downed the rest.

His radio crackled.

"Hawke?"

"Copy." Hawke pulled his logbook closer and picked up his pen.

"The vehicle is registered to Arnold and Laurel Bertram. Five-nine-seven-two-six Leap Road, Eagle."

"Phone number?" Hawke planned to call and see what was going on.

Dispatch rattled off the number and Hawke signed off. He picked up his phone and dialed the number. The phone rang several times before a breathless female voice answered.

"Hello?"

"Mrs. Bertram?" Hawke asked.

"Yes. Who are you?" Her tone revealed irritation.

"I'm State Trooper Hawke. Do you know why a pickup registered to you and your husband is sitting at Freezeout Trailhead?"

"Freezeout? What does the pickup look like?"

"It's a Ford F-one-fifty. Brown. Looks like a model older than two-thousand."

"That's Arnie's pickup. He left here Thursday headed to Spokane for an Ag Conference. I didn't expect him back until tomorrow." Her voice grated with irritation.

"Have you spoken with him since he left?" Hawke didn't like the scenario his mind was conjuring up.

"No. No reason to. I can take care of things while he's gone, and he doesn't like talking on the phone." Her voice didn't hold any kind of concern.

"Why would he leave his vehicle out here at a trailhead?" Hawke didn't understand how the man would have ended up here instead of at a conference in Spokane. This was a different direction than he would

9

have taken.

"How should I know. He's been mumbling and acting out of sorts for a while now."

"Do you have a number where he could be reached at the conference? Or the number of where he is staying?"

"Nope. He was attending the Ag conference at the Doubletree Hotel. At least that's what he told me. Now that you found his vehicle still in the county, I'm wondering just what he's been doing all weekend. It sure isn't helping me get the last of the hay in."

"Aren't you worried something might have happened to him?" Hawke asked.

"I couldn't get that lucky. When you find him, tell him he might as well be ready to be served divorce papers."

The call ended. Hawke stared at his phone. Most women would have been near hysterics about what had happened to their husband. He would definitely dig deeper into the marriage. But first, he needed to get someone to call the Doubletree and ask if an Arnie Bertram was there.

Hawke called his superior, Sergeant Spruel, head of the Fish and Wildlife Division of the Oregon State Police in Wallowa County.

"Spruel," the sergeant answered his phone.

"It's Hawke. I have a suspicious vehicle at Freezeout Trailhead." He went on to tell Spruel about the phone call with the wife. "Could you contact the hotel and see if Arnold Bertram arrived?"

"I'll do that right away. I'll ask Sheriff Lindsey to send a deputy to ask Mrs. Bertram more questions," Spruel said.

"I'm going to have a look around the vehicle. See if I can tell if one person, or more, drove here in it. Can you have that deputy get an extra set of keys for the vehicle and bring them up here? I'd like to take a look around the inside." Hawke had another thought. "Also have the deputy ask the wife to look and see if any camping gear is missing."

"Hawke, you can't take on a missing person case. We need you to keep tabs on the hunters."

Spruel knew him too well. Once an oddity like murder or missing person came across his path, he had to see it to the end.

"I'll work on this during my off-hours. Which is now." He had to admit, it was good timing. He'd been working more or less around the clock the last four days, checking out hunters in the Hat Point Hunt area. He now had two days off. That was enough time to determine if the man had come to harm or had just disappeared on purpose.

As soon as Hawke finished his call with Spruel, he checked the ground around the vehicle. He found it odd there weren't any tracks. It had been a dry week with very little dew each morning. If a person, or persons, had exited the vehicle there should have been at least a portion of a track. When he couldn't find any details to show an imprint, he slowly lowered to his hands and knees. A joint popped and he cursed getting old. At fifty-four he was a senior trooper and had been working in Wallowa County, the home of his ancestors, for the last fifteen years with the Fish and Wildlife Division. He leaned down, his head level with the ground, and scanned the area for what shouldn't be there. That's when he detected broken grass in a sweeping back and forth motion and dirt swirled as if by a branch. Someone had purposely hidden the tracks. Whoever had exited the vehicle hadn't wanted their footprints to be found.

Hawke stood and glanced around to see if anyone else had returned to the area. He spotted some people moving about in a camp, and a group rode horses out of the trees. He started questioning the people at the camp and moved on to the mounted group who'd just entered the camping area.

Only a few had noticed the pickup sitting by itself. One of those was a man who had joined his hunting party on Thursday and was packing up to leave.

"Was the Ford here when you arrived on Thursday?" Hawke asked.

"I got in after dark on Wednesday. Left work early in Lewiston to get here before dark but had a flat tire on the way," the man, who'd identified himself as Charlie Gribner, said.

"Do you remember seeing any lights or anything where the vehicle is parked?" Hawke wanted to establish when the vehicle had arrived. Mrs. Bertram had said her husband left for Spokane on Thursday. He'd have to ask for an exact time.

"I don't remember anything other than rolling out my sleeping bag in the back of my truck and going to sleep." Gribner thought a minute. "I do remember hearing what sounded like a small engine sometime during the night."

"Small engine? Like a chain saw?"

"No. A motorcycle. Not a big one like a Harley. Maybe a Yamaha? Definitely an off-road sound to it."

"This was Wednesday night?" Hawke asked,

wondering if the wife had been lying about when her husband had left.

"More like early Thursday morning," Gribner replied.

It was dark by the time the deputy arrived with the keys to the Bertram vehicle. Hawke had talked to everyone and had spent more time studying the vehicle after taking down statements. He'd found two tie-down straps in the bed of the pickup and a spot of oil. He'd dabbed up the oil and put it in an evidence bag in case this turned into more than a missing person.

"Here's the keys. Spruel said the man was registered for the conference and never showed up." Deputy Corcoran held out the keys.

"I'm not sure if he is missing on purpose or due to foul play." Hawke grasped the keys and opened the driver's side door, clicking the unlock button. "Check out the other side."

Corcoran hurried around to the passenger side. He opened the door and stared at Hawke. "What are we looking for?"

"Anything. Scrap of paper, mail, food wrappers." As Hawke talked, he scanned the dash. There wasn't a parking permit. On the floor, he found a cigarette butt. While waiting for the deputy, he'd stuffed a pair of gloves and evidence bags in his pockets. He pulled out the gloves, shoved his hands in, and then picked up the cigarette butt, placing it in an evidence bag. They could compare it to DNA from the missing man.

He'd heard back from Sergeant Spruel. The Wallowa County Search and Rescue were headed his way to start searching for the man at first light. It would take that long to get everyone rounded up and make the drive to Freezeout.

Normally, Hawke would have been in on the search, but his gut was telling him they weren't going to find the man or any clues in the wilderness. He wondered if the man had planned a disappearance or if he'd come to harm, as they gathered the bits and pieces that could prove crucial in this investigation.

Deputy Corcoran took all the evidence he and Hawke had collected and headed to the Sheriff's Office where a State Trooper would collect the evidence and take it to the Oregon State Police Forensic Lab in Pendleton.

Hawke and Dog dozed in the front seats of the OSP vehicle waiting for Sheriff Lindsey and the volunteer search and rescue members to arrive. He wanted to get home, take a shower, and sleep in his own bed. However, he wanted to fill the sheriff and searchers in on what he suspected.

As daylight broke over the hills to the east, four more pickups and horse trailers pulled into the trailhead clearing, making space a valuable commodity in the small area. Mules and horses were unloaded and readied for the trek into the wilderness. Two men and a woman were setting up a base camp.

Sheriff Lindsey and Deputy Alden stood beside Hawke.

"Spruel said you've been out in this area the last four days, any idea where we might need to look?" Sheriff Lindsey asked.

Hawke shook his head. "I didn't see any sign of a man by himself backpacking or just hiking. But I was focused on the people running around with guns. I didn't know about this before I went in and didn't ask anyone if they'd seen a man by himself. Sorry, I'm not much help."

"I wouldn't mind you coming along. You have your horse here already." The sheriff motioned to Jack and Horse standing slack hipped by the trailer.

"Honestly, it looked like someone tried to cover their tracks leaving the vehicle. To me, that means you aren't going to find Mr. Bertram out there. I'm going to focus on talking to people and whatever forensics can discover from his vehicle." Hawke waved at the trees. "But knock yourselves out, I hope you do find him just getting away from it all."

Deputy Alden scanned Hawke's face. "You don't think he's alive."

"I'm not saying he is or he isn't, but I have a gut feeling he isn't out there."

"We'll keep that in mind as we look." The sheriff and deputy wandered over to the group saddled and ready to head out.

Hawke sighed. He usually jumped at the chance to go with a search and rescue group. However, this morning he wanted a shower and a few hours of sleep in his own bed. He loaded up Jack and Horse.

At the cab of the pickup, he opened the door and Dog jumped into the OSP vehicle, taking his place in the passenger seat.

"Let's go home and take a nap. Then we'll go talk to Mrs. Bertram and her neighbors."

Chapter Two

By the time Hawke arrived home, it was close to ten. After taking care of the animals and unloading his camping supplies, half the day was nearly gone. He climbed the stairs to his one-room apartment over the horse arena with Dog on his heels.

He had lived in the apartment for fourteen years. It was the perfect setup for him. And provided a paddock and run for Jack, Horse, and Dot, his young gelding. His landlords, Herb and Darlene Trembley, took care of his horses, and sometimes Dog, when Hawke was away on work or visiting his mom at the Confederated Tribes of the Umatilla Reservation.

The other good thing about renting from the Trembley's...they knew everyone who lived in Wallowa County and usually were on top of the gossip.

Hawke tossed food in Dog's dish, stripped, and walked into his shower, scrubbing off four days' worth of sweat and bug spray. When he came out, he felt refreshed and hungry.

Before taking off to get something to eat and talk to Mrs. Bertram, Hawke filled the horses' water trough. He stood with his arms on the fence, enjoying the sunshine, and the scents of horses, hay, and a fall day. The sipping of his horses and mule drinking the water as the trough filled was a sound he enjoyed. Hawke felt the presence of his landlord before the man spoke.

"Hawke, catch anyone not behaving?" Herb asked, walking up and patting Horse on the neck as the mule drank.

"A few." Hawke turned the faucet off and faced Herb. "Do you know anything about Arnie and Laurel Bertram?"

"Arnie? Why would you ask that? I don't think he's hunted a day in his life." Herb studied him.

"I found his truck at Freezeout Trailhead. Looks like it's been there since early Thursday morning. Does he backpack?"

Herb snorted. "That man is too lazy to hunt or hike. He has a section of land out in the Leap area. His wife does most of the farming."

"That explains her attitude when I called after finding their pickup. She said he'd gone to an Ag conference in Spokane. We called and he never arrived there." Hawke sighed. He hoped search and rescue found the man, but he had that niggling feeling the man wasn't in the forest.

He had another thought. "Did Bertram go to the Ag conferences often?"

"Don't know. You'd have to ask Laurel. Or their daughter, Jennifer. She and her husband live in Imnaha."

"The husband's name?" Hawke would check in

with Spruel, then go see the wife and then the daughter.

"Reed Kamp. Word is he's been trying to set up a hemp growing operation." Herb shook his head. "I don't know if it's truly to grow hemp or to hide his pot smoking."

Hawke didn't agree with the new Oregon law allowing a person over the age of 21 to grow marijuana for personal use. It made it harder to keep tabs on the illegal growers. "Great. See you later."

"You doing anything fun on your days off?" Herb asked.

His landlords always knew his schedule and too damn much about his personal life, but he also knew they were pretty good about keeping all of that to themselves. At least he hoped so. "Too early to tell."

He walked over to his personal pickup and whistled for Dog. "Come on, boy."

The animal spun away from the cat he'd cornered. The feline's hair stood up straight down its hunched gray back.

"You shouldn't harass the cats so much," Hawke said, opening the vehicle door for Dog to jump in.

Once seated, Dog looked him in the eyes, and his lips curved up at the ends as if he smiled.

"Yep, you were harassing that cat on purpose." He scratched the dog's ears and started up the vehicle.

《》《》《》

After a quick late lunch at the Rusty Nail and visiting with Sergeant Spruel at the OSP office in Winslow, Hawke headed out to the Leap area. This was farm ground north of Winslow. He found the Bertram farm and turned into the long driveway running alongside a field that had just been mowed and baled.

The house, barn, and shed at the end of the lane were in good repair. Arnie Bertram couldn't be that lazy from the tidiness of the place.

Two dogs, a heeler and a border collie, ran from different directions, barking and wagging their tails. Or in the case of the heeler with a docked tail, his backend wiggled.

Hawke noticed a backhoe parked beside what looked like a freshly dug trench. He parked in front of the house. It was mid-afternoon, he'd hoped to catch the wife taking a break.

The front door of the house opened and a woman in her late fifties, possibly early sixties, glared at him from behind the screen door.

"I don't buy nothin' from anyone having to drum up business going door to door."

"I'm not a salesman. I'm Trooper Hawke. I called you last night about your husband's pickup at Freezeout."

She studied him. "How come you aren't in uniform?"

Hawke drew his badge, hanging on a chain around his neck, out from under his shirt and showed it to her. "It's my day off, but I had some questions I wanted to ask."

"I told that deputy all I knew last night. I bet that fool husband of mine decided he'd had enough of working the land and took off someplace where he could relax all day." She didn't budge from the screen door that still remained closed.

"Why would he leave his vehicle in a remote area like Freezeout Trailhead?" Hawke didn't understand this woman's reasoning, at all.

"The last few years, I stopped trying to figure out what was going on in his head."

"Does he have dementia or Alzheimer's?" Hawke had witnessed a couple of people he'd worked with over the years in the state police slowly forget everything that had meant something to them.

"No. The doc said it was just old age and his body wanting to rest." She snorted. "He's never done enough work to need to rest. Who is here putting up the hay by myself?" She stared at him as if she expected an answer.

"You don't have anyone to help you?"

"Do you think I could afford to pay someone to help? I have been taking care of this place since the day I married that good-for-nothing husband of mine. The only good thing I got out of it was our sweet Jenny. And now she's hitched herself to that good-for-nothing pothead."

It appeared the women in this family tended to fall for the complete opposite of themselves.

"Do you think your daughter might have an idea of where your husband has gone?" Hawke wanted to get in the house and have a look around, but she was keeping the door shut tight.

"I called her after the deputy left last night. She doesn't know where he is either. She said she talked to him on Wednesday. He'd called to ask if she needed anything from Spokane." The woman snorted, again. "As if he had a few hundred dollars to throw around buying things for other people."

"This place looks prosperous. You and your husband have kept the buildings in good repair."

"I can't stand a building that looks like it hasn't

seen a paintbrush in years. That was all me, hanging from a ladder, keeping everything in good condition. The only thing Arnie did was pick the paint up from town." Pride slackened her hard features.

"Do you think your husband could be wandering around the Hat Point Area?"

She stared at him. "You think he's lost or something happened that he can't find his way home?"

"That's one explanation for his vehicle being at the trailhead." He studied the woman. Did he see a flicker of hope? Maybe she didn't dislike her husband as much as she said. He'd come across men and women who grumbled about their significant others because they didn't know how to express how they really felt.

"But why would he even be there? He hated hiking. Anything that used energy."

"He's never said anything about wanting to look around that area? Was he going to ride with anyone to the conference?" He decided to see if maybe the man had taken off with someone and just left his vehicle in a remote area to not be caught too soon.

"No. He always drives to these conferences by himself. Says he likes the time alone. Didn't room with no one either that I know of. The bills always showed the full price for the room and his food never went over the money he took with him." Her gaze latched on to something over Hawke's left shoulder.

The screen door shoved open.

Hawke stepped back just in time to avoid being struck in the face by the screen.

"Sic 'im!" she shouted at the dogs. The two cow dogs took off at a run toward a vehicle pulling up beside Hawke's pickup. "That bully Ed Newton isn't going to get his hands on this property."

A tall, heavy-set man in his sixties stepped out of his suburban and kicked at the two dogs. "Get! Get! You better call off these mongrels or I'll sue you for everything you got if one bites me!" the man shouted.

"Mrs. Bertram, call the dogs off," Hawke said, walking toward the man.

The woman whistled and the dogs ran back to her and the house.

"Who are you?" the man asked, as Hawke stopped in front of him.

"State Trooper Hawke. And you are?"

The man's gaze ran the length of Hawke. "How come you aren't in uniform?"

"It's my day off." He went through the motions of showing his badge. "And who are you?"

"Ed Newton. I own the land adjacent to this place. Came over to see if Laurel needed anything. Heard her husband's pickup was found abandoned." The man's narrow-set eyes held a steady gaze on Hawke.

"I don't think now is a good time for you to be coming around." Hawke motioned for the man to return to his vehicle.

"I just wanted to talk to Laurel about something her husband and I had been visiting about."

It wouldn't have surprised Hawke to learn the man had once thought about going into politics. His words oozed through his slimy smile like most politicians Hawke knew.

"I don't care if Arnie and you were talking about us selling. That was just his old age and tiredness talking. He'd never sell this place." Mrs. Bertram walked around Hawke and stood with her arms crossed and her face set like granite.

"Is that what you wanted to talk to Mrs. Bertram about? Selling?" It angered Hawke the man was over here trying to wear the woman down when she didn't even know the whereabouts of her husband.

"Arnie and I were negotiating the terms on Wednesday. He was going to give me his answer when he came back from Spokane." The man narrowed his eyes. "Funny how he didn't come back from that trip."

"What are you saying?" Hawke asked, watching Mrs. Bertram's face redden. He couldn't tell if it was embarrassment or anger.

"I'm just saying that he told me he'd give me a decision when he came back from the conference, and now, he's missing, and Laurel, here, is telling me there is no way he'd sell." Newton patted his pockets and pulled out a cigarette. "He didn't say anything about talking it over with his wife."

The woman lunged at Newton, knocking the cigarette out of the man's hand as she tried to slap his face.

Hawke grabbed her by the arms. "Mr. Newton, you are on private property, and I suggest you leave."

The man grinned, showing his incisors. "There's nothing you can do about it, Laurel. You might as well work with me."

The woman spat, hitting Newton in the middle of his round stomach. "Get off my land!"

"Go." Hawke nodded toward the man's vehicle.

One last smirk at Mrs. Bertram and Newton walked back to his SUV. Before he drove away, he said, "I'll get this land one way or the other."

Hawke released the woman as dust obliterated the

sight of the vehicle. "What did he mean by that? 'He'd get the land one way or the other?'"

She shook herself like a dog ridding its coat of water. "His family homesteaded a large part of this area. He's been trying to find legal documents that say our land had been taken from his family and not rightfully sold." She shook a fist in the air. "I'll die before I'll see this place in the hands of Ed Newton." The woman stomped back to the house and disappeared.

Hawke climbed into his pickup, patted Dog on the head, and drove down the lane to get back to the main road. From the hint of dust hanging in the air, he determined Mr. Newton lived to the east. He'd go have a talk with the man. If he wanted the land bad enough, it was hard telling what he might do.

Chapter Three

"Well, well, State Trooper Hawke, I didn't expect you to follow me home," Mr. Newton said, opening the screen door to allow Hawke inside. "Mary, we have company!"

Hawke entered the 1800s two-story farmhouse. The rooms had floral wallpaper, lace curtains, and hardwood floors. The furniture was all twenty-first century.

"Have a seat. My wife will be right out with coffee and cookies." Newton lowered his hefty body down onto a large recliner.

Hawke took a seat on the leather couch. "Mr. Newton, I'd like to know if Arnie Bertram said or did anything unusual when you saw him on Wednesday?"

A petite woman with gray hair cut in what Hawke knew to be a latest style, according to his friend Dani Singer, walked into the room carrying a tray with a coffee pot, cups, and a plate of cookies. She placed the tray on the coffee table in front of the couch and sat down on the end opposite of Hawke.

"I'm Mary Newton." She held out her hand.

Hawke took her small hand in his. "State Trooper Hawke."

Her left eyebrow rose. "I see. What has Ed done now?"

Hawke glanced at the man. His eyes had gone dark and a grimace tweaked his lips. Either the woman was making a joke at her husband's expense or he was in trouble most of the time.

"Nothing, that I'm aware of. I understand your husband was with Arnie Bertram on Wednesday, the day before he disappeared." Hawke accepted the cup of coffee the woman handed him.

"Yes, Arnie and Ed sat here, in the living room, discussing terms for us purchasing the Bertram place." The woman didn't bat an eyelash as she rose, walked over to her husband, and handed him a cup of coffee.

"You heard the discussion?" Hawke asked, hoping to draw more information out of the woman.

"Yes. I serve coffee and sit in on all of Ed's conversations with the neighbors." She picked up the last cup on the tray and settled her back against the couch. Sipping the coffee, she watched him.

Hawke glanced back and forth between the couple. "Arnie Bertram was talking to you about selling his place?"

The woman nodded.

"He was. He was tired of farming and tired of his wife." Newton gave his wife half of a smile. "I'm glad my Mary isn't as argumentative as Laurel. I swear that woman will argue with the Lord when she gets to the pearly gates." Newton raised his cup to his lips and sipped.

Hawke shifted his attention to the woman. "What do you think of Mrs. Bertram?"

"She's a hard worker. Had to be. Arnie isn't much for farming or any kind of work." She picked up the plate of cookies and offered it to him.

"How did he, or they, end up with a farm if he isn't a farmer or a worker? Farming is hard work." Hawke turned his attention back to Newton.

"He inherited it from an uncle on his mom's side. About a year before he married Laurel?" The man questioned his wife.

"Yes. I believe he'd just started dating Laurel when he'd received the farm." Mrs. Newton slid the plate of cookies across the coffee table, away from her husband. It was apparent she planned on making him work for his calories.

"He would have sold it then if Laurel hadn't told him she'd do all the work. I have to admit, she has worked hard and raised a fine daughter on that land. Too bad Jenny has her mother's taste in men." Mrs. Newton picked up a cookie.

"I don't understand what you had to gain by approaching Mrs. Bertram about selling when we aren't even sure where her husband is." Hawke studied the man, nibbling on an oatmeal cookie.

"I just wanted to make it clear, that if for some reason, Arnie isn't found, it was his wish to sell his farm to me." The man finished his cookie and spread his hands. "I'm the logical person."

"But from what his wife said, she isn't interested in selling." Hawke thought it callous of the man to even approach the woman when they had no idea where her husband was or if he was even alive.

"She may change her mind. Who knows?" Mr. Newton stood. "I need to be in town for a meeting."

Hawke stood and headed for the door. "Where were you Wednesday night?"

The husband and wife glanced at each other. "We were at a water board meeting in Eagle," Mr. Newton said.

The woman nodded.

"What time did you come home?"

"We left town around nine and I imagine we arrived here around nine-thirty?" The man continued to peer at his wife.

"Yes, I believe that's what time it was," she added.

"Thank you." Hawke stepped out the door and put his hat back on his head. There was something off about those two. He walked out to his pickup and slid inside. As he wound his way back to Winslow, he called Spruel.

"Hawke, it's your day off. Go do something fun."

Hawke chuckled. "I am. I'm driving around with Dog, thinking about where we're going to go hiking. Any chance you could get me an address for a Reed and Jennifer Kamp?"

"I know that is the missing man's daughter and son-in-law. Why do you want to talk to them?" Tapping on a keyboard came from Spruel's side of the conversation.

"Curiosity." He went on to reveal what he'd learned so far. "I have a hunch either Arnie Bertram disappeared to escape having to deal with his wife's wrath when she found out he'd sold the farm, or someone not wanting the farm sold made him disappear."

"You mean homicide?" Spruel said.

"I don't want to think that of his family, but Mrs. Bertram loves that land even if she does complain about all the work." He could tell her grumbling was just who she was. She enjoyed growing things and keeping things tidy.

"Sheriff Lindsey reported that search and rescue haven't seen anything so far. We may have to wait until forensics finishes with the vehicle to know more," Spruel said. "Here is the address for the Kamps." He rattled it off and Hawke wrote it down. "It wouldn't hurt to see what the daughter thinks might have happened to her father. That might give us an idea if we need to keep searching or not."

"I'll see what I can learn." Hawke ended the call and headed his vehicle out of Winslow and east on Highway 82. It was close to dinner time when he drove through Alder. Rather than stop here, he'd stop at the Imnaha store, grab something to eat, and then head to the Kamps place.

It seemed ironic that Bertram's vehicle was left at Freezeout Trailhead less than ten miles from his daughter and son-in-law's farm.

Dog sat in the passenger seat, his head resting on the open window as Hawke crossed the bridge into Imnaha and parked in the small lot to the side of the store. This was an unincorporated community of about a dozen residents. However, up and down the Imnaha River there were close to eighty households. They relied on the staples the store stocked and grabbing a meal and a beer from the Store and Tavern.

Hawke parked at the side of the building, leaving the windows down halfway, and pouring a bowl of water for Dog. He nodded to two hunters sitting in a pickup in front of the store and continued to the door. Stepping into the building was like entering a taxidermist shop. Mounted elk, deer, and moose heads lined the upper walls of the establishment. Memorabilia filled in the gaps on all the flat surfaces. A large black barrel stove, with a stovepipe like a pillar, stood in the middle of the room. Folded bills were stuck to the ceiling like large spit wads.

It was a long open building. The bar, with stools to sit and eat or drink, were along the left side. Behind the wood stove sat a pool table. The right side had groceries on stocked shelves behind five tables for people to sit and eat or have a drink. The back of the building had a storeroom and restrooms.

Hawke walked over to the bar and sat down.

"You haven't stopped in here for a while," the owner, Tyler Lockhart, said.

"I've been through here, just not on a day off." Hawke took a seat at the counter.

Tyler poured a glass of iced tea and placed it in front of Hawke. "Heard there's a missing person in Freezeout."

As a rule, Hawke didn't talk shop with anyone outside of law enforcement and the Trembleys. However, he did want to learn more about the Kamps and if anyone had seen Bertram's vehicle early Thursday morning. "I'll have a hamburger basket with fries," he said, before taking a sip of the tea.

"No comment as usual about what is happening in this community?" Tyler wasn't the type to take anything personally.

"Not really. We found an abandoned vehicle. It's being checked over by forensics. Search and Rescue started looking when we discovered the abandoned vehicle had been headed for Spokane four days ago." He raised the glass to his lips.

"Search and Rescue having any luck?" Tyler held his order in his hand as he watched Hawke.

"Not so far."

The door jingled and an older couple walked in, headed for the shelves of food.

"I'll get this started." Tyler disappeared into the kitchen behind the counter.

Hawke sipped his tea and studied the sayings, photos, pictures, and head mounts adorning the walls.

The couple walked up to the cash register with half a dozen food items in their hands.

Tyler returned, conversed with the couple who it turned out were locals, and after the two walked out the door, the owner stood across the counter from Hawke. "Word is it's a local man who's missing. Can you tell me that much?"

"He's not someone from Imnaha." Hawke decided to ask about the daughter. "You see Jennifer and Reed Kamp much?"

Tyler studied him for thirty seconds. "Yeah. They come in once a week for a burger. Be right back." He disappeared through the kitchen door.

Hawke drained his glass and waited. Five minutes later, Tyler walked out of the kitchen with a burger basket, brimming with crispy fries. "Thanks." Hawke picked up a knife to cut the burger in half.

Tyler refilled his drink and leaned a hip against the

31

counter. "Why did you ask about Jenny and Reed?"

"I'm headed out to talk to them."

The man frowned. "Officially?"

"Yeah. It's technically my day off, but I have some questions that are bothering me."

Tyler studied him. "This have anything to do with the missing person? I know it's not either of them. They were in here Saturday night celebrating a grant they got to continue growing hemp for fiber."

"I was under the impression they had already established a hemp farm." Hawke bit into the burger and wasn't disappointed. Tyler used local beef and knew how to cook the meat to the right juiciness.

"They do have an established farm, but growing hemp isn't a cheap business."

Hawke studied the man. "How do you know?"

"My cousin tried to raise it in the Willamette Valley. He went broke. But he didn't put in for the grants like Reed does. He's smart enough to realize it will take lots of money before he starts turning a profit."

Hawke had finished one half of his burger while Tyler talked. He waited for the man to finish and asked, "Okay, as a couple, what do you think?"

"What are you really going out to see them about?" Tyler had become suspicious.

Hawk sighed. "It's Jennifer's father that is missing."

"Really?" The store owner leaned on the counter with his forearms. "You mean he parked at Freezeout and walked into the wilderness?"

"That's what we are trying to establish. I wanted to talk to the Kamps about his frame of mind the last time they talked to him." Hawke picked up the other half of his burger.

"He seemed fine when he and the missus stopped in here a couple weeks ago."

Hawke stopped the sandwich before it reached his mouth. "Mr. and Mrs. Bertram come this way often?"

"Yeah, I think they came out and visited with Jenny and Reed at least once a month. Arnie more often than the missus." Tyler refilled Hawke's iced tea as the door jingled.

This time it was visitors asking questions and for directions. Tyler stood over by the cash register visiting with them.

Hawke finished off his burger and half of the fries thinking the missing man knew this area well if he visited often. Could he be hiding out in the area? But why had he covered up his tracks? Was it so no one could follow him? More and more questions swirled in his head as the people left and Tyler wandered back to him at the counter.

"You want any dessert? Mandy made fresh peach pies this morning." Tyler held up a pie with a golden-brown crust.

Hawke folded the paper in the basket up around his fries. Dog would like the treat. "I'll take a piece of Mandy's pie. You are a lucky man to have a wife who can bake like she does."

"Don't I know it! These pies are what people remember about this place. It also helps the fruit is from here. Makes for good advertising."

Tyler placed a slice of pie in front of him.

Hawke's mouth watered just looking at the brightly colored peaches and hint of spice. He knew what to expect before he savored the first bite, but his tongue was still surprised at the rush of flavor. "Mandy should sell these in Prairie Creek."

"She thought about it but worried making them in large batches might change the flavor." Tyler had dished himself a piece.

Taking his time, savoring every bite, Hawke finally finished the pie. He placed money on the counter. "Thanks for the good food and the conversation."

"Anytime. Next time you're here officially, you might talk to Judd Bishop. Last time he was in, he complained of hearing dirt bikes running around his place in the middle of the night."

"I'll check into it. Thanks." Hawke picked up the paper with the fries and headed out to his vehicle. Dog stretched halfway out of the driver's side window, sniffing the air.

"Yeah, I brought you a snack. Get out of the window." Hawke waited for the dog to move back to the passenger side before he opened the driver's door and slid in. He handed the fries, paper and all, to Dog and started up his pickup. "Time to talk to the Kamps."

He headed the vehicle as if going back to Prairie Creek, then took a left on the upper Imnaha Road. The same road that went by Freezeout. Twenty minutes later he passed by Freezeout Road. His foot eased off the accelerator as he wondered if the Search and Rescue had learned anything. He sped up. There would be time to check in with them after he talked to the Kamps.

Traveling another ten miles beyond that road, he spotted the large drying shed and two fields of twelve-foot-high hemp plants. He pulled in the driveway, taking in all that he saw as he drove up to the house.

There is a fine line between hemp and marijuana. Hawke wanted to make sure the Kamps were legitimately growing fiber hemp.

Four barking dogs ran from all directions toward his vehicle. Dog's hair bristled. A low canine grumble filled the cab.

"It's okay. They are just protecting the property. It's their job, like protecting this pickup and the Trembley's is your job." He patted Dog on the head and switched off the ignition. Once the vehicle had stopped and no longer rumbled, the four sat down in a row five feet from the driver's side door.

"Guess I'm going to see how much bite is with their bark." Hawke opened the door and placed a booted foot on the ground. While cowboy boots had saved him when smaller dogs took a bite at him, he doubted this quartet of mongrels would go for his ankles.

"Killer, Viper, Jaws, Angel, get over here!" A male voice called from over by the drying shed.

Chapter Four

Three of the dogs turned and jogged over to the shed. One continued to show its teeth.

"Angel, get over here!" the man shouted in a gruffer tone.

Angel gave Hawke one hard look with a fang showing and walked slowly toward the man and the shed.

Hawke glanced over at Dog. "You better stay put. I'd hate to have to pull you out of a dog pile." He placed both feet on the ground and shut the door.

The man, he presumed was Reed Kamp, walked toward him.

"Evening. How can I help you?" the man asked in a welcoming tone, much different than how he'd dealt with the four dogs now heeling behind him.

Hawke held out his hand. "State Trooper Hawke. Are you Reed Kamp?"

"I am." The man shook hands. "Why are you

looking for me?"

"I'm looking for both you and your wife. I have some questions about her father."

Kamp shifted his attention to the dogs. "Stay. Be good." He motioned to the house. "Come on inside. Jenny is canning today."

The man headed to the house. Hawke walked beside him, glancing over his shoulder once to see what the mongrel pack was doing. They were busy sniffing and peeing on his pickup tires. That was going to piss off Dog.

At the house, Kamp went around to the back. "This porch is screened. Helps to keep out the bugs around here."

Hawke nodded, following the man. The aroma of fruit hung in the air as they entered first the porch and then the kitchen. Heat was the second thing Hawke experienced. Hot, humid heat nearly took his breath away. A more petite version of Mrs. Betram stood at the stove stirring a steaming pot.

Her eyes widened at the sight of him standing in her kitchen.

"Jenny, this is the state trooper your mom called about earlier." Kamp faced Hawke. "Would you like something cold to drink?"

"Sounds good." Hawke wasn't sure whether to take a seat at the small kitchen table or ask if they could talk outside.

Kamp filled three glasses with what looked like lemonade. "Come out to the gazebo when you can," he said to his wife and handed a glass to Hawke.

They exited out the back porch and took a left. Hawke saw the screen-enclosed hexagonal structure under a large willow that had been trimmed to keep limbs from resting on the structure.

"I built this for Jenny last summer. She wanted a place where she could enjoy the outdoors without getting eaten up by the bugs or worrying about rattlesnakes." Kamp opened the screen door and waited for Hawke to enter before he closed it and took a seat at a small round table with four dainty metal chairs.

Hawke sat across from him. "Sounds like Mrs. Bertram has told you her husband is missing?" He started the conversation, unsure when the woman would join them and wanting to feel out the man when his wife wasn't around.

"Yeah, I'm pretty sure it was before you drove away from the house. She was unhappy. Wanted to know if we had any idea where Arnie could be. We saw him last week. All he talked about was the conference and he was working on a plan to give him and Laurel an easier life." Kamp took a sip of his lemonade.

"Did Mrs. Bertram ever mention she thought her husband might have another woman?"

The man's eyes widened. "Did he? I mean, I never thought he had the guts or a roving eye, but hey, some men do get fed up with their wives." He plopped the glass down on the table and raised both hands. "Not me! I love Jenny and would never do anything that would hurt her."

Hawke ignored his dramatics. "But you think Arnie might have been ready to leave his wife?"

"I don't know. He did say he was planning to make both their lives better. To me, that sounds like he planned on them having a better life together, not apart." Kamp picked his glass back up and sipped.

Hawke nodded. That would be what he would presume as well. "Did he give you any hint at what he had planned to make their life better?"

"Nope. I thought maybe it was something he was doing while at the conference. You know, maybe getting a job with one of the companies that promotes there."

"You're the first person I've talked to who has linked Arnie and work in the same sentence."

Kamp laughed until he had tears running down his cheeks. When he pulled himself together, he said, "I can understand. He is not the most ambitious person."

"From what I've gathered, Mrs. Bertram does all the work at the farm. Do you think she'd be upset if the farm was sold?"

The man sat up straighter. "Is there someone interested in the farm?"

"Not my place to say. I want to know your thoughts on your mother and father-in-law."

The screen cricked open. "He loves them both." Mrs. Kamp glided across to the seat next to her husband and picked up the lemonade, drinking a third of it, before placing the cup down and staring at Hawke. "What are you trying to do? Dig up dirt on my parents?"

"No, I'm trying to figure out what happened to your father. Do you think he could have gone hiking to clear his head?"

She peered at him. "I have never seen him camp or even own camping gear."

"Do you have any idea of why he would leave his pickup at Freezeout Trailhead?" Hawke studied the woman. The trailhead wasn't that far from where the daughter lived. Could the two have worked out something to get him away from Mrs. Bertram?

"None what-so-ever. As far as I know, he's never been there before. As I said, he isn't into nature. And he doesn't like farming. He only kept the farm because Mom enjoys it so much."

"What about another woman? Think your father would cheat on your mom?" Hawke caught the smirk on Kamp's face before he studied the wife.

"He might have thought about it. Mom is a bit of a cold fish. Well, when it comes to people. She loves animals and plants. But my father is spineless. He wouldn't step out on my mom or confront her, that would take too much energy." The woman's eyes widened. "Don't get me wrong. I love both my parents. They are just two very different people, who, I think while they love me, they don't really love one another anymore. Father has someone who will work the farm he doesn't want to work, and Mom has someone who lets her do what she wants without meddling. Oh, she complains about doing all the work, but she really wouldn't have it any other way. When I offered to help, she always told me, only she knew the right way to do things."

Hawke studied the woman. She had enough of her mother's drive to can and take care of her husband, but enough of her father's laidback easiness to not care that her parents were who they were.

He shifted his attention back to the husband. "Did you ever ask your father-in-law to help you out financially?"

"Where did you hear that?" Kamp bristled and sat back in his chair as if Hawke had backhanded him.

"I'm just asking. From your response, I'd say you have."

Mrs. Kamp jumped in. "Father would tell us when he came into money, he'd help us out, but that was all. And what good would Father's disappearance do us if that were so?"

She'd already jumped to the fact Hawke had asked the question wondering if the Kamps were after money from the man's death.

"Maybe you and your mom had planned to split the money from the sale of the farm?" Hawke studied both of them.

Mrs. Kamp broke into a hearty laugh.

Mr. Kamp smirked.

When she stopped laughing, Mrs. Kamp said, "My mother would never sell that farm. It's all she knows."

Hawke had a bad feeling from what the neighbors said and what this couple had told him, that the wife could have had something to do with her husband's disappearance. "Who are some of the people or places where your father would visit?"

The woman's brow wrinkled. "Ever since I can remember his best friend has been Milton Freyer. He lives in Eagle. Father likes to go to Al's in Eagle in the mornings to visit with the other farmers. Other than that, I don't know."

"Thank you for your time." Hawke finished his glass of lemonade and stood.

"If you have any more questions, we'll be right here. We're getting ready for harvest," Kamp said, also standing.

Hawke nodded and exited the gazebo. The four dogs were lounging in the shade of the trees around the perimeter of the yard. They raised their heads but didn't make any move to herd him away.

At the pickup, Dog didn't even look at him. The animal sat in the passenger seat, face forward.

"Hey, I didn't even touch one of them. Come on, sniff me and see." He held his hands out to the dog, who pretended he wasn't even sitting in the cab. Hawke scratched behind Dog's ears. "As soon as we stop somewhere, you can hop out and pee all over the tires and hide their scent. I promise."

Dog gave him a sideways look, and Hawke was pretty sure the animal smiled.

Hawke started up the pickup and they headed back toward Imnaha. He pulled onto Freezeout Road. Since he was in the area, he might as well see what Search and Rescue had discovered, if anything. He followed the narrow dirt and rock road up through the trees and private land for three miles. It was slower driving than the graveled Upper Imnaha Road. The righthand side was a drop off down into a narrow, wooded canyon.

Crossing the last cattle guard, he pulled into the trailhead parking area and stopped beside the van being used as the incident command post. Dog jumped out and immediately raised his leg on the back tire. Hawke grinned and walked over to Sheriff Lindsey.

"What are you doing back here?" Lindsey asked, looking up from a map. "I thought you didn't want to join our search."

"I was in the area and wondered if you'd found anything." Hawke stopped close enough he could get a look at the map.

"We did a hasty search and brought in a canine. The canine couldn't pick up a scent. I'm starting to think you were right about this being a bastard search."

Hawke nodded. "The person we're looking for isn't here. How much longer are you going to stick this out?"

"We better give it another twenty-four hours. But I doubt we are going to find anything other than goat hunters." Lindsey tossed a pencil down on the map. "Waste of time and manpower but without anything else to go on…"

Hawke glanced at the spot where the missing man's vehicle had sat. "Let's hope forensics comes up with something that will help us figure this out."

"At this point, that's our only hope." The radio crackled and the sheriff answered.

Hawke walked back to his vehicle. Dog had peed on every tire several times. "Is it your property again?"

The animal stood by the door, waiting to hop in.

"I guess so." Once he was close to Imnaha and had a signal on his phone, he called Sergeant Spruel.

"Spruel."

"This is Hawke. Could you look up the address of a Milton Freyer in Eagle for me?"

There was a long, drawn-out sigh on the other end of the call. "What have you discovered so far?"

Hawke recounted what he'd learned, including what Sheriff Lindsey believed.

"We should have something from forensics by tomorrow. That might help." Spruel tapped keys on his computer. "Here's the address."

Chapter Five

By the time Hawke arrived back in Alder, it was after ten. The lights of the Treetop Diner shown like a beacon on a lighthouse. It was a good place to get some coffee to help him keep his eyes open the rest of the way home. Also, he might learn more about what was going on in the law enforcement world since it wasn't far from the courthouse and sheriff's office.

"Hey, Hawke. Where you been hiding?" Janelle, a bleached blonde waitress with a raspy smoker's voice, asked.

"Checking out hunters. It's that time of year." He turned the coffee cup on the counter in front of him right side up, and she filled it while handing him a menu.

"Don't I know it. The whole town is crawling with campers and trailers hauling ATVs. Not to mention men." She stood with her pen poised over her order pad. Her smile proved she liked the idea of men all over town.

"I'll have a piece of chocolate pie." Hawke handed her the menu and scanned the café for anyone he knew. Looked like he'd picked a bad time to run into anyone in law enforcement. There were two older couples and a booth full of teenagers.

It was Monday night.

"Did you hear there is someone missing at Freezeout?" Janelle asked when she spun back with a slice of pie on a plate.

"I did hear that. What have you heard?" Gathering gossip and not having to cook were the two reasons he ate out a lot.

"Well, a farmer from out at Leap is missing. They think he walked into the wilderness to die." She nodded as she talked.

"Who thinks he wanted to die in the wilderness?" Hawke thought that at first, too. But now he wasn't so sure. Having talked to the family members, the man didn't seem suicidal at all.

"Deputy Corcoran and Ralph were talking about it."

Ralph was the nighttime deputy jailer. He was young and had the hots for the forty-something waitress who smoked like an old-time coal locomotive.

"You can't always believe what you hear." Was all Hawke would say. He had a pretty good idea Mrs. Bertram and her daughter wouldn't like this kind of rumor spreading.

A bell dinged and Janelle spun to the window behind the counter and picked up four plates. She juggled the plates as she walked over to the table full of teenagers.

Hawke studied the teens but couldn't place any of

them. That was a good thing. It meant he hadn't met them through his work.

Janelle returned with the coffee pot in her hand and refilled his cup. "I also heard you've been spending a lot of your days off at Charlie's Lodge." Her free hand sat on her hip as she stared at him.

He shrugged. It was none of her business what he did on his days off. He'd never given her a single sign that he was even remotely interested in her. Since his divorce twenty-five years ago, he'd shied away from women and commitments. Much to his mother's dismay. That was until he met Dani Singer two years ago. Now he spent a good deal of his non-working time with her. And yes, it was at Charlie's Lodge. She'd inherited the run-down lodge from her uncle and had turned it into a unique get-away for families and business groups.

He finished eating, slipped money under the edge of his plate, and left.

In his vehicle, Dog started sniffing and ended up nearly in Hawke's lap.

"Back off, or you won't get this crust." Hawke eased the dog back to the passenger side by pushing on his chest. "Sit."

Dog plopped his butt down on the seat. Drool appeared on his lip. The animal's pink tongue lapped at the drool as Hawke unwrapped the crust and held it toward the dog.

One bite and the crust vanished. Dog licked his lips and stared at him as if more would magically appear.

Hawke patted his head. "That's all for now. I'll feed you when we get home." He pulled out his phone and dialed the number Spruel gave him for Milton

Freyer. There was no sense driving all the way to Eagle tonight if the man wasn't at home or he had already gone to bed.

The phone rang several times and the answering machine came on. Hawke didn't leave a message. He'd get up early and have breakfast at Al's Café in Eagle in the morning. That way he could talk to the other farmers Arnie Bertram met there, and if he was lucky, he'd run into Milton Freyer.

《》《》《》

It was rare for Hawke to have breakfast at Al's. He usually stopped at the Rusty Nail in Winslow where he worked out of the OSP building that also housed the Department of Fish and Wildlife offices.

He was surprised at the number of vehicles parked around the café. He had to circle the block twice to find an opening. "Stay," he told Dog, rolling the windows down halfway.

Standing in the door of the establishment, Hawke scanned the room for a place to sit. There were two open stools at the counter and one small table in the back.

"Hawke, what are you doing here so early in the day?" Lacie Ramsey, one of the co-owners of the café, asked as she walked up to him with a menu and pot of coffee.

"I need breakfast and wondered if you could tell me which group of men Arnie Bertram sat with when he came in?"

"Oh! Are you helping look for him? It's so sad he's gone missing. Follow me." She led him over to a group of four men, dressed in jeans and long-sleeved work shirts. Their ages looked to range from mid-thirties to perhaps eighty.

"Gentlemen, this is State Trooper Hawke, he wants to ask you questions about Arnie." Lacie pulled a chair over from another table and placed the menu on the table in front of the chair. Then she filled a cup with coffee and walked away.

Hawke studied the group. They were as curious about him as he was about them. He sat down and started with the man to his right. "Could I get all of your names, please?"

"Dave Tilden, I live east of Eagle." The man was in his thirties, short and stocky.

"Cy Grover, I live in Diamond Prairie." Hawke made mental note to ask him about Milton Freyer. This farmer was in his sixties, weather-worn, but his eyes were watchful.

"Deke Justice. I have a place closer to Winslow." He was a man in his fifties. Tall, slender, with a graying beard and a ponytail.

"I'm Alfred Zahn. I live in town now." He was the oldest of the group. His gnarled hands and wizened face showed he'd put in his years of hard work on the land.

"I'm pleased to meet you. I understand Arnie Bertram is a usual member of this group."

Heads nodded.

"He's missing and I wondered if you might have some insight into what might have happened?" Hawke had his notepad open on the table.

Lacie appeared at his elbow, filling everyone's cup. "Did you plan to order?"

"Bacon, eggs, toast," he said, not even looking at the menu.

"I'll have Burt get that going." She disappeared.

Alfred cleared his throat. "We were just talking about Arnie."

Hawke glanced around the table. "Did you know his pickup was found at Freezeout Trailhead yesterday?"

"Heard that from Laurel when she called me asking if I knew what Arnie was up to," Deke said. "That was the first I'd heard of him being missing. We all thought he was at the conference in Spokane he'd been talking about for a month."

Everyone bobbed their head.

"Did he ever talk like he wanted out of here, his marriage, his life?"

This time the men shared glances.

"What was it he wanted to change?" Hawke asked.

"He'd been talking a lot about traveling. Seeing more than the places he'd been to for Ag shows," Dave said.

"That's the only reason he went to them. It was a way to travel somewhere without Laurel saying they had work to do on the farm." Cy picked up his cup of coffee.

Hawke studied the men. "Do you think he would have disappeared and left everyone wondering where he went?"

They all shook their heads.

"No. He would have wanted to tell us all about it. He wouldn't have disappeared." Deke glanced at the other men and they all agreed.

"Any ideas why his pickup was found at Freezeout Trailhead? Does it have any meaning?" Hawke could tell these men were as perplexed as he was.

"It doesn't make sense," Cy said. "He would make

a weekly trip out to see Jenny and Reed, but he's never mentioned Freezeout."

"What did he think of his son-in-law?" Hawke asked.

"Arnie liked Reed. Though he was a forward thinker. He was glad Jenny found a man who had ambition." Alfred laughed. "Arnie knew he didn't have any ambition. I think that's why he put up with Laurel always calling him lazy. He didn't want his daughter to be as unhappy as his wife."

Hawke snatched onto that tidbit. "Laurel is unhappy?" He already had that notion by the way she spoke yesterday.

"Has been nearly every day of her marriage, I'd say," Deke offered. "At least from what Arnie has said, and what my wife, Ginger, has thought from talking to Laurel."

"Why stay married if they were both so unhappy?" Hawke wondered this all the time when he came across a married couple who seemed miserable. This day and age, it was easy to get out of a marriage you weren't happy in. His wife dumped him long ago when he'd arrested her brother for drugs.

Alfred shrugged. "Arnie didn't like work but wanted the farm. Laurel likes working the farm. Guess that was enough for a while."

"Do you have any idea if Arnie had another woman in his life?" Hawke asked as Lacie set his plate of food in front of him. The aroma of the bacon started his stomach grumbling.

Lacie didn't hurry off. "Arnie was in here a month ago with a woman. It wasn't Laurel. This woman was short, thin. I don't think I've ever seen her before."

"What time of day?" Hawke asked. "Any other usual customers in here at the time?"

The woman scrunched her face in thought. "It was early for dinner. Maybe four-thirty? Not a lot of people. Miracle was working that day. It was before school started. I can ask her if she remembers anything about the woman."

"I'll ask her. Can you get me Miracle's phone number, please? And can you remember if there were any other customers?" Hawke was writing all of this down.

"I'm not sure. It was a month ago. I didn't think that much about it. Arnie tends to come in all hours of the day and will sit with anyone who wants to talk. But I remember I hadn't seen the woman before." Lacie filled everyone's coffee cup and walked away.

Hawke raised his first bite of breakfast to his mouth when Lacie returned with a small piece of paper.

"Here's Miracle's information."

Hawke nodded and chewed. He swallowed and glanced around the table. "Any of you have an idea who the woman might be?"

"Like Lacie said, Arnie talks to anyone who will listen," Cy said.

Chapter Six

After his conversation with Bertram's friends, Hawke sat in his vehicle and called the number Lacie gave him for the young waitress, Miracle.

"Hello?" an older woman's voice asked.

"Ma'am, I'm State Trooper Hawke. I'd like to talk to Miracle."

"What did she do? I've been telling her that group she hangs out with is trouble."

"She hasn't done anything. I have some questions I'd like to ask her about someone she served at Al's Café." Hawke wondered about the young woman's friends.

"She's in school right now. You can call or come around, after four. She'll be home then."

"Thank you. I'll do that." Hawke ended the call and started his vehicle.

"Let's go have a chat with Milton Freyer," he said, scratching Dog's ears before pulling away from the curb.

Churlish Badger

«»«»«»

Hawke pulled up to a run-down farmhouse on Diamond Prairie. A woman in overalls and a flannel shirt stepped out of a small barn. She studied him through squinted eyes as he parked and stepped out.

Two border collie mix dogs ran up to him yipping and wagging their tails. He scratched their heads and waited for the woman to walk over.

"Can I help you?" she asked, standing twenty feet back.

Hawke drew his badge out from under his shirt and introduced himself. "I would like to talk to Milton Freyer."

"I'm his wife. He's out in the field raking." She pointed to the east. "We can walk or you can hop in my side-by-side."

"If I can let my dog out, I'd prefer to walk." Hawke always took the healthier route. At his age, he needed to keep in shape to stay out in the field on his job.

"My dogs are friendly."

Hawke opened the vehicle door and Dog hopped out. He sniffed noses and butts with the two dogs and the three started running around playing.

"It's this way," Mrs. Freyer said, motioning with her hand and heading down a dirt road beside the barn.

"I'm here to ask your husband about Arnie Bertram." Hawke left it at that.

"We couldn't believe it when we heard. What was his pickup doing at Freezeout? We've both known him our whole lives. We all grew up and went to school together."

"That's what I'm trying to find out. Can you or your husband think of any reason he would have driven

53

to Freezeout?"

"None. He only went to Imnaha to see Jenny and Reed. He never talked about ever going anywhere other than straight there and back. He was more interested in the cities than the wilderness."

Hawke heard the old Farmall before he saw the tractor with a frontend rake going around the field.

"What about his marriage? Are you and Laurel friends?" He had a feeling he knew the answer from what others had said.

"I tried to be friends with her. After all, Arnie, Milton, and I have been friends since before their marriage. Laurel isn't from around here. Arnie met her in college. Not to gossip, but we all think she married him for his land. They had Jenny, but neither one of them has been happy for a long time. It must be awful to be married to someone and be lonely."

Hawke had thought the same thing.

They walked up to the gate. Mrs. Freyer hollered and waved her arms when Milton had the tractor aimed in their direction. He pulled the rake up and headed across the field toward them.

Milton Freyer was a tall, broad man with a long face and eyes that sparkled with merriment. When the tractor stopped in front of Hawke and Mrs. Freyer, the man stepped off the mid-size tractor and walked over, his hand held out.

Hawke shook hands as the woman made introductions and said why Hawke was there.

"Good. I'm glad someone is looking for Arnie. I can't believe he has disappeared on purpose. He would have told me if he planned to take a trip." Milton waved to a cottonwood tree twelve feet from the field.

They walked over to the shade of the tree. Mrs. Freyer stepped behind the tree and pulled a folding chair out. She opened the chair and sat. Milton settled on the ground next to her.

Hawke followed their lead and also sat on the ground. Dog ran over, his tongue hanging out, and laid down next to him.

"When was the last time you saw Arnie?" Hawke asked, pulling out his notepad.

Milton studied his wife. "I think it was the Tuesday before he was headed to Spokane."

"Yes. He came by to see if we had anything to go to our son. He lives outside of Spokane." Mrs. Freyer smiled. "He's doing well up there."

Hawke nodded. "Did Arnie say anything to you about selling the farm?" So far all he had were the Newton's statements he had planned to sell.

"He'd been talking about it more and more lately. Selling the farm so he and Laurel could travel to see the places he'd been making a list of." Milton shook his head. "I kept telling him Laurel wouldn't care for traveling. She barely leaves the farm. It's almost as if she's afraid if she leaves someone will come in and take it away from her."

"What about another woman? I've heard he has been seen talking to a woman at Al's Café in Eagle." Hawke didn't know if this was anything important since it appeared the man talked to anyone who would listen. But if the co-owner of Al's brought it up, it had to have been something out of the ordinary.

"Another woman? Like cheating on Laurel?" Milton shook his head. "Arnie may not be ambitious, but he is loyal as a dog. He would never cheat on

Laurel."

"Not even if it meant he'd have a traveling partner?" Hawke asked.

"I would pity the woman who came between Laurel and the farm," Mrs. Freyer said.

"Don't you mean, Laurel and Arnie?" Hawke studied the woman.

"Arnie and the farm are one and the same to Laurel. Without him, she wouldn't have the farm."

"Does she have mental issues?" Hawke had wondered at the woman's hostility toward him and her husband.

"I don't think it's mental as in needing help, but she's kept to herself, other than Arnie and Jenny, and has thrown herself completely into farming that land." Mrs. Freyer's eyes softened with sympathy. "She really should get out more and socialize."

"Arnie's tried to get her to go with him to meetings and town, but she refuses." Milton's gaze roamed over his land. "I love my land and my family, but I don't obsess over it."

"What do you think she would do if she learned Arnie had been talking to someone about selling?" Hawke watched the two exchange a glance.

"I'm sure she wouldn't be happy," Milton said.

"Would she get violent?"

"Do you think she killed Arnie?" Milton asked.

"I'm just gathering information to help the investigation." Hawke could see the husband and wife had no doubt Mrs. Bertram would be angry with her husband if he sold the farm.

《》《》《》

Hawke headed toward Winslow. He wanted to

speak more with Mrs. Bertram, which meant heading back to the Leap area.

His phone buzzed. "Hawke."

"It's Spruel. A preliminary report came back from forensics. There were traces of blood on the driver's side floor of the vehicle. They believe it was on the shoe of whoever drove the vehicle to Freezeout."

"Is that the only place?" Hawke's mind started whirling. If someone with blood on the sole of their shoe drove the pickup to Freezeout as a decoy, Arnie Bertram's body was somewhere else.

"They found a trace of blood ground in dirt in the bed of the vehicle. And the oil you found in the bed of the vehicle is motorcycle oil."

Hawke thought about the man at the camp area who said he heard what sounded like a motorcycle. Whoever left the vehicle, drove away on a motorcycle that had been in the back of Bertram's pickup. This had been a planned and thought-out disappearance.

"Is it Bertram's blood?"

"It is the same blood type. A deputy has been sent to the Bertram farm to get a DNA sample."

"I was headed that way with more questions. I'll meet him there." Hawke disconnected the call before Spruel could remind him it was his day off.

He wanted to see Laurel Bertram's reaction when they told her they'd found blood in her husband's abandoned vehicle.

Chapter Seven

Hawke arrived at the Bertram farm before the deputy. He pulled up to the house as he had the day before. The same border collie and heeler greeted him with wagging tails.

Today the hay that had been in the field was stacked next to the first two cuttings. The backhoe sat beside the haystack.

"Where's your mistress?" he asked the two dogs as he scratched their heads. When he stopped scratching them, they trotted toward the barn.

Hawke followed. The barn door stood open. He walked into the dark interior. "Mrs. Bertram?"

He continued through the barn, following the dogs, who trotted to a door in the back of the building.

Standing in the sunshine, Hawke blinked several times until his eyes became accustomed to the brightness. He spotted the woman working in a garden. Walking up to the well-tended patch of vegetables, he cleared his throat.

The woman straightened, clutching her chest. She whipped around and glared at him. "Sneaking up on a person is a good way to give them a heart attack."

"I didn't mean to sneak up. I just followed your dogs." Hawke studied the woman. She appeared more than startled. She also seemed disappointed. Had she been expecting someone else when she'd spun around?

"What do you want?" She walked through the plants and over to where Hawke stood at the edge of the garden.

"I have some more questions and there is a deputy coming to get a sample of your husband's DNA."

"Sample of his DNA? Why?" Mrs. Bertram studied him. "What did you find?"

"There were traces of blood on the floorboard of his pickup." He wasn't giving away his speculation about the motorcycle.

"Blood? Floorboard of the pickup? I don't understand. Why would there be blood?" She stared at him as if she were trying to read something on his face.

"We believe someone may have harmed your husband. Would you know of anyone who your husband hasn't been getting along with?" Hawke ignored the whining dogs and studied the woman.

She shook her head. "Arnie got along with everyone. That was part of his problem. He wouldn't stand up for us with anyone. If the seed company said we owed more than they had originally quoted, he'd find a way to pay rather than talk to them. And the fertilizer company switched our blend and he didn't even argue that it was wrong for the crop."

"There isn't anyone you can think of that would

want to harm him?" Hawke knew she was the only one who might have had a grudge, but she stood there shaking her head.

The sound of tires on gravel sent the dogs running and barking toward the front of the barn.

"That should be the deputy." Hawke motioned for her to walk ahead of him.

She walked slowly around the side of the barn, between it and the house.

Deputy Alden bent beside his county car petting the dogs. He stood when he caught sight of them.

Hawke followed the woman up to the deputy.

"This trooper says you need a DNA sample of my husband's. What would that be?"

Deputy Alden listed the personal items that would work.

"He would have packed most of those for his trip. Didn't you find them in his pickup?" she asked.

Hawke answered her, "There wasn't a suitcase or anything else in the vehicle."

Her eyes widened then shut. Without another word, she led them into the house and down the hall to a bathroom. Mrs. Bertram stopped in the doorway and stared.

"What's wrong?" Hawke asked.

"His stuff is here. All of it. I-I hadn't noticed. This is his bathroom. I don't come in here except to clean it." Tears glistened in her eyes. "I thought he'd left for Spokane."

Hawke pulled the woman out of the doorway, and Deputy Alden ducked in to collect what he needed.

"Why did you think he'd left? Didn't you see him off?" Hawke drew her into the living room and sat her in a chair.

"I was out baling. The alfalfa has to be baled when there is dew or the leaves will fall off the stems. The pickup was here when I went out at one to wait for the dew to come on and it was gone when I came in around ten in the morning. I just figured he'd left. I didn't even look in his room to see if his suitcase was gone."

Hawke studied her. She appeared stunned that all this time she hadn't known where her husband was.

He pulled out his phone and called Spruel.

"I just discovered Mrs. Bertram was out baling during the time frame Mr. Bertram disappeared. Since blood has been found in his vehicle, it might not hurt to have forensics come out to the farm and see if we can find where he might have been attacked."

The woman next to him inhaled. "Attacked? You think he might be…dead?" The devastation was slowly replaced with elation.

Hawke listened to his superior say he would get a forensic team out as soon as possible. The call ended. The elation on the woman's face had to be her realizing the farm was hers and she would never have to worry about losing it. "We don't know what has happened to him, but if the DNA from his personal items matches the trace of blood we found in his vehicle, we'll know he has come to harm."

"Does Jenny know about the blood?" Mrs. Bertram had suddenly become all business.

"No, Ma'am, you are the only person who knows about it."

"I should let her know." Mrs. Bertram stood.

Deputy Alden entered the room. "I have what forensics needs."

"Spruel is sending a forensic team out here to check for a possible scene of the crime." Hawke followed the deputy out to his vehicle and filled him in on what he'd just learned.

"Do I need to stay here until forensics arrives?"

Hawke stared at the house. "Do you think her surprise at seeing her husband's belongings was sincere?"

Alden studied him. "What do you mean? Don't you?"

"It was either sincere, or she was stunned to realize she hadn't covered her tracks well." Hawke glanced at the deputy. "From everything I'm hearing, Mrs. Bertram is the only person who stands to gain from her husband's death. I'll wait here for forensics and do some snooping."

"Knock yourself out." Deputy Alden slid into his vehicle and drove away.

Hawke walked up to the door and knocked.

"Come in!" Mrs. Bertram called out. She was on the phone. He could tell by the conversation it was her daughter.

When she ended the call, Hawke said, "I'm going to stick around until forensics arrives. Do you mind if I let my dog out?"

"That's fine. I need to get back to the garden."

"Do you mind if I look around? Maybe I can find where forensics needs to gather evidence."

"I don't care. I'd like to know what happened to my husband." She walked to the door. "Do you plan on looking around in here?"

"If you don't mind."

"Just don't touch stuff. You can look but don't

touch." She walked out of the house. The two dogs followed her back to the garden.

Hawke did a quick look at the missing man's bedroom and the bathroom. Nothing out of place. His suitcase was packed with clothes and sitting on the floor of the closet. How had the wife not noticed?

He opened a door that appeared to be the main bedroom. A bathroom was connected. Everything in both rooms were items a woman would use or wear. They lived in the same house but they were not living like a husband and wife. That drew Hawke's thoughts to the woman Arnie had been seen with at Al's Café. Had he decided to sell the farm and leave his wife?

Hawke exited the house and let Dog out. The animal immediately began reinstating the pickup as his by peeing on all the tires.

Grinning at his canine friend's diligence to make sure the world knew the Dodge was his territory, Hawke headed for a shed that sheltered the tractors and farm equipment.

Dog soon caught up and passed him, ducking into the shed ahead of Hawke. A cat charged out with Dog on its tail.

"Sit!" Hawke ordered.

Dog slid to a stop and plopped down on his butt.

"No chasing cats. This isn't the Trembley's. You need to mind your manners."

Hawke stepped into the shed and waited for his eyes to adjust. He scanned the area. There were two tractors, a baler, several implements he wasn't sure the name of, but he knew their functions. What he was looking for was a motorcycle. He continued moving through the equipment. At the far end, he spotted a tarp.

It didn't appear to be just tossed to the side. He tugged and the front tire of a motorcycle was revealed.

Could this be the one that drove away from the parked pickup? He pulled the tarp all the way off and knelt beside the bike. He touched the ground under the motor to see if it dripped oil. There was an oily spot on the ground. His heart pounded. He'd direct forensics in here to take a sample of the oil.

Dog whimpered and dug at the side of the shed.

"I told you to be considerate. Stop digging." Hawke walked over and used the flashlight app on his phone to light the ground. He saw dark splotches leaking through the gaps in the board siding.

"Let's look outside." Hawke, followed by Dog, walked around to the outside of the building. There was a dark mark on the blade of a horse-drawn plow that stood next to the building and the ground appeared saturated with a dark substance. Hawke strode to his vehicle and gathered his small pack with a few evidence bags, gloves, and luminal spray.

Back at the plow, he sprayed the dark substance and draped his coat over the blade to put where he'd sprayed in darkness. A peek under the coat the area glowing. Blood. He had found the possible point of the attack on Arnie Bertram. Had his wife really been out baling or had she shoved her husband, discovered he was dead, and staged the elaborate disappearance? If so, why hadn't she cleaned everything up?

Hawke wandered back to his vehicle and called Spruel to update him on what he'd discovered.

"Where is Mrs. Bertram now?" Spruel asked.

"Tending her garden. She told me to look around as if she didn't have a care. She is either a good actor or she doesn't know that her husband was attacked here. But what I don't understand is where his body ended up." Hawke stared around the farm. There was a newly dug trench that appeared to go from the pump house to the back of the corral. He'd seen the backhoe sitting next to it on his first visit.

"Let's go check that out." Hawke motioned for Dog to follow him. They walked over to the freshly dug dirt and studied it. If the trench was open when Bertram was killed, the body could have been dumped in and then covered.

If the woman ran all the farm equipment, she would know how to run the backhoe. But why hadn't she covered up all the evidence?

Hawke spent the rest of the afternoon waiting for the OSP Pendleton Forensic team and then showing them what he'd discovered. Luckily, Sheriff Lindsey had sent a deputy out to keep an eye on everything. When Mrs. Bertram heard what he'd found, she'd become adamant she had nothing to do with any of it. She'd been out baling. She'd tried to get in the middle of everything the Forensic team was doing. Deputy Corcoran finally took her into the house.

After he was sure Forensics knew all the things he'd discovered, Hawke headed for Eagle. It was after four and he hoped to find Miracle at home.

Chapter Eight

Miracle Durham was at home. Mrs. Durham was also there and not letting Hawke do his job.

"Mrs. Durham, could you find something to do in another room?" he finally asked.

The woman flustered and narrowed her eyes. "Miracle is a minor. I have the right to hear what she has to say and what you ask her."

"That would be fine if you would be quiet and let me ask and let her answer. So far, all you've done is chastise your daughter when all I want to do is ask her some simple questions that have nothing to do with anything she has done."

"I'm going to call your superior." The woman stood.

"Go right ahead." Hawke rattled off the number for Sergeant Spruel.

The woman huffed and walked out of the room.

"I thought she'd never leave," Hawke said.

Miracle giggled.

"Miracle, I need you to think back to the day Mr. Bertram and a woman were at Al's Café. Do you remember that day?"

The teenager nodded. "Yeah. Jimmy Polk came in that day. He said something mean as he left, and Mr. Bertram told me not to mind what Jimmy said. He said all teenage boys didn't know what they were talking about."

Hawke nodded. "Do you remember anything about the woman?"

"Yeah. She looked about Mr. Bertram's age. Small, petite. Long gray hair with highlights, pulled up on the sides. I guess she was pretty for her age."

"Have you seen her before? In the café or around town?" Hawke wondered if it could have just been a family friend.

"No, I don't think I've seen her. She was kind of snooty. The type of person who doesn't usually come into Al's. Just regular people come in."

Hawke understood what the girl meant. Al's was a place for the local farmers and townsfolk to hang out and get a meal. If a person thought themselves better than the common county residents, they would eat at one of the fancier restaurants in Alder or Prairie Creek.

"Did you happen to hear any of their conversation?" Most people eavesdropped. He knew waitresses did. His friend Justine, who waitressed at the Rusty Nail, had told him it eased the monotony of the day. Especially if it was a slow day. However, unlike most waitresses, Justine didn't gossip. What she heard stayed with her unless she thought Hawke needed to know in his capacity as an Oregon State Trooper.

"They were talking about property and vacations. Mr. Bertram named off Los Angeles and New York as places he wanted to see. The woman said something about, if you sell you can visit those and lots more."

Hawke studied the girl. "The woman was pushing Mr. Bertram to sell?"

"Yeah, I think so. Do you think she is a real estate agent?" The girl's face lit up. "I can look at the realtor's websites and see."

She had a good idea. It would be helpful to know if Bertram had been talking to a realtor rather than selling to the neighbor. Hawke held out his card. "Give me a call if you discover she does work for a realtor." He stood. "Is there anything else you can think of?"

"Mr. Bertram acted like he didn't see Alfred when he came in. Those two and Dave, Cy, and Deke sit together nearly every day. I thought it was odd that Mr. Bertram kind of hid when his friend walked in."

Alfred hadn't mentioned seeing his friend with another woman when Hawke had talked to the men. "Thank you. You have been very helpful."

"I hope you find Mr. Bertram. He's a nice man. Always tips well." Miracle sat in her chair, plucking at the hem of her shirt.

"We're trying to locate him. Thank you for talking with me." Hawke pointed to the business card he gave her. "Call if you figure out who the woman is."

Her face brightened. "I will."

Hawke left the Durham home and headed toward Winslow. He'd grab something to eat at the Rusty Nail before going on home. Maybe he'd take Dot, or Polka Dot, as his friend Kitree named his young gelding, out for a ride tomorrow.

Churlish Badger

Surprise and pleasure heated Hawke's body as he drove into the Rusty Nail parking lot. Dani Singer's older model suburban sat in the lot. While they'd bumped egos and were suspicious of one another at their first meetings, they were now what younger people called, boyfriend and girlfriend. But being as he was over fifty and Dani was in her late forties, they just called themselves friends when introducing one another. However, they were friends with benefits. He grinned thinking about how he now slept in Dani's room when he visited the lodge she ran in the Eagle Cap Wilderness. And when she was off the mountain picking up clients or supplies, he spent the night at her place outside of Eagle.

He walked into the Rusty Nail and didn't flinch when he spotted Dani talking with Justine. The two had named themselves the Hawke Fan Club. At first it annoyed him, but now he thought it was amusing. Both women weren't the gossipy or chummy type so it made sense they would become friends. That it happened to be because of him…didn't matter anymore.

"Hawke, I should have known you'd show up with Dani down off the mountain." Justine stood as if getting back to work.

"This is a pleasant surprise." His gaze landed on Dani. "Looks like I won't have to eat alone."

She returned his smile and kicked the chair across from her out as an invitation.

He sat, continuing to study the woman across the table. He'd known many Native American women who grew more beautiful with age. Dani was one of them.

"Are you ready to order or do you want to see the

menu?" Justine asked, returning with a glass of iced tea.

"I'll have the chicken fried steak and a salad." He picked up his tea and drank, not taking his gaze from Dani's face.

"I'll get that in. Dani, your meal will be up shortly."

The woman across the table from him nodded. "Thank you, Justine."

"How come you didn't call and let me know you were down in the valley?" Hawke asked, placing his glass on the table.

"I've only been here an hour. I flew in to pick up clients in the morning, grabbed items at the store that Sage needed, and stopped here for dinner on my way home. I planned to call after I was settled in."

"Glad I decided to stop for dinner. I wouldn't have wanted to come back out if I'd gone home." He picked up his drink and sipped.

"Have you been citing lots of hunters?" she asked, picking up her water.

"It's been a pretty good batch of hunters so far. Mostly following the rules."

The door jingled and Deke Justice walked in with a woman and two pre-teen children. The family settled in a booth. Deke glanced around. His gaze landed on Hawke. The man said something to his wife and stood.

Hawke watched as Deke crossed the room and stopped at the side of his table.

"Ma'am," Deke said, nodding at Dani. "Trooper, I'd like to talk to you." His gaze drifted to Dani and back to Hawke. "In private."

"I'll be right back," Hawke said to Dani and walked outside with the man.

They stood to the side of the door.

"What did you want to talk about?" Hawke asked, wondering what the man would have to say that he didn't want to be said in front of anyone.

"I don't think everyone was being truthful with you when you came by Al's this morning."

Hawke studied the man. "What do you mean?"

"I happen to know that besides Milton Freyer, Arnie spent a lot of time at Alfred's place. Sometimes overnight because Laurel was mad at him. I think Alfred knows more than he's saying. But you didn't hear this from me. It took me a long time to get included in the morning coffee klatch at Al's. I don't want to do anything to get tossed out."

"Thanks for the information. I won't say anything to anyone." Hawke motioned for them to both go back inside.

Once he was seated at the table, Dani studied him with questioning eyes. Hawke nodded to the plate in front of her. "Eat. Mine will be along soon."

"What are you caught up in now?" she asked, picking up her fork.

"I found an abandoned vehicle at a trailhead. No one knows where the owner of the vehicle is. His wife thought he was at a conference. Didn't know he was missing for four days."

"And you have an idea about what happened to this missing person." She forked a bite of salad into her mouth.

"I have several scenarios playing in my head. The problem is finding the truth." He went on to tell her what he'd learned so far.

Justine arrived with his dinner, stopping the

conversation. Not that Justine hadn't been caught up in his investigations before. She knew how to keep a secret, even when her father and sister had been suspects and turned out to be murderers.

Hawke liked discussing his work with Dani. She was interested in what he did and understood duty, having been a career pilot in the Air Force. While she mentioned he was putting himself in danger, she never told him to stop investigating. She also understood his need to find a missing person or a killer.

"Thank you. Smells and looks delicious." Hawke picked up his knife and fork and went to work cutting up the steak and mixing it with the potatoes and gravy.

When Justine refilled their drinks and retreated, Dani asked, "Do you think he's still alive?"

Hawke shook his head. "I doubt it."

Sadness dulled her eyes before she lowered her gaze to her dinner.

"Let's talk about something else. When do you plan to close down the lodge for winter?"

They talked about the lodge, how well Tuck and Sage could handle things when Dani was gone, and when she'd be taking up permanent residence in the valley during winter.

After the meal, he and Dog followed Dani back to Eagle. He called Herb Trembley and asked him to feed his animals tonight.

"Are you so caught up in Arnie Bertram's disappearance you aren't coming home until late?" Herb asked.

Hawke let out a slow sigh. He didn't like telling anyone, not even his landlords, how deep of a relationship he had with Dani. But they knew he wasn't working. "I'm staying with a friend tonight. But I'll be there early in the morning. I have to work tomorrow."

"Ahhhh. Dani must be in the valley. I'll take care of things." Herb ended the call.

Hawke shook his head grinning. He really had the best landlords anyone could want. He parked his pickup next to Dani's SUV. Dog ran up the stairs to Dani's place which was over a garage. Even his dog liked coming here.

Chapter Nine

The next morning, after a quick breakfast with Dani, Hawke knew he should hurry home to feed his animals, get in his uniform, and head out to Wenaha and check hunters. However, since he was in Eagle, it made sense to visit Alfred Zahn. He drove up to a large lot in town. The man and his wife had moved to town five years ago after turning the farm over to their son and his family. Two years later, Mrs. Zahn died and now Alfred spent his days tending to the flowerbeds and visiting with people at Al's Café.

The man's yard was a burst of colors. Hawke had only seen this many varieties of flowers at The Oregon Garden in Silverton. He'd gone to the garden with, now Lieutenant Carol Keller, the lead OSP officer in Pendleton. Back then she was a Police Academy

Recruit just like him. She'd suggested it would be a nice place to take a breather when they were finally given a couple days off from training. Hawke had enjoyed getting out in nature, and he'd enjoyed the color, but he found it odd to grow so many plants that didn't have a use other than to be pretty.

Alfred straightened from behind a rose bush. "Can I help you?"

"I hope so." Hawke walked over to the man. "When I was in Al's yesterday, Lacie and a waitress said they remembered seeing Arnie sitting with a woman. The waitress believes they were talking about Arnie selling the farm. Do you know anything about this? Maybe who the realtor was?"

Alfred's shoulders drooped. "I promised Arnie I wouldn't tell anyone. He wanted it to be a surprise for Laurel. I told him if he didn't ask her what she wanted, he may be in for a surprise."

"Because Laurel doesn't want to sell?" Hawke knew the answer but wondered why her husband of thirty or better years thought she would.

"Yeah. He thought if he got her away from the farm, she'd be the sweet inquisitive young woman he'd met in college." Alfred snorted. "That sweet inquisitive young woman was looking for a husband. One with land and who was easy to manipulate."

"She married Arnie for his land and not because she loved him?" Hawke asked, to keep the man talking.

"My Ruthie figured it out straight away. But Arnie wouldn't hear it. He was smitten and liked the idea his new wife was willing to do the work. Arnie has always had an aversion to work. A dreamer. That's what he is."

"Do you think Laurel might have heard he was

planning to sell?" Hawke didn't like putting ideas in a person's mind, but he wanted to know what the woman was capable of without asking.

Alfred shrugged. "It's a small community. I know Arnie told Myra not to call his house or come by until he'd talked to Laurel. But knowing Myra, she probably told someone she was working on a big deal and let it slip whose farm she was selling and someone told Laurel. While she doesn't get out and mingle with the womenfolk, she does know quite a few people."

"Myra who?" Hawke would get a photo of the realtor and ask Miracle if she was the woman Arnie had been talking with.

"Myra Bittle. She works at Wallowa Valley Realty in Alder." Alfred thought a minute. "You might want to call and see if she's in. Arnie made some kind of comment she liked to meet clients out of the office." His face above his beard grew redder.

Hawke ignored the innuendo that the woman may have been playing hanky-panky to get listers and buyers. "Do you know if they had signed any papers?"

"I'm not sure. I know Arnie was still mulling it over Wednesday night when he came by here."

Hawke jumped on that information. "What time did he arrive and when did he leave?"

"I think it was close to seven when he showed up. He was excited about going to Spokane and said he would make his mind up by the time he returned. He didn't say if it was to sell or to ask Laurel about selling." Alfred snipped a dead rose. "I sure don't think he ran off. He wouldn't have had any money to see the things he wanted to see. I have a really bad feeling I won't see him again."

"We should know something soon," Hawke said. "Thank you for the information."

He walked back to his vehicle, slid behind the wheel, and scratched Dog's ears. "I have the same feeling as Alfred. But where is Arnie's body?"

Hawke headed home. He needed to get dressed and call in that he was on duty.

He wanted to have a talk with Myra Bittle, but it was too early to try to call the realty office and he didn't have her personal phone number. Alder would be on his way to Wenaha. He'd stop in on his way through.

《》《》《》

At Wallowa Valley Realty, Hawke asked to see Myra Bittle.

"Myra isn't in. She called in sick on Thursday and said her doctor told her to take a vacation. She won't be back until the twentieth. I can give you her cell number," the woman at the reception desk offered.

Hawke wrote the number down in his notepad and returned to his vehicle. Inside, he dialed the number. Voicemail picked up.

"Ms. Bittle, this is Oregon State Trooper Hawke. I would like to talk to you about your dealings with Arnie Bertram. Please give me a call." He left his phone number and shoved his cell phone into his pocket.

"That's all I can do about that," he said to himself. Hawke pulled away from the realty office and hit the drive-thru at the Shake Shack. He ordered a burger, fries, and a strawberry milkshake. On the drive out to Wenaha, he ate the fries and drank the milkshake but saved the burger for later.

He passed Flora and Troy, taking 62 into the

Wenaha/Tucannon Wilderness. With Arnie Bertram's disappearance on his mind, Hawke had decided to just do day trips, not pack in and camp. That way he could spend his nights following leads.

Today he'd drive the roads and check out camps since he was getting a late start.

The first group he came upon were sitting around a dead campfire, drinking and talking. There wasn't a mountain goat, elk, or deer hanging from any trees.

He stepped out, introduced himself, and opened his logbook.

"I'm checking to see what hunters are seeing and if they've had any luck hunting."

The oldest-looking man in the group spoke up. "So far we haven't seen any elk. Did see a mountain goat hung up in a camp farther down the road."

"Thank you. Have you been hunting the whole area or a section?" He made note of the number of hunters. "And what do you have tags for?"

"We've been mainly hunting here in the east side of the area." The older man nodded to two of the other men. "Me, my two boys, and the pipsqueak over there have bow tags for elk." He motioned to a boy who looked just old enough to have his hunting license.

"And the rest of you? Did you bring rifles or bows?" It was against the law for someone without a tag to be carrying a rifle or to have a rifle if they were bow hunting.

The other three all raised their hands. "We're the dogs and mules," one of the younger men said.

Hawke nodded. He understood they helped look for the elk and would help pack out any that might be shot. "Good luck and be safe." He noted the group in his logbook and walked over to his vehicle.

Down the road another two miles, he came across a camp where a mountain goat was hanging. There were two pickups and a camp trailer. The camp was empty. He called out, "Anyone here? I'm State Trooper Hawke."

The camp trailer didn't move and no one appeared at a window or the door. He walked over to the animal hanging in the tree. It was wrapped in gauze and had been skinned and cleaned. There wasn't a tag on the body. He looked around for the head and couldn't find it.

Instead of making a circle, he'd come back this way. He needed to see a tag for the animal. Taking the next forest service road, he meandered out through the pine trees and drove as close as he could get to an area where the cliffs along the Wenaha River were a favorite of the mountain goats and sheep. He stood on the edge, using his binoculars, to see the animals and if any hunters were traversing the ravine.

The problem with shooting a mountain goat on the side of the cliff was the fall it could take. Tumbling down the side of the canyon would bruise the meat and possibly ruin most of the animal.

He spotted a group of three hunters nearing the top of the ravine. Two had guns slung over their shoulders. One of those and the third man were dragging a goat.

Hawke wandered down the top of the rim to where the men would appear.

To his surprise, the one not carrying the goat was a woman. From a distance, with a hat and sunglasses, along with all the camo clothing, he hadn't noticed it. But her long braid and feminine face revealed it the minute she locked eyes with him.

"Trooper," she said, stopping.

The two men continued up over the rim and placed the mountain goat on the ground in front of them.

Hawke introduced himself and asked to see their hunting licenses. After writing down the information on the woman and one of the men. He nodded to the goat. "Who tagged it?"

The woman cocked her hip and stared at the man who'd shown his license. "He shot it. Got in front of me so I couldn't take the shot, then insisted I put my tag on it, so he could shoot another one."

"Hillary," the man said in an ominous tone.

"It's the truth. Isn't it Paul?" She stared at the other man.

Paul let out a sigh. "That is the truth, Trooper. Max tried to make Hillary put her tag on the goat. She refused. At this moment its not tagged."

Hawke studied Max. "It sounds like you shot the animal."

When the man didn't say a word, Hawke held out a hand. "May I see your rifle?"

Hillary handed hers over. It had a faint gun powder smell and no stippling of powder around the hole in the barrel. He handed it back and reached toward Max.

"Fine. I shot the goat and I'll tag it." He pulled out his wallet, flipped it open, and held up the tag.

Hawke stood by the animal while the man notched the tag and tied it to a leg on the mountain goat.

Hillary grinned from ear to ear. "Paul, will you go back out with me later?"

"Glad to," the man said, ignoring the glare he received from Max.

"Did you see any other hunters down there?" Hawke asked.

"No, but we heard a couple shots upriver about two hours ago," Hillary offered.

"Thanks. Safe hunting." Hawke walked back toward his vehicle. A grin crept onto his lips. He was glad he came across the group. The woman would get her chance to shoot a mountain goat, and the man, who it seemed liked to skirt the laws, had to do what was right. That was what he liked most about his job. Keeping order in the way the creatures of this county were harvested. His ancestors had lived off this land for centuries and there had been plenty for them and the newcomers. Yet, it had been taken away from them. Now, after over a hundred years of forced abandonment of the land they loved, the Nez Perce were slowly purchasing land in the county to benefit them and the animals that had been a huge part of their survival for so many years.

Back in the vehicle, Hawke headed down another road that would take him back to the empty camp he'd found earlier in the day. Bumping over the dirt road, dodging potholes, he tried to eat the burger. After hitting his nose instead of his mouth three times, he tossed it out the window for the birds. His stomach could wait.

As he neared the camp with the hanging mountain goat, he spotted two other vehicles and another goat hanging from a tree. Five men, who appeared to be in their thirties, sat in camp chairs drinking beer.

He didn't take his gaze off the men as he pulled up and parked beside a newer Dodge. Hawke turned off the ignition, grabbed his cap and logbook, and stepped out.

Two men disappeared into the camper and the other three watched him walk over to the goats.

"I'm State Trooper Hawke with Fish and Wildlife. Could the two who tagged these please come over?" He watched as none of the men made a move, other than to take another drink of their beers.

"I was by here earlier and couldn't find a tag on the smaller of the two."

Nothing. It was five to one, and he knew the odds weren't on his side. Given they weren't cooperating, he was pretty sure they either didn't have tags or they planned on getting more animals than they had tags for. "You know the rules state I need to see your tags. If not, you will need to stop at the ODFW in the county and have them check your tags on your animals."

No response. Not a problem.

"Have a good day," he said and walked back to his vehicle.

Laughter followed his departure, but he'd have the last laugh. He wrote down all the makes, models, and license plates before leaving. As soon as he had a radio signal, he called dispatch and asked that the vehicles be pulled over and searched before leaving the county, he had reason to believe they were poaching. That meant a County Deputy would be stationed at the only road heading south and a State Trooper would be stationed on the only road heading north. The only other way out would be east. And he doubted any of the vehicles with license plate frames boasting auto dealerships on the west side of the state would go that way home.

If he was lucky in the next couple of days, he'd get to pull one or more of them over. Divide and conquer and you lived to fight another day.

His tires turned onto Highway 3 and his phone buzzed. He didn't know the number.

"Hawke."

"Trooper Hawke, this is Miracle. I found the lady who was with Arnie at the café. It is Myra Bittle from the Wallowa Valley Realty." Her young voice held pride.

He didn't want to shatter her triumph. "Thank you. That is helpful. If you think of anything else, let me know."

"I have!" she said excitedly.

"What's that?" he asked, wondering what else she could have overheard.

"After school today, when I was working at the restaurant, Arnie's wife came in. She looked mad. She sat down at a table with the Newtons. She told them there was no way they'd get their hands on her farm now."

Hawke thought this over. Did she know her husband was dead and she would inherit the farm? "Thank you. That's good to know."

"Do you want me to keep listening?" she asked, as if this was the most exciting thing she'd ever experienced.

"No. This is good. I don't want you to get in trouble."

"Lacie doesn't care. She wants to know what happened to Arnie too."

Hawke grimaced. He didn't need the staff at Al's Café getting themselves in over their heads thinking they were helping him.

"What you gave me is enough. Thank you."

"Okay. But if I do hear something, I'll call." She ended the conversation, he believed to keep him from telling her to stop completely.

Still nothing from Myra Bittle. It was after six. He didn't want to bother Spruel at home. Entering Alder, Hawke pulled through the Shake Shack. This time he ordered the chicken strip basket and iced tea. Once he had his food, he pulled into a parking slot and opened his laptop. He wanted to know more about Myra Bittle.

Before he had a chance to type in her name, he glanced at his inbox. Emails from Spruel. They were forwards from forensics. He opened the first one.

Chapter Ten

The first forensic report stated the blood found on the floorboard of Arnie Bertram's pickup matched the blood found at the farm. The DNA samples Deputy Corcoran sent to forensics matched the blood. The DNA on the cigarette butt found in the vehicle didn't match Bertram.

Someone else had driven the vehicle. Someone who smoked.

They now knew that Arnie Bertram didn't leave on his own. He had been assaulted on the farm, but the lack of blood in his vehicle led Hawke to believe he'd never left. Whoever killed him drove the pickup to Freezeout to make it look like he'd gone on his trip to the conference. But why leave the vehicle where it would be found?

He skipped through the document to the oil he'd sampled in the back of the pickup. It matched the oil dripping from the motorcycle found in the Bertram barn. Hawke eased his hunched shoulders back against the bucket seat. All the evidence was pointing to Laurel

Bertram, whose alibi was baling all night. It would have taken her two and a half hours to drive to Freezeout. Then leave the vehicle, unload the motorcycle, and cover the tracks. All of that would have taken at least half an hour. Then the two and a half hours back to the farm. That was five and a half to six hours the tractor and baler wouldn't have been running. He thought about the closest neighbors besides Newtons. Would they have noticed if the woman had been baling?

Did she have an accomplice? Her daughter? Or son-in-law? One of them could have driven the pickup to Freezeout while she baled.

Who else would have benefitted from Arnie's death? So far, no one.

Hawke had thought the wife uncaring, but she'd also seemed as if she believed the man was just off living it up for a while. Though her eyes did light up at the mention that with her husband gone, she'd have the farm to herself…

This conjecturing wasn't going to get him anywhere. He closed the forensic reports and did a check for Myra Bittle. She lived in Alder. On the side of town that had money. He wondered if she really was on a vacation at her doctor's request.

Finishing off his dinner, Hawke got out and put the trash in a trash can, then buckled back up to drive across town and see if Myra was at home.

《》《》《》

At Ms. Bittle's house, Hawke got out and walked up to the door. He rang the doorbell and listened. A bird squawked from somewhere inside, but he didn't hear a television or any appliances running. He walked around the side, peering in the windows. A light in the living room came on. No one was there.

"She must have timers on her lights," he mumbled and continued to the back of the house. A back door slammed from a house next door. Hawke walked over to the wood fence and called over.

"Hello? I'm State Trooper Hawke. Could I have a word with you?"

A gate halfway down the fence line opened and a woman in her forties stepped through. "Trooper? What are you doing in Myra's backyard?"

"I'm trying to get in contact with her. Do you happen to know where she is?"

"I'm feeding Lucifer, her Macaw, while she's gone. She didn't say where she was going, only that she needed to rest. I have her cell phone number." The woman pointed toward her house.

"I have that. I just thought I might catch her home. Has she gone off like this before?" He thought it curious that she disappeared after a man she had been working with also disappeared or was murdered.

"This is the first time it was sudden. She goes on vacations about every three months. I didn't think the real estate business here was that good." The woman said it in a confiding tone.

"Does she have any friends who might know where she went?" Hawke pulled out his logbook.

"Not that I can name. I see several different men come and go at different times of night, but I don't know their names. She has a cousin who lives in the county, but I'm not sure who she is. Myra just calls her Cousin."

"What is your name?" Hawke asked.

The woman gave her name and Hawke wrote it in

his book.

"When did you last talk to Myra?"

"About a week ago."

Hawke studied the woman. "Is that when she asked you to look after her bird?"

"No. I received a text Thursday evening asking me to take care of Lucifer."

"Did she text you often?"

"No, not really. Usually only when she'd come home from her trips. She'd just say I'm home and I knew not to worry about the bird."

"Thank you." He held out one of his cards. "If she comes home, would you contact me or give her this card to give me a call?"

"I can leave it on her table when I take care of Lucifer tomorrow."

"Thank you." While Hawke would have liked to have a look around in the woman's house, he had no reason other than his own curiosity.

On the drive home, he decided to stop in and talk to Sergeant Spruel first thing in the morning.

《》《》《》

Hawke pulled up to the State Police Office in Winslow. He planned to do a drive through the Chesnimnus and Sled Springs area to check bow hunters with elk tags. He'd circle down through Imnaha. That way he'd be covering three of the areas open for bow hunters to bag an elk.

Inside the building, the smell of fresh-brewed coffee drew him to the breakroom. Ivy Bisset, their newest trooper to the county, was pouring herself a cup.

"Hey, Hawke. I didn't see your trailer. Aren't you going out on some trails today?" Ivy was a patrol officer and didn't work Fish and Wildlife.

"Headed to Chesnimnus and Sled Springs. I'll do drive-bys."

"Have fun. I'm on patrol. I got your info on the vehicles from yesterday. I'll keep an eye out."

"Be careful, they don't respect authority. That's why I want them stopped. It was five against one yesterday out in Wenaha."

She saluted and headed out the door.

Hawke grinned. She was feisty, he'd give her that. Hopefully, not too feisty for her own good. He filled a cup and headed to Spruel's office.

"Come in," Spruel said, before Hawke even knocked.

Hawke stood by the door, waiting for the sergeant to finish writing.

"Tell me you are going to check hunters today," his superior said, not looking up.

Hawke grinned. "I'm headed out to check the Sled Springs and Chesnimnus area."

"Good." Spruel raised his gaze to Hawke. "What did you find out when you weren't working." The man cocked an eyebrow.

Hawke relayed everything he'd learned so far ending with, "The wife is looking good for this." He scratched his head. "But it is puzzling that the realtor Bertram was talking with is also missing. Well, according to the people I talked to she was told by her doctor she needed a rest."

"And you plan to look into this? You know this is the County's missing person. You don't need to do anything." Spruel leaned back in his chair.

Hawke shrugged. "You know I can't let something

like this go. We need to find the body."

"What if there isn't one? What if there was an altercation? Bertram got away and he's hiding from his attacker?" Spruel picked up a paper. "We can't do anything without a body or knowledge there is a body, more than the blood at the farm. According to forensics, it wasn't enough to say one hundred percent the person is dead."

"Yeah, I saw that." Hawke put his hand on the doorknob. "I'll ponder all of this while I'm checking hunters."

Spruel grinned. "Good idea."

Hawke left the building feeling as if he was missing something important. Like a body. Where could it be? It had to still be on the farm. But without proof to get a warrant, or Mrs. Bertram's consent, they couldn't take cadaver dogs in and search.

He slid in behind the steering wheel of his vehicle and started it up. An hour later he was bouncing around on the back roads through Sled Springs. He came upon a camp with an elk hanging in a tree.

The woman at the camp showed him the tag on the animal. She told him her son shot it and tagged it, and he was out helping her husband find one to shoot. Pulling a bow out of the back of the pickup, she said it was her son's. He'd left it behind because he'd tagged his elk already.

Hawke thanked her for showing him and moved on along the road.

At noon, he stopped and ate the sandwich he'd brought with him and drank a bottle of water. He'd crossed Hwy 3 and headed to Chesnimnus. A quick swing through that hunt area and he'd head through the

Imnaha area. He didn't plan to go to Freezeout. There wouldn't be anything there. He was fairly certain the body was at the farm. But he had a niggling feeling he'd missed something at Freezeout.

He stopped at a few camps along the way. It seemed the hunters weren't having as good of luck this year as in the past. Cutting across Fence Line Road to Lower Imnaha Road, his stomach started growling. Guess he'd stop at the store in Imnaha and grab something to eat. He'd always found it interesting when he drove around, he became hungry easier than when he was out riding the mountain on a horse. Must be boredom that triggered his stomach.

Half an hour later, he parked in front of the Imnaha Store, noting the other vehicles parked around the building. A couple from out of state and some that appeared to be county residents given the local car dealership on the license plate frame.

Stepping into the store, all heads turned at the sound of the tinkling bells. Their gazes remained on him as they took in his uniform.

"Hawke, what can I do for you?" Tyler asked, after finishing a transaction with a couple in their mid-fifties.

"Any chance you can cook up a burger? I've been out checking bow hunters and need something to eat." He sat at the counter as the other customers resumed their browsing.

"I can get that started. Anything to drink?"

"Iced tea, please."

Tyler placed a glass of iced tea in front of Hawke and disappeared through the kitchen door behind the counter.

Hawke spun on his stool, reading the signs he read

every time he came in and watching people make comments about the money tacked to the ceiling and the stuffed wildlife.

Hawke spun back to the counter and sipped his drink.

The door jingled.

Before he could look over his shoulder, a shrill female voice asked, "What are you doing here?"

Thinking it was someone talking to him, he spun and found Jenny Kamp with her hands on her hips staring at someone Hawke couldn't see because of the barrel stove.

The person responded in a quiet voice Hawke couldn't hear. He didn't know if the person talking was male or female or why they would upset Jenny so much.

"I don't care if you're just out for a drive. There are a lot of places in this county you could have gone other than here." Jenny didn't seem to care that she now had half the customers in the store watching and listening.

If she didn't want whoever it was to be here, why was she making such a scene? This intrigued Hawke. He decided to get a look at the person.

Standing, he took two steps to his left. Sitting at a table on the other side of the room, he recognized the person the distraught young woman wanted to leave.

Mrs. Newton. Why would Jenny be against this woman taking a drive to Imnaha?

Hawke walked over to the older woman. Jenny's eyes widened at the sight of him. Which made him wonder about her not seeing the State Police vehicle parked outside.

"Mrs. Newton. Mrs. Kamp. Anything I can help you with?" he asked.

"No!" Jenny said, backing up and running out the door.

Mrs. Newton looked up at him over her shoulder. "Why do you think you scared her off?"

"Why didn't she want you visiting Imnaha?" he countered.

The woman shrugged. "How would I know."

"Maybe because you and your husband are trying to push her mother into selling the farm before we even know what happened to Arnie?"

The woman didn't even flinch. She either had nothing to do with the man's disappearance or was more calculating than he'd thought from their first encounter. He didn't think she'd killed Arnie. She was too small, frail. But her mind and her cunning, he could see her masterminding something.

All the facts though pointed to Laurel. He wondered what this woman had to say about her neighbor. "Do you have time to sit down and answer some questions for me?" he asked, heading back to the counter.

His burger in a basket sat next to his half-full iced tea. He slid onto the stool and wasn't surprised the tiny woman had followed him. "Want something to drink?"

"I'll have an Arnold Palmer, please," she said to Tyler.

Hawke had tried the half-iced tea, half-lemonade drink once. He hadn't cared for it. He bit into his burger and chewed while the woman waited for her drink and then sipped.

He swallowed and asked, "A week ago Wednesday

night, do you remember seeing or hearing Laurel Bertram baling hay?"

"I believe when we were coming home from the meeting that night, we saw her headed out to the field with the tractor and baler."

"Do you know if she was out there all night?" Hawke asked, before taking another bite of his sandwich.

"I can't tell you. You've been to our place. The field she was baling is on the far side of where our properties meet. I never hear the machinery when she's harvesting." The woman sipped her drink. "Have you found Arnie?"

Hawke studied the woman. What was she fishing for? "No. We have alerts out to all the agencies looking for him." He took a drink of iced tea and asked, "Where do you think he is?"

She shrugged. "I hope he's off having the time of his life. Lord knows he's not had a blissful marriage."

Changing the subject, he asked, "Why didn't Jenny want you here?"

The woman kept her eyes downcast, peering into her drink. "Like you said, because her mother thinks we are trying to steal the farm."

"Are you?" He bit into his burger, watching her.

She stirred her drink. "We are willing to pay her the going rate for that land. She's just too stubborn to see it's the best thing for her."

"From what I've seen, Laurel Bertram loves that land and will do anything to keep it."

The woman stared him in the eyes. "That's what I think too."

Chapter Eleven

Hawke decided to visit Judd Bishop before he left Imnaha. The man's place was on the way toward Prairie Creek. He hoped the stop didn't take too long. It was getting late, and he wanted to check on his theory Arnie Bertram's body had to be at the farm. Since the chilling statement by Mrs. Newton, Hawke felt he was right that the man's body was there. And it had been hidden by his wife.

He pulled up to the Bishop house. Two small dogs ran out, barking like he was a monster invading their territory.

"Hey, boys. Just here to talk," Hawke said softly and crouched to allow the animals to sniff his hand.

"What are you doing out here, Trooper?" a bearded man asked, stepping down off the front porch.

"Tyler told me you had some dirt bikes here last week? Anything you want to tell me about?"

The man ran a hand over his beard. "It was last

Wednesday, well probably more like early morning Thursday. Around three-thirty or four. I didn't have glasses on when I looked at the clock. It was the noise that woke me up."

"Were they on your property? Did you see tracks?" Hawke pulled out his logbook.

"No. The more I think about it, I haven't heard it since. I think it was just one rider and they were on the road. I think the wind was blowing just right to make it sound like it was behind the house. I couldn't find a track anywhere." The man shrugged. "I was griping before I had the facts."

"It never hurts to check things out. Thanks." Hawke drove home wondering if the dirt bike wasn't the motorcycle the killer rode back to the Bertram farm.

«»«»«»

It was too late to make a call on Mrs. Bertram. Hawke headed home.

"Hawke, got a minute?" Herb called to him as Hawke started up the stairs to his apartment.

He faced his landlord. "Is this something we can discuss in the morning?"

The man smiled. "How about you come to the house. Darlene made peach cobbler today."

He never turned down Darlene's cooking. "Sounds good."

They walked over to the house, neither one saying a word.

Herb held the door open for Hawke. Dog pushed by him, knowing he was welcome in the Trembley's kitchen.

"Hawke, good to see you," Darlene said, walking out of the pantry.

"He'd like some of your cobbler," Herb said, going to the cupboard and grabbing small bowls out.

Darlene placed a dish with tan crust and oozing peaches on the table. "Sit. I'm sure you're tired."

Hawke grinned. They may be his landlords, but they had become his best friends over the fourteen years he'd lived above their arena.

Once his bowl was overflowing with cobbler and vanilla ice cream, Herb set a glass of milk in front of Hawke and sat down with his serving. "What I was coming to tell you…" he started, took a swallow of milk, and continued. "I heard today that Laurel Bertram showed up at the bank asking for a loan against the property so she can put in a greenhouse."

With a forkful of cobbler halfway to his mouth, Hawke asked, "Haven't they taken out loans before?"

Herb shook his head. "No. Arnie didn't want to lose the property if they couldn't pay it back. He wouldn't have anything to do with loans against the property."

"Is this greenhouse something Laurel's been wanting? May have argued over with Arnie?" This was more evidence against the wife.

Darlene spoke up. "Jenny comes to the quilting club once in a while. A couple years ago, she mentioned her mom wanted a greenhouse but her dad was against it. Jenny thought it would be good for the community since her mom wanted to grow vegetables to sell."

Hawke nodded as he slipped another bite into his mouth. The woman wasn't waiting for proof her husband wasn't coming back. Did that mean she already knew he was dead?

"What do you make of it?" Herb asked.

Hawke studied the man. His landlord knew he didn't reveal law enforcement information if it could put someone in danger. This was one of those times. He didn't need Herb or Darlene asking questions that could make Laurel think she needed to kill someone else.

"I think it's interesting." He continued to eat his dessert.

"Do you think Laurel killed Arnie?" Herb asked.

Darlene slapped Herb on the arm. "Don't go saying such things. You don't know it to be the truth and shouldn't go saying it out loud anywhere."

"What she said." Hawke pointed his spoon at Darlene.

"Do you have any other suspects?" Herb asked.

Hawke shoved the spoon into his dessert and drank some milk before asking, "Do either of you know a Myra Bittle?"

Herb's face fell. "Never met her. I've seen her ads in the paper. She's in real estate."

"Several women at the hair salon have mentioned her," Darlene said. "And not in a very flattering way."

Hawke shifted his attention to Darlene. "Do you happen to know if she's always lived here? A neighbor mentioned a cousin."

"I do think she's a local. But honestly, I don't remember her from before she started selling real estate." Darlene stared at her husband. "Though her photo in the paper did look familiar. Do you want me to ask around about her?"

Hawke didn't think it would get his landlord in trouble asking about a realtor. "Just don't mention I'm interested. I'm sure you can come up with a reason to find out more about her."

Darlene smiled. "I'll visit with people tomorrow and see what I can come up with."

Hawke finished off his serving of cobbler. "Thank you. It was delicious."

Darlene blushed and Herb smiled. His landlord knew he was a lucky man to have a wife who could cook and drive a tractor. She also helped supplement the farm by boarding horses and giving riding lessons.

"I'll head out early in the morning, again. Lots of hunters that need to know we are keeping a presence in the hunting areas."

"Be careful. There are too many hunters from out of the state and county who don't know the difference between a person and a deer." Herb wore a scowl. He'd quit hunting three years ago when an arrow hit the tree beside him while he was out hunting.

"I mostly drive around and talk to the people at camps. Not a problem there." Hawke left the house with Dog on his heels. Darlene had placed a small bag with two steak bones in his hands before he walked out the door.

Up in his apartment, Hawke gave Dog one of the bones and then took a shower, speculating on what he did know about Arnie Bertram's disappearance.

《》《》《》

Hawke called Sergeant Spruel on his way to check hunters in the Wenaha area. His counterpart in the Fish and Wildlife Division was headed to Zumwalt and the area he'd checked the day before.

"I have a feeling the body is on the farm. Can you call Sheriff Lindsey and D.A. Lange to see if there is enough evidence to do a search?" Hawke had thought about the body every time he woke during the night. It was there, somewhere.

"I'll see what they say. One of the vehicles you asked to have detained turned out to have an elk and no tag or hunting license on the person in the vehicle. Good call."

Hawke grinned. He knew that the group of hunters were up to no good. He'd pass by there again today and see how many were still hanging around.

Before he was out of cell service, he called Jenny Kamp.

"Hello?" the woman answered.

"Mrs. Kamp, it's State Trooper Hawke. I was wondering why you were so upset yesterday about seeing Mrs. Newton in Imnaha?"

She sighed. "That woman and her husband have been harassing my mother about selling the farm. Mom calls me every day saying they've been by or called, asking if she'd like to sell. I don't understand why they are being so pushy now. When I saw Mrs. Newton, I thought she was going to come to our house and try to persuade us to make my mom change her mind."

"Do you have that much sway in your mother's thinking?" Hawke asked, not believing there was anyone who could make Mrs. Bertram change her mind.

"Not really. I do know she wants Reed's business to take off and offered to give us the money to help."

"Where would she get the money for that?" Hawke wondered if the husband had been socking money away for when he was ready to travel.

"I don't know. She just said, if we needed it, she could get money for us."

"Would she mortgage the farm to do it?" Hawke asked.

There was a long pause. "I wouldn't think she'd risk the farm. Not the way she cares about it. But there are some upgrades she's wanted to do for years that Dad wouldn't let her get a loan for."

"Do you have any idea where your father may have gone?" He'd act like the man had just done a disappearing act rather than tell the daughter he was most likely dead.

"If he's hurt, he would have come here."

"What makes you think he's hurt?" Hawke asked, turning off Hwy 3. He pulled over to the shoulder and parked to keep from losing the conversation.

"Mom told me you found blood and the CSI were all over the place taking samples. How did he get hurt?"

"Didn't your mom have an idea?" Hawke watched a pickup go by. It was one of the ones he had tagged to pull over. "Can you hold, please?" He grabbed his radio and called dispatch.

"Dispatch, Hawke."

"Copy."

"One of the vehicles I requested be pulled over, just turned onto Hwy 3 headed south from the Flora turnoff. See if a county or state vehicle can intercept and pull over."

"Copy."

Knowing another one of the men who'd thought they'd bested him would be pulled over, made Hawke smile.

"Are you still there?" he asked into his phone.

"Yes. Who are you pulling over?" the woman asked, a bit of awe in her voice.

"Some men who are hunting illegally. Did your mom have any idea how your father might have gotten hurt or what happened to him?"

There was a long enough pause, Hawke didn't think the woman was going to answer him.

A burst of air whistled through the phone. "She said he's been seeing another woman. She thinks the woman was married and her husband beat Dad up. Then he and the woman ran off."

Now Hawke could understand Laurel Bertram's anger at her husband when he'd called about the missing pickup. If that was what had happened. But how could a motorcycle from their barn be returned after the pickup was left at Freezeout?

"Does she have any idea the name of the woman?" Hawke wondered if it was Myra Bittle. As far as he knew there wasn't a husband.

"I don't think she does. Or if she does, she didn't want to tell me." There was the sound of a door shutting. "I have to go."

The line went dead. Who didn't she want to know she was talking to him? Her husband or her mother?

Hawke shoved his phone in his pocket and put the vehicle in gear. He'd make sure he came out in the Leap Area at the end of the day and ask Mrs. Bertram some questions.

Chapter Twelve

Laurel Bertram sat atop the backhoe when Hawke pulled up to her house. He saw how well she ran the machine as she dug a trench from what looked to be the pumphouse toward the garden area.

He stepped out of his vehicle and waited for her to stop digging and climb down off the equipment.

Her dogs bounded out from the barn when the backhoe shut down. They veered his direction, barking when they caught sight of him.

"Hey, guys. Friend here," Hawke said, bending slightly to scratch the dogs behind their ears.

"You're all decked out in a uniform today. Does that mean you have something official to tell me about my husband's disappearance?" Mrs. Bertram asked, stopping a good ten feet back from him.

"Nothing new. Just more questions." Hawke pulled out his logbook. "What time did you say you went out to bale hay?"

"I told you all of this before." She shoved fisted hands on her hips.

"I know. I'm trying to do a timeline to figure out when your husband was assaulted over there by the barn." He shifted his attention to the side of the building.

"I went to bed around eight. Arnie had gone off to Alfred's house right after dinner. I got up at one, dressed, grabbed a snack I'd made after dinner, and went straight to the tractor."

"Where was it parked?" Hawke asked. Noting it was parked by the now tarped, stacked hay.

"It was over there, by the fuel tank. I'd filled it up before dinner, preparing to bale later."

Hawke walked toward the house. "Did you come out of the front or back door?"

"Back door. That's where my boots were." She followed him to the back of the house.

He stopped and faced her. "Didn't you wonder if your husband had come home?"

"We don't sleep in the same room. When I walked out and saw his pickup, I figured he was in bed asleep." She didn't seem the least bit embarrassed to talk about their sleeping arrangements.

"You didn't just peek in to see if he was in his bed? I know you thought he might have been fooling around with someone else."

Her face reddened and her eyes sparked with anger. "I didn't care if he fooled around with someone else. He knew there was no way I'd give up this farm."

Hawke studied her. "Did you know he'd been talking to a realtor about selling?"

Her head whipped around and she stared at him.

"A realtor? I only knew that scum Ed Newton was after the place." She smiled. "Arnie would never sell to Ed. Ed bullied him in school. Arnie talked about how he hated being neighbors with that bully."

This was different than what both Mr. and Mrs. Newton had said about their visit with Arnie Bertram. He believed the wife.

"Walk over to the fuel tank like you did that night." Hawke followed her. There was never a clear line of sight to the side of the barn where the blood was found.

At the fuel tank, he asked, "Was there a full moon?"

She thought a few seconds. "No. I used a flashlight to get from the house to here. Then the lights on the tractor."

"Show me how you drove to the field." He followed her along the opposite side of the barn and down the dirt road to the field. It was a quarter-mile from the house.

"Did you see any lights back at the house while you were baling?"

She studied him. "Have you ever baled?"

He had to admit he'd bucked hay but never made the bales.

"When you're baling you have to watch the row to make sure you straddle it, that it all goes into the baler, and then keep an eye on the twine tension and watch to see if the bale comes out tied and tight." She shook her head. "I didn't have time to look at a house that I believed was calm and quiet."

The two dogs that had followed them, set off barking and running into the field.

"What about the dogs? Were they with you or at

the house?"

"They were out here catching mice." Her gaze followed the two dogs running around the field.

He studied the woman watching the dogs, trying to figure out how to ask if they could do a cadaver search.

She faced him. "Where do you think my Arnie is?"

Hawke peered into her eyes. "I believe we'll find his body here, on the farm."

"I thought as much." She sighed. "How do we find out?"

"There's a search and rescue member who has a cadaver dog. I can have them out here tomorrow." He saw a myriad of emotions swimming in the woman's eyes. The most prevalent was determination.

"Fine. I'd like to know if he left me for another woman or if he was taken from me." The woman strode to the house.

Hawke pulled out his phone and called Spruel.

"It's Hawke. Mrs. Bertram has agreed to a cadaver dog. Can you make that happen tomorrow?"

"I can make the call. Not sure when they'll get here. Sheriff Lindsey will have to contact them," Spruel replied.

"Let me know when they will be here. I'd like to be present during the search." Hawke knew it would pull him from his duties, but he wanted to see the woman's face when her husband was discovered. Her questions had him thinking she didn't have anything to do with it, but her actions since his disappearance had Hawke wondering if she was that good at hiding her true feelings.

He had one more question for her. Hawke jogged over to the house, catching up with the woman before she entered. "When was the last time someone rode that motorcycle in your barn?"

She spun around. "What?"

"The motorcycle in your barn. When was the last time anyone rode it?"

Laurel stared at the barn, her eyes blinking. "The Honda? I don't know. A few months ago. Arnie had the Honda before we got married, said he felt free when he rode it. But the last few years, Reed would take the motorcycle for a spin now and then, saying the motor needed to run or it would seize up."

"Thank you." Hawke walked back to his vehicle. Reed Kamp knew about the motorcycle. But how did he return the bike to the farm if he was the one to take the pickup to Freezeout? It made more sense for him to take the motorcycle to his place and hide it.

«»«»«»

Saturday morning, Hawke headed toward the Hurricane Creek Trailhead to check in with hunters going in and out of that hunt area. He wanted to do his job but be available to head to the Bertram farm when he had word of the arrival of the cadaver dog.

He was almost to Alder when his phone buzzed. It was Jenny Kamp.

"Hawke."

"Trooper Hawke, this is Jenny Kamp. Mom wanted me to be there today while they look for my father." She hiccupped. "I'm not sure I can."

"I'm sure your mom could use your support if they do find a body."

"You are positive my father is dead and he's there?" Her voice rose an octave.

"The facts point to his not leaving the farm."

Sobbing and sniffing echoed through the phone. "I was sure he left with a woman. Not...not...you know, being dead."

"What woman?"

"Whoever mom thought he was fooling around with." Her tone had sharpened, there wasn't fear or sorrow in her voice.

"You don't have any idea who that could have been?" Hawke wondered at how the woman kept dragging in someone else. Was it to throw them off her mother or perhaps her husband?

"No. Just that mom caught him talking on the phone with a woman and then someone said they saw the two together at a restaurant."

"Where? What restaurant?" He wondered if it was Myra Bittle and they had been talking about selling the farm rather than a relationship. He wished someone knew where she'd gone on her vacation.

"I don't remember if the name was even mentioned." She backtracked.

"Who told you about their meeting?" Hawke wasn't going to let her make accusations and not give proof.

"I don't remember. It was someone at a meeting. What time will they be at my mom's to search?"

She'd deftly changed the subject.

"I haven't heard. But it would be good for you to be there."

"I'll try." She ended the conversation.

Hawke turned his vehicle before entering Alder and took the backroads over to Hurricane Creek Road. Why had the woman called him? He knew there had been an ulterior motive. She wouldn't just call him to see if she should agree to her mom's request. Bringing up the other woman felt like she'd been trying to draw attention away from her family. Did she know something about her father's death?

He wondered if there was anyone who could vouch for Mr. and Mrs. Kamp's whereabouts the night Arnie Bertram went missing?

《》《》《》

Shortly after noon, Hawke received the call he'd been waiting for. The cadaver dog, his handler, and a deputy were headed to the Bertram farm.

Hawke was sitting on the tailgate of his vehicle, drinking water and waiting for someone to come down the trail to question. He hopped off, closed the tailgate, and climbed into his vehicle. It would take him a good hour and a half to get to the farm. He'd wanted to be there when they started but that wasn't going to happen.

Driving fast, he dodged potholes and wished this was an emergency so he could run his lights. Instead, he kept a steady foot and hurried back to the pavement and then onto the highway.

He didn't want to miss seeing the look on the mother and daughter's faces when the body was found.

Chapter Thirteen

Sheriff Lindsey stood beside Deputy Corcoran as Clint Mosby and his German Shepard, Artemis, walked away from the area near the barn where the assault had happened. Laurel and Jenny stood by the house watching.

Hawke walked up to the sheriff. "Are they just getting started?"

Lindsey glanced at him and then back at the Search and Rescue member and his dog. "Yes, only been here about thirty minutes. Clint wanted to know why he was called out to look for a body and then let the dog sniff around where the assault occurred."

"Good." Hawke nodded and watched the dog walking around sniffing both the air and the ground. He'd watched this dog work before on search and rescue missions and knew it had a good nose.

"Looks like Mrs. Bertram's been doing more digging," Deputy Corcoran said.

"Yeah, I noticed that too." Hawke nodded toward the sunken trail of dirt that had looked freshly dug the first time he'd visited the farm. "I wonder if the body is in that trench?" He glanced over at the women. They were watching intently. He caught Laurel flicking her gaze toward the trench, then back to the dog.

"Sheriff, why don't you suggest that they look along the trench?" Hawke tipped his head slightly toward the sunken dirt.

"What are you up to?" Sheriff Lindsey asked.

"A hunch. I think Mrs. Bertram knows the body is in there. She keeps looking that direction." Hawke waved a hand toward the dog and handler. "Go ask Clint. I'm going to go talk to the women."

Corcoran got a nod from his superior and headed toward the handler and dog.

Hawke walked over to the Bertram women. "Afternoon. I hope this won't be too much of an imposition for you."

Laurel glared at him. "I know you suggested this last night, but I didn't think you'd get someone here so soon."

Ahhh, had she needed more time to move the body? "I told you they might be here today."

The woman didn't hear him. All her attention was focused on the man and dog walking toward the sunken trench running from the pumphouse to a corral. She started wringing her hands and her face paled.

"Is there a reason you don't want the dog to sniff around that trench?" Hawke asked.

Jenny glared at him. "What are you talking about? Mom has nothing to hide. If you find my father here, someone else did it." She put an arm around her

111

mother's shoulders.

"Where's your husband? I would have thought he'd be here to comfort you." Hawke watched both their faces.

The mother continued to watch the dog.

Jenny glanced toward the dog and back at him. "He had a prospective buyer coming to see how we raise and care for the hemp."

Laurel flinched as the dog began digging.

"Grab the shovels," Sheriff Lindsey said to the deputy.

Hawke motioned to the house. "Why don't you two go in there until we see what we have."

Jenny nodded and turned her mother to walk into the house.

Hawke bounded off the porch and snagged a shovel out of his vehicle. The three law enforcement officers and the handler began digging in the area the dog had dug. Eight feet down they encountered clothing. A plaid flannel shirt.

"Time to call in forensics." Sheriff Lindsey stepped back and pulled out his phone.

Hawke used his hands to uncover the face before he, Clint, and Corcoran also stepped back to not contaminate the crime scene any more than necessary.

"Is that Arnie Bertram?" Hawke asked the deputy.

"Yes, it's him," Deputy Corcoran said.

Sheriff Lindsey rejoined them. "I'll go tell the women." He glanced Hawke's direction. "Want to come with me?"

"Wouldn't miss it." Hawke fell in step beside the sheriff.

"What made you suspect the body was here?"

Sheriff Lindsey asked.

"Several things really. Something happened here to either injure or kill someone. DNA said it was Arnie. But the vehicle used to throw everyone off only had a small amount of blood. He never left here. Unless it was in another vehicle. I couldn't find a connection with anyone other than his friends and family who could have taken him away from here."

They stepped up to the door and it opened.

"What did you find?" Jenny asked.

Hawke looked beyond her to the older woman, sitting in a chair, wringing her hands.

"We'd like to tell you both at the same time," Sheriff Lindsey said.

"Yes, of course." Jenny backed up, allowing them to pass into the living room.

Hawke stood slightly to the side of the sheriff, watching the woman in the chair.

"Mrs. Bertram, I'm sorry to inform you that we have found your husband."

Her head moved back and forth slightly. "My husband?" Surprise and relief fluttered in her eyes before she glanced down at her hands. "How did he get there?"

"I think you know," Hawke said, quietly.

She shifted her gaze up to his face and glared at him. "I couldn't kill my husband."

"Why is it you became scared when the dog went over to sniff the trench? The closer he moved to the spot where he started digging, the more nervous you became."

"The whole thing is upsetting. The tension. I just wanted you to find whatever and be done."

Hawke exchanged glances with the sheriff.

"Mrs. Bertram, I'd like you to come to the Sheriff's Office with me. I'd like to ask you some questions." Sheriff Lindsey put out a hand as if to help the woman to her feet.

Jenny jumped between them. "Is she under arrest?"

"Not at this time," Sheriff Lindsey said.

"Then she'll not be going anywhere. You can't make her leave with you." Jenny looked fierce and determined. It was a 360 from the fragile, quiet woman Hawke had met at her home. Had she known her mother had killed her father? Had they conspired together to hide the body and move the pickup?

"You're right. I can't make your mother go with me, but by her not coming, I will dig deeper into finding the truth." Sheriff Lindsey stared at both women for several minutes before walking to the door.

Hawke wasn't willing to leave that easy. "If you didn't kill your husband, you have more to gain by helping the police than by refusing."

Laurel stared at him but didn't say a word.

Jenny waved at the door. "We aren't going anywhere. You need to leave."

He studied the two women one more time and walked out to where the other officer stood.

"What do you think?" Sheriff Lindsey asked.

"She insisted she couldn't kill him, but I saw her watching. She knew he was buried there." Hawke rubbed a hand over his face. "Something isn't adding up."

"You want me and Artemis to sniff around some more?" Clint asked. "After driving four hours to get here, we don't mind putting in a little more time."

Hawke glanced at the sheriff who shrugged. He took that as he didn't care. "If you want, it wouldn't hurt."

"Corcoran, stay here until forensics arrives. Hawke, are you taking off?" Sheriff Lindsey asked.

"I think I'll see if I can find a neighbor who can verify whether or not Mrs. Bertram was baling all night when her husband was killed." Hawke hadn't met any of the neighbors, other than the Newtons.

"Knock yourself out. I have a party to attend." Sheriff Lindsey walked over to his vehicle and drove away.

"Any suggestions?" Clint asked.

"Not really. This is the only area that made the woman nervous when you and Artemis walked over to it." Hawke slapped Corcoran on the back. "I'll be back after I talk to the neighbors. I want to see what all forensics digs up."

He walked over to his vehicle and climbed in. He pulled up a map and discovered only the neighbors to the Bertram's north may have noticed the woman baling all night. He set out in search of their driveway.

《》《》《》

Mr. and Mrs. Klein invited Hawke in when he introduced himself. They had a century-old farm that looked as worn and weathered as did the husband and wife who sat in matching recliners smiling at him. They were in their eighties and while spry enough to greet him, he didn't see either one of them doing the work required on this farm.

"Do you live here alone?" Hawke asked.

"Our youngest son, Jerome, lives with us. He's out with friends tonight," Mrs. Klein said.

"Does he go out often?" Hawke asked, hoping he might have seen something on Wednesday night.

"Every Saturday night. He says after working here all week and hanging out with us, he needs to talk to other people." The father didn't seem to agree with his son's needs.

"Did he happen to be outside a week ago Wednesday night?" Hawke asked.

"Wednesday? A week ago?" The woman studied him as if he had a calendar on his face.

He didn't want to put ideas in their heads but he wanted to give them some context. "It was the night Mrs. Bertram was baling hay."

The woman smiled. "That would be the night before Jerome was in a grouchy mood in the morning. He complained he couldn't sleep because the wind had carried the noise of the Bertram's baler our direction and it kept him up all night."

"Did you hear the baler?" Hawke asked.

Mr. Klein shook his head. "We don't hear a thing once we take our hearing aids out. Best sleep we've ever had, once we went deaf." The man laughed.

"When do you expect Jerome to return?"

"I'm not sure. It's always after we've gone to bed," Mrs. Klein said.

"Does he have a cell phone?" Hawke hoped he could contact the man.

"No, but he is most likely in Alder at the High Mountain Brewery." Mr. Klein frowned. "Don't know why he thinks he has to go out in public to drink."

"Thank you. If I don't catch up to him tonight, would you have him give me a call tomorrow?" Hawke handed Mr. Klein one of his business cards.

"Sure. I can do that. It was nice meeting you," the old man said and waved a hand for his wife to show Hawke out.

Hawke followed the woman to the door. "Thank you for taking time to talk with me."

"It's nice when people come by. Joe and I don't get out like we used to."

Out in his vehicle, Hawke called Deputy Corcoran to tell him he was headed to Alder and would appreciate a call when forensics arrived.

"Have Clint and Artemis found anything else?"

"Yeah. Another spot with blood. Close to the front of the barn. I marked it and will have forensics take a sample. You think she struck him there first, he tried to get away around the side of the barn, and she attacked him again?" The deputy's voice rose with excitement.

"We won't know until the blood is examined. But I'd like to see the area. Can you take photos in case forensics disturbs the area before I get there?"

"Sure. See you when you get here." The deputy ended the call.

Hawke started his vehicle and headed for Alder. With any luck, he'd know by the end of the night if Mrs. Bertram had an alibi for her husband's death.

Chapter Fourteen

An hour and a half later, Hawke pulled into the High Mountain Brewery in his pickup with Dog in the passenger seat. He'd stopped off at home to change out of his uniform and look less threatening when he struck up a conversation with Jerome Klein.

"Sit tight," Hawke told Dog as he rolled the windows halfway down and slid out.

Striding up to the door of the brewery, Hawke scanned the vehicles. He found Desiree Halver's beat-up Toyota pickup where the employees parked. A grin spread across his face. He'd helped Desiree's family out with a trespasser years ago, but they still thanked him every time they saw him. Desiree was always helpful when he came here without a description of the person he wanted to question.

His stomach started rumbling as the aroma of burgers and steak floated out the doors when he stepped through.

Because it was a brewpub, it was a seat yourself type of environment. He glanced around, spotted Desiree at the bar, and walked up to it.

The young woman's face lit up at the sight of him. "Hawke! Haven't seen you around here in a long time."

"I've been busy."

She nodded. "Hunting season. What brings you in here tonight?" She poured two glasses of beer and made a drink while talking to him.

The waitress waiting for the order looked him up and down and smiled. "You're the cop who caught a poacher on my uncle's place last year."

"Who is your uncle?" he asked. While he was happy to be the face of the Fish and Wildlife in the county, he didn't like to be thought of as a hero. That's the look he saw in the young woman's eyes.

"Dale Ussery."

He remembered that stakeout and how he'd ended up investigating a car on fire with a body inside. "I'm glad I could help him out."

"Here's your order," Desiree said, shooing the waitress away. "Sorry about that."

Hawke shook his head. "That's okay. Any chance you know Jerome Klein?"

"As in, can I point him out?" she studied his face. "Is he in trouble with the law?"

"No. I just need to ask him questions to see if he can give someone an alibi." Hawke's stomach grumbled. "And would I get food quicker here at the bar or a table?"

"What would you like? I'll put the ticket up and bring it to you wherever you end up."

He'd been a fan of this young woman ever since

he'd helped the family. But the way she came through when he needed her help, he wanted to suggest she go to school for Criminal Justice.

"I'll have a steak, baked potato, and salad with ranch."

"And an iced tea?" She handed him a glass filled with tea.

"You know me too well."

She pointed over Hawke's right shoulder. "The man in the blue striped shirt with the gray hair and Vanessa Barber hanging on him. That's Jerome."

He nodded and stood, carrying his drink with him. At the table, he cleared his throat to get the couple's attention. They were close to his age by the gray in the hair and faint wrinkles on their faces.

"Can I help you?" Jerome asked, in a not-so-friendly tone.

"I hope so. May I?" Hawke took the seat before either one responded. "I'm Hawke, a state trooper." He motioned to his attire. "I'm off duty, but since I ran into you, Jerome, I'd like to ask you a couple of questions about your neighbor."

The man's glare faded and was replaced with interest. "My neighbor? You mean Arnie Bertram, who is missing?"

"Oh, I heard about the man who is missing. He's your neighbor?" Vanessa asked, peering at Jerome.

Hawke wondered at the couple's relationship. "I'm more interested in what you can tell me about his wife."

"His wife? Jerome, have you been two-timing me?" The woman pushed to her feet and swung an arm at the man's head.

Jerome had quick reflexes to ward off her hit and

sat her back in the chair. "No. You know I only meet you on my night out." He glared at Hawke. "Why did you come in here and start trouble?"

Hawke put up his hands. "I didn't mean anything that implicated he and Mrs. Bertram were anything other than neighbors." He peered into the woman's eyes.

She nodded.

"I need to know if you remember hearing Mrs. Bertram out baling a week ago Wednesday night."

"The night before Arnie left for the conference?" Jerome asked.

"Yes." Hawke didn't like serving a person information but it seemed like the only way to get to what he wanted to know.

"I remember I couldn't sleep. I guess I should say, I fell asleep around ten. Then about two, I woke up and heard the baling. The sound doesn't always drift our way but that night the wind was blowing toward our farm."

"Did you stay awake after you heard the sound?"

"Yeah. For some reason, that night the sound didn't lull me to sleep. It irritated me. I remember getting up and thinking I wish she'd stop. But I know you have to bale when the conditions are right."

Desiree arrived with Hawke's dinner.

"Thanks." He picked up his utensils and studied the couple. "Mind if I eat here?"

Jerome and Ms. Barber exchanged a glance. Jerome's head started to bob, but the woman put her hand on his arm, halting the motion.

Hawke hid a grin as he cut into his steak. The juice ran out and his mouth watered. But instead of putting a bite in his mouth, he asked, "Did you notice anything out of the ordinary the next day?"

Jerome shook his head, then nodded slightly. "About seven-thirty or eight in the morning, I heard a motorcycle on the county road."

"Did you still hear the baler running?"

The man studied the wall ahead of him for several seconds. "Yeah, I'm pretty sure I did hear the baler still thumping away. The sound the packing arm makes is so rhythmical, like a heart beating, that when it stops everything seems dead."

Hawke decided he'd let the man learn about his neighbor's death from the news or gossip. He focused on the motorcycle. "Don't you hear quite a few motorcycles running up and down the road?"

"Not really. Usually, the only time is when Reed is visiting Arnie and Laurel. He takes Arnie's old bike out for a spin."

"Does he do that often?" This was the second person who linked Reed Kamp to the motorcycle.

"I'd say about once a month during good weather."

"Have you ever witnessed Arnie and Laurel fighting?" Hawke ate his dinner between questions.

"Are you trying to say she killed him?" Jerome stared at Hawke.

"No, I'm gathering information about the couple. It's been mentioned Arnie may have had a woman friend."

Vanessa, who had been studying other patrons, whipped her head around. "You think he was fooling around? With who?"

Jerome narrowed his eyes. "It's not good to gossip."

"I'm not. I'm gathering information." The woman smiled and kissed Jerome on the nose.

Hawke wondered again about the relationship between the two. He pulled the conversation back to the topic he was interested in. "Have you seen or heard anything about another woman?"

"No. I pretty much guess that Laurel would kill Arnie if she thought he was fooling around." Jerome didn't seem to understand what he'd just said.

"This Arnie is missing and you think he had a lover?" Vanessa grabbed Jerome's arm. "And you say his wife would kill him if he did have a lover?" She tapped his temple with a finger. "Don't you see? She killed him to keep him from running off with someone else."

"Don't jump to conclusions," Hawke said. "Jerome was just using a figure of speech. I'm sure he didn't mean she would actually kill her husband." Even as he tried to tell the woman she was jumping to conclusions, he had a strong hunch that might be what happened to Arnie Bertram.

《》《》《》

It was nine by the time Hawke walked out of the brewery. His phone vibrated as he handed Dog his steak bone.

"Hawke."

"This is Corcoran. Forensics arrived about fifteen minutes ago. They've gathered the blood from the second spot the dog found and have lights set up around the body." He said something to someone else and came back, "The funny thing is, Clint says his dog is trying to dig at the head of the body. Like there might be another one underneath."

"I'll be there in forty-five. Have you called Lindsey and filled him in?"

"Yeah. He grumbled about he'd leave the party early and get ahold of Lange. See if they couldn't get Mrs. Bertram brought in on suspicion of murder."

Hawke liked the idea of bringing the woman in for questioning. It would be more intimidating, and they might get more answers out of her. But after talking to Jerome Klien, he wasn't so sure she'd killed her husband. "Sounds good. I'll be there soon."

He had to obey the speed limits in his own vehicle, but this time of night there were very few cars on the road to slow him down. Hawke pulled into the farm and out of the beam of the large lights that had been set up.

Deputy Corcoran hurried over to his vehicle. "Looks like there is another body down there. Forensics pulled Arnie out of the trench and that dog went crazy digging. Dug another two feet and we saw a hand."

Hawke glanced toward the house. A shadow stood in the window. From the shape, he believed it was Laurel Bertram keeping tabs on what was happening.

"Make sure no one leaves here," Hawke said, tipping his head toward the house.

Corcoran nodded. "I'll keep an eye on things."

The sound of gravel under tires heralded the sheriff's car. It stopped alongside Hawke's pickup.

Sheriff Lindsey eased out and stood by the door of his vehicle with a paper in his hands.

Hawke walked over. "Is that a warrant for her arrest?"

Lindsey nodded. "When Deputy Corcoran called me about a second body, that made Judge Vickers sign pretty damn quick." He glanced at the lights and people digging. "Any idea who it is yet?"

"I just arrived myself. Mrs. Bertram has a pretty good alibi for the night her husband was killed. Unless the autopsy puts his death before midnight on Wednesday." Hawke walked beside the sheriff over to the trench and large hole.

Two forensic team members were in the hole digging with hand trowels. From what they'd uncovered so far, it appeared the body was that of a woman.

Hawke pulled out his phone. They knew of a woman who had taken off unexpectedly. He texted Darlene. *Could you take a picture with your phone of the photo of Myra in the paper and send it to me?*

I learned something about her today. Want to know it now?

No. Just send the photo. I'll talk to you when I get home.

Ok.

He waited a few minutes while the team uncovered more of the woman, showing her face. His phone vibrated and he looked at the message. He hated it when he was right.

"That's Myra Bittle," he said, showing the photo to Sheriff Lindsey.

"How does she fit into this?" the sheriff asked, studying the photo and the face still sprinkled with bits of dirt.

Hawke told him about her trying to get Arnie to sell the farm through her. "I believe she came here to talk to Laurel, believing Arnie was stalling because he didn't want to sell. When I think he was still trying to find a way to talk his wife into it. Anyway, she probably came out here to talk to Mrs. Bertram. Who wouldn't be happy to know that her husband was talking to a realtor about selling the farm."

"Do you think this woman triggered both the deaths?" Lindsey asked.

"We won't know until you talk with Mrs. Bertram." He nodded toward the house.

"Guess now is a good time to take her in." Sheriff Lindsey strode three steps away and faced Hawke. "You want in on the questioning?"

"Are you going to do it tonight?" He wanted to go home and get some sleep. He had another shift to work tomorrow. But he also would like to know what the woman had to say.

"No. I'll do it about ten tomorrow. Give her some time to sit in jail and think about the right thing to do." Lindsey spun back around and strode to the house.

Hawke gazed down at the woman slowly emerging from the dirt. Had she been so eager to make the deal that she hadn't done her legwork to know that Mrs. Bertram loved the farm and would never sell?

Chapter Fifteen

Hawke and Dog parked beside the arena. "Are you going with me to the house or do you want to stretch your legs?" Hawke asked as they exited the pickup.

Dog ran out beyond the runs and disappeared into the dark.

"Guess that answers my question."

A soft nicker drew him over to the stall where his three equines stood with their heads over the gate.

"You three bachelors are a sorry sight," he said softly, before walking to the room where the feed was kept and grabbing three alfalfa cubes to feed them. Back at the gate, he handed one to Horse. The mule had been given the name Horse to hopefully make him behave more like a horse and less like a stubborn mule. So far, for the most part, it had worked. "You're a good old boy," he said, patting the animal on his neck.

Then he handed the young appaloosa, Dot, a cube. The gelding was the perfect match for the trail riding

Hawke did. Darlene had found the four-year-old for him.

Jack nudged his arm. "Don't worry Jack. I saved the best cube for you." He fed the older gelding and patted his neck, before scratching around the base of the animal's ears. "Of all the horses I've had, you have been my ears and eyes on the mountain. You will always get the best treats and the most scratches." Hawke scratched him one more time and swiped his hands together to get rid of most of the dust.

Time to talk to Darlene and see what she'd found out about the dead woman. He walked over to the back door of the Trembley house and knocked.

"Come in," Herb called.

Hawke turned the knob and shoved the door open. The kitchen was as fragrant and humid as the Kamp kitchen had been when he'd first visited.

"I've been canning applesauce all afternoon," Darlene said, wiping her brow with a towel and smiling.

"Have a seat," Herb said, placing a glass of iced tea on the table. "I'll get some cookies."

Darlene finished taking full jars out of a large pot of steaming water and placing them on a towel on the counter. "That's the last batch," she said, wiping her face again and sitting down at the table.

Herb placed a plate of cookies on the table, a glass of iced tea in front of his wife, and sat with a glass of milk.

"What did you discover about Myra Bittle?" Hawke asked, deciding not to say the woman had been found and was a victim of homicide.

"She was born in the county. Became an orphan

and was in several foster homes before being adopted. Her adoptive family left here when she was around twelve. Then after she married Mr. Bittle and became a widow, she returned to the county and started selling real estate. No one could place her with any man. Janie, over at the real estate office, said that Myra had a competitive nature. Always trying to bring in more sales than the other realtors."

"Does she have children? Any relatives in the county?" Hawke picked up a cookie and nibbled on it, waiting for Darlene's answers.

"From what I could dig up, no kids. Someone said they thought she had a cousin still living here, but no one seemed to know the name." Darlene sipped her drink.

"Maiden name?" Hawke asked.

"No one was sure. Either Smith or Jones or Thomas. I got a different answer from each person I talked to." She downed half the glass of tea.

"I'll look her up in the computer and see if I can figure it out. Thanks." He started to stand and decided after all her work, Darlene deserved to know about the woman. "We found her tonight."

"Oh, then you can ask her these questions," Darlene said, biting into a cookie.

"I'm afraid not. We need to find her next of kin."

Darlene choked on the cookie.

Herb patted her back. "You mean she's dead? Where did you find her?"

Hawke shook his head. "I can't tell you that. And you can't tell any of these people you talked to until it comes out in the news."

The woman regained her voice. "Was she

connected to Arnie Bertram?"

"In a way. I'll tell you all about it when I can. Thanks for the drink, cookies, and information." Hawke stood this time and walked out of the house. He hadn't planned to upset Darlene. He just thought letting her know was kinder than her hearing it on the news.

«»«»«»

Sunday morning, rain poured out of the sky as if the Creator used large buckets to fill up Wallowa Lake and it splattered over the whole county. Hawke crawled out of bed, put his uniform on, and fed his crew. They were all appreciative of the food and shelter out of the rain.

"Dog, you be good and stay out of trouble," Hawke said, walking out from under the shelter of the barn and arena. He dashed to his work vehicle and slid in. After going to his room over the arena last night, he'd opened his computer and looked up Myra Bittle. He'd found a bio on her at the real estate website. The only helpful information was her move from Sacramento, California back to the valley. He'd sent a request to the courthouse in Sacramento for files on Myra Bittle.

When he pulled out onto the highway, he called in that he was on duty and headed to Winslow to update Sergeant Spruel. Hawke would let the man know he'd be sitting in on the questioning of Laurel Bertram this morning before he went out to check hunters.

His stomach started growling as he entered Winslow. Wouldn't hurt to get a good breakfast. Hard telling when he'd get back in this evening. He pulled into the Rusty Nail and parked. There were more cars than during the week. Second thoughts about eating in the café had him sitting in the vehicle, undecided.

Gurgling in his stomach made up his mind. He shut down the engine and slid out. Walking around to the door, he peered in the windows. He only recognized a few locals. Most of the clientele wore hunting vests and had thick coats draped over the backs of their chairs. The rain had brought hunters into town for a warm meal.

The door jingled when he opened it. All eyes stared at the door. The locals raised a hand. Some hunters smiled; others looked the other way. He'd see if he could learn anything from them before he, or they, left the café.

Justine smiled, turned a coffee cup right-side-up on the counter, and slid a menu in front of the cup. "Didn't expect to see you in here today. Shouldn't you be out chasing hunters around? Oh, wait. All the hunters are in here having breakfast." She laughed at her own joke.

"That's the way it seems. Seen any of them before?"

"The older group in the corner have been in here every morning this week. I think they aren't hardcore hunters." She grabbed a coffee pot and filled his cup. "What are you having today?"

"Is Merrilee cooking?"

"Yes, I am. Just cuz I'm old don't mean I can't hear everything said out there." The cranky woman in her seventies, who owned the Rusty Nail, poked her head up to look through the window from the kitchen. Her thin reddish-orange hair stuck out like down on a baby bird.

"Morning, Merrilee. Since you're cooking, I'll have pancakes, eggs, and bacon. You make the best pancakes." He smiled and saw the glint of good humor in the woman's rheumy eyes.

"Don't write it down, I'll remember." The old woman ordered Justine.

The younger woman rolled her eyes at Hawke and set off to refill coffee cups.

Hawke spun his stool and studied the people in the cafe, who were mostly male. He decided to have a chat with the group of older men in the corner first. Standing, he caught the attention of several men at a table not far from the counter. He decided to chat with them before they took off.

"Morning gentlemen," he started. "Looks like you're in the county hunting. Have you had any luck?"

"Not much. We've only been here a couple of days," one of the men said. The others nodded.

"What hunt are your tags for?" Hawke studied each man as they looked at the man who had spoken first.

"We have the Hurricane Creek hunt. Thought we'd go in from the Lostine River side, then the rain started pouring down and we decided to grab breakfast and see if it lets up."

"Smart move. That country can be treacherous during a downpour like this. Good luck." He moved on over to the group of older men.

"Morning. I was wondering if you are here hunting?" Hawke asked.

The men glanced around at one another.

One of the men, puffed up his chest and acted cocky. "Is that what we look like? Hunters? There a law against being a hunter?"

"No, there is no law. But I'm with Fish and Wildlife and I'd like to know where you've been hunting and if you've had any luck."

One of the other men slapped the cocky one on the arm. "Shut up, Ted. Yes, sir. We have been up here hunting. At least that's what our wives think."

The others chuckled.

"We've been sightseeing and checking out this country. Every fall, since we all retired, we do this in a different area of Oregon. It gives us a break from the wives, and we get to see parts of the state we wouldn't get to see otherwise."

Hawke nodded. "Enjoy your sightseeing. Today might be a good day to check out the Nez Perce Center in Eagle or the Josephy Center in Prairie Creek."

"Thanks for the tip."

"You're welcome." Hawke wandered back to his place and found his breakfast waiting on the counter for him.

When Justine wandered by to refill his coffee, he said, "Thanks."

"No problem. Are you going out in this rain today?"

"Yes. After I stop by the Sheriff's Office." He started eating so she wouldn't ask him any more questions.

Halfway through his meal, the door jingled. He didn't turn around to look. No need. He recognized the booming voice.

"Hey Justine, how about a cup of coffee and cinnamon rolls for all of us." Ed Newton had entered the Rusty Nail.

From how friendly he was with Justine, the man must frequent the café often. Hawke wondered what his friend could tell him about the man. Itching to see who he was with, Hawke about dropped his cup of coffee when the couple came into view. Reed and Jenny Kamp.

Jenny had to know that her mother was being held at the county jail. She had been at the house when her mom was taken away. Why would she and her husband be sitting down with a man who had made no apologies for wanting her parents' farm?

When the woman took her eyes off her husband and scanned the room. Her gaze landed on Hawke and fear replaced the adoration that had been there while watching Reed.

Yep. That was a clear sign she hadn't wanted to be seen talking to this man. Hawke couldn't resist. He stood and walked over to the table.

"Don't you think this is a little premature?" he said, staring at Newton. The Kamps were in his peripheral vision.

"I don't know what you're talking about?" Newton tried to look confused but he didn't pull it off.

Hawke waved a hand toward the younger couple. "Trying to get these two to sell the farm to you when they are dealing with Jenny's mom being in jail and her father's death."

"That's what I thought." Jenny leaned toward her husband.

He put an arm around her shoulders. "I went to the farm to pick Jenny up this morning and Ed drove in behind me, saying he wanted to buy us breakfast." He glanced at the older man. "He didn't say anything about selling the farm."

The older man smiled and held both hands out, palms up. "This is just a neighborly attempt to ease their hardship."

Hawke didn't believe it for one second. He studied all three and went back to the counter to finish his cold meal.

When Justine came by to refill his coffee, Hawke touched her wrist to get her attention. She leaned closer.

"Does Ed Newton come in here frequently?"

She nodded. "He's full of hot air. Blusters about how well his farm is doing and all that, but always buys the cheapest thing on the menu."

Hawke let that sink in. "You think he has enough money to buy out his neighbor?"

She shook her head. "I'd be surprised if he did."

This was interesting. Why did he keep hounding the Bertrams if he didn't have the money to follow through?

"Thanks for breakfast." He stood and peered through the kitchen window. "As always, delicious pancakes, Merrilee." Hawke always left a hefty tip. Merrilee had been running the place with minimal help since her husband ran out on her over ten years ago. It was her livelihood.

"Don't be a stranger," Merrilee called out.

He waved and walked by the table with Newton and the Kamps. They were deep in a discussion, that for once Newton wasn't broadcasting to the world.

Unable to stand and eavesdrop, Hawke hurried out the door and drove to the OSP Office.

Sergeant Spruel stood outside his office door when Hawke walked into the OSP side of the building they shared with Fish and Wildlife.

"Heard they brought in Mrs. Bertram. Did she kill her husband?" the sergeant asked.

Hawke shook his head. "I'm on the fence. A

neighbor heard the baler running all night long. She couldn't have driven her husband's pickup to Freezeout and still had the baler running. However, I believe that two people had to be involved. She could have killed him and the other person drove the pickup out and the motorcycle back. But she was nervous about the cadaver dog getting close to the trench where we found Bertram's body and that of Myra Bittle, the real estate agent."

"Two bodies in a trench on her property? That's pretty damaging."

"Yeah. I'm going to sit in on the questioning. Then I'll head out north and check hunters." Hawke pivoted to head out the back of the building.

"Between OSP and County, they pulled over all the vehicles you'd requested. Only one had a valid tag and license. Good call."

Hawk spun back around, a grin on his face. "Thanks. Their hostility toward me was obvious. That meant they were doing something they shouldn't have been."

It was moments like this that he understood his calling to be a game warden in this county. He'd brought to justice men who were ignoring the laws put in place to keep the wildlife thriving in his ancestors' home.

Climbing into his vehicle, he thought about Laurel Bertram. He found it hard to believe she'd killed her husband. She'd been too interested in what had happened to him. He also believed what she'd said about her husband not planning to sell to the bully Ed Newton. The only other people who seemed eager to sell the farm were the daughter and son-in-law. But would Jenny have killed her father and then placed the blame on her mother?

He didn't understand the family dynamics. Hadn't had a chance to look into them. Something he needed to do. Perhaps another visit with Milton Freyer, Arnie's best friend, was needed. He could circle through the north country and end up in the Eagle area tonight.

Chapter Sixteen

At the Sheriff's Office, Hawke walked in through the front. The woman behind the counter waved him on back.

"They're in the interview room."

He glanced at his watch. He was ten minutes early. Had they started without him?

Opening the door, he found Sheriff Lindsey and District Attorney Benjamin Lange with their heads together over a file.

"I thought maybe you started without me," Hawke said, putting his hat on the table and taking a seat alongside the sheriff.

Lange studied him. "I understand you started this hunt for the victim."

"I saw a vehicle that appeared abandoned and started checking, yes." Hawke and the D.A. had a history. A bit contentious until Hawke saved the D.A.s butt when a poacher using a tag with the D.A.'s name on it was killed.

"And now we have two bodies." Lange returned his gaze to the file.

"What are you reading?"

"Preliminary report from Dr. Vance," Sheriff Lindsey said. "The only mark on Bertram is where his head hit the plow and faint bruising on his chest. Vance thinks it could be impressions where he was pushed backward. Dr. Vance found bruising and a laceration on the woman's head. She thinks the woman was unconscious when she was put in the trench and died of asphyxiation. She'll know more after she autopsies both victims."

Had whoever killed Ms. Bittle felt emboldened by getting away with it and decided to take out Arnie which appeared to have been a harder death? Or was it the other way around....

A knock on the door had them all craning over their shoulders to see who it was.

A female deputy Hawke hadn't met, poked her head in. "I have Mrs. Bertram."

"Bring her in," Sheriff Lindsey said.

The door opened wider, and the two women walked in. Mrs. Bertram's hair was more disheveled than normal. Dark circles under her eyes highlighted the puffiness of her face. Her hands trembled as she sat in the chair across from them.

The deputy took up a stance at the door.

"Mrs. Bertram, please state your full name for the video camera." Sheriff Lindsey pointed to the camera in the corner of the room.

She peered at the camera and gave her full name.

"This is District Attorney Lange. He is sitting in on

this discussion to determine if we have enough evidence against you for a formal arrest." Sheriff Lindsey softened his gaze. "Do you understand your rights as they were read to you last night?"

She nodded.

"Could you answer verbally, please?" Sheriff Lindsey asked.

"Yes, I do."

"We'd like to hear your side of the story about how your husband ended up buried in a trench." Sheriff Lindsey placed a photo of Arnie Bertram as he lay in the trench before forensics pulled him out.

She turned her face away. "I-I didn't put him there."

Hawke placed his forearms on the table and leaned forward. "I don't believe you killed him. I talked to your neighbors and they said you were baling all night long."

She nodded.

"But I don't understand how you wouldn't have noticed the blood at the side of the barn. Surely your dogs would have brought it to your attention. And then there is the fact that your husband's suitcase and personal items were all still in the house."

She started to open her mouth, and he held up a hand.

"I know you had separate beds. But in the four days, until we discovered he was missing, you never once used the bathroom with all of his stuff in it? And then there would be the freshly dug dirt on the trench. You, a farming woman, would have noticed the dirt had been disturbed."

He leaned back. Waiting.

She didn't say anything.

Sheriff Lindsey opened up the file and pulled out another photo. This one was of Ms. Bittle in the trench. "What about this body found under your husband's. Any idea how she ended up in the same trench?"

She didn't even look at that photo. Her hands began wringing and an eyelid twitched.

The sheriff started to say something. Hawke touched his arm and asked, "Did Ms. Bittle come to the farm to ask you why you were holding up the sale?"

Laurel slowly brought her gaze up to his.

He continued, "She did. She came to the farm. Said Arnie wanted to sell the property but wouldn't without your agreement. Was that all it took for you to lash out at her?"

The woman's head vibrated back and forth. "She said Arnie was excited to sell the farm and go traveling." A lopsided smile appeared on her lips. "Travel? Do you know how many years he's talked about traveling? But did he help with the farming so we could possibly set aside money for that? No!" She slapped a hand on the table causing the D.A. to startle.

"He could sell the farm without your consent, couldn't he? Your name isn't on the deed." Hawke was guessing at this but it made sense of why she'd be worried he would sell the place out from under her.

"He inherited it right before we married, but he never had my name added to the deed. It was almost as if he knew one day he'd want to sell and I wouldn't." She shifted her gaze to Lange. "Isn't there some law that after a person works the ground for so long the property becomes theirs?"

"You would have that as a case if you hadn't had

your husband's permission to farm the land. Since you just confessed that he let you do all the work, you can't use that as a reason to take over the property." D.A. Lange relaxed in his seat for the first time since the woman entered the room.

"Damn him! Damn his lazy ass!" She glared at the D.A. as if he were the husband she was cussing out.

Hawke cleared his throat, garnering her attention. "What did Myra Bittle say that resulted in you hitting her?"

"I told her Arnie wouldn't sell without my agreeing. And that woman said, she already had his signature and he'd invited her to go with him." Laurel's eyes narrowed. "I wasn't about to lose my farm and my husband to that skinny woman. I picked up a two-by-four and let her have it." Her hands shook. "Arnie showed up, and there I was standing over that woman with a board in my hands. He asked me what I'd done. We got in an argument." Tears slid down the side of her face. "He said he wasn't planning on going anywhere with anyone but me. He said the woman was lying about that. And he'd only talked to her about what the place was worth. He hadn't agreed to sell." She stared at Hawke. "He told me to go in and rest, he'd take care of her."

"When I saw the fresh dirt in the trench when I came outside later that night, I knew what he'd done with her. He didn't tell me. I didn't see him again."

Hawke glanced at the sheriff and D.A. If Dr. Vance was correct with her assumption the woman had died of asphyxiation, Mrs. Bertram didn't kill her. Arnie Bertram did by putting her in the trench. Laurel could be held on assault charges but not murder.

D.A. Lange motioned for them to go out of the room. All three stood and exited.

Out in the hall, Lange shook his head. "I don't think she killed the woman or the man. I can't make murder charges stick."

Sheriff Lindsey nodded.

"Looks like we're back to figuring out who wanted Arnie dead. I plan to talk to his best friend tonight when I get done with my patrol." He settled his gaze on Lindsey. "It wouldn't hurt to look into the Kamps' financials. They were talking with Ed Newton this morning at the Rusty Nail. Seemed odd they would be befriending the neighbor who wants to purchase the Bertram place."

"I'll get on that. Anything else?" The sheriff pulled a small notepad out of his breast pocket.

"See if you can dig up information on Myra Bittle. And you know, it wouldn't hurt to have more information on the Newtons."

"I'll get someone to check into all of that." Sheriff Lindsey headed to his office.

Lange faced Hawke. "Who do you think looks good for the Bertram homicide?"

Hawke shrugged. "I'm not sure. I'll let you know if I get any inklings. The facts didn't add up for Mrs. Bertram to have killed him but the evidence all pointed to her. Which makes me wonder if she wasn't set up for her husband's death…" Hawke started down the hall and spun back around. "I'll let you know what I find." He pivoted and headed out of the County Office.

The sooner he made his rounds of the north country, the sooner he could talk with Milton Freyer and Alfred Zahn. He had a feeling the two men who grew up with Arnie would know more about his past life than anyone else.

《》《》《》

It was after dark when he finished checking tags and licenses through the Sled Springs and Wenaha areas. He came down Promise Road and crossed the highway to Diamond Prairie. His stomach was grumbling but it would have to wait. He'd listed several questions he wanted to ask Milton Freyer and his wife.

At the Freyer farm, he parked and waited for the two dogs to come out and greet him. Their barking would rouse the people inside the house. It was after eight and he wanted them to have time to gather themselves if they were sitting around watching television in their pajamas.

He didn't like embarrassing people. It made it harder to get their cooperation.

Milton opened the door as Hawke walked up to the porch. "Trooper, what are you doing out so late?"

"I have some more questions about Arnie Bertram. Do you mind if I come in?" Hawke waited for an invitation.

"Come on in. The missus is putting on a pot of coffee."

Hawke didn't want any coffee on his empty stomach. He followed the man into the dining room. A plate of cupcakes sat in the middle of the table.

"Help yourself. Cheryl bakes more than we can eat." Milton took a seat at the head of the table.

Hawke sat to the left of the man and gladly plucked a cupcake from the plate. He had it half-eaten when Mrs. Freyer arrived with a pot of coffee and three cups.

"Thank you. These cupcakes are delicious," he

said, after chewing and swallowing the rest of the dessert.

"Thank you. They're made from scratch, not some box." She sat down opposite Milton.

"What kind of questions do you have for us?" the man asked.

"First. Have you heard we found Arnie's body?" Hawke wanted to make sure the people knew they weren't giving away any confidences by talking to him.

Milton nodded. A tear glistened in his eyes. "Heard they'd found him and Laurel was hauled off. Did she kill him?"

"She says she didn't. What I've determined through my investigation, I don't think she did. I would like to know everything you can tell me about Arnie. From the time he went to college and came back home. Possibly even his teen years."

Milton stared at him. "Why do you want to know that much history?"

"I need to know who would want him dead."

Chapter Seventeen

Milton shook his head. "I've been thinking on that myself the last few days. I can't think of a single person who hated Arnie enough to want him dead."

"You never know what can push someone to kill another. Tell me about Arnie in high school." Hawke pulled out his logbook to take notes.

"His family had a place just down the road from here. We'd ride the bus to school together and had most of the same classes." Milton glanced at his wife. "We all went to football games and basketball games together."

"You and Arnie weren't on the teams?" Hawke thought the large man would have been an excellent athlete.

"Too much work to do at home to be gone for practice and all the games. Not that I didn't want to, but..." He shrugged. "The farm came first."

"Same with Arnie?" Hawke asked, taking notes.

Mrs. Freyer laughed. "No. He didn't want to run and get sweaty. He'd work well enough on the farm with his father prodding him, but he never liked work of any kind."

"He read a lot. He said he went places in books." Milton shook his head. "I never took to reading. Just did what I had to for my schoolwork." The man raised a hand with one finger up. "Ed Newton used to give Arnie fits about his nose being in a book."

The woman shivered. "Ed was the biggest bully in school. Back then you just all ganged up on the bully and showed him some respect, but a month later he'd be back to his pushing people around. He was big for his age back then. He did all his growing in Junior High."

"Did they get into anything that carried over into their adult years?" Hawke asked.

"Not that I know of. I'm sure Arnie would have told me if they were having trouble." The man took a sip of his coffee and placed the mug on the table firmly. "They were having it out over that land. Ed believed it had been stolen from his family by Arnie's uncle. But I can tell you, Ed's family had to sell and Arnie's uncle had come back from the war with all his money saved up and bought it. He farmed it for fifty years until his death and then it went to Arnie. He was the only nephew the uncle had."

"Only nephew? Were there nieces? Any that might take exception to Arnie getting the land?" This day and age, he could see an angry female cousin thinking the lazy Arnie didn't deserve to get the farm just because he was male.

Mrs. Freyer nodded. "Trudy moved to Portland

after high school, and Arnie's sister, Carla, was never interested in farming. I can't see either of them wanting the farm. Or caring what Arnie did with it."

Hawke wrote down the names even though these two, who were knowledgeable about Arnie's family, didn't seem to think the women were a threat.

"What about college? That's where Arnie met Laurel?" Hawke wondered about someone as lazy as Arnie going to college.

"Arnie went to Eastern Oregon College in La Grande. He figured doing schoolwork was less work than helping out on the farm." Milton grinned. "I have never seen anyone as adverse to work as Arnie."

"And yet, you two were friends." Hawke studied the man.

"He was like a brother to me. He might not have liked physical labor, but he was smart and listened when a person had a problem. All those books he read helped him see things beyond this county and the small lives the rest of us lived." He glanced at his wife. "We cherished his friendship."

"Did he ever speak of anyone at college who gave him trouble?" Hawke wanted to get to Alfred Zahn's before it was too late.

"No one that gave him trouble. He only talked about Laurel. He brought her home his second year for Thanksgiving. She was pretty and sweet and seemed to hang on his every word." Mrs. Freyer smiled. "They were a nice couple. Then that spring, his uncle died and they both left college to run the farm."

Milton cleared his throat. "More like they made decisions about the farm and Laurel did all the work."

"Even from the beginning?" Hawke knew in his

culture, when his ancestors still roamed this area, it was the job of the women to gather roots and berries and do any cultivating of crops. The men hunted and fished. But with the white world, the men insisted on being the money makers and taking on the harder chores.

"Yes. It was almost like they'd made the decision before they moved back here." Milton held his wife's gaze.

None of this was helping Hawke get any closer to what he wanted to know. "Thank you for your time. I'd like to have a chat with Alfred before he calls it a night."

"You might as well forget going to see him. He goes to bed at eight and gets up at four in the morning. Old farming habit he hasn't kicked." Milton stood.

"Then I guess I'll be visiting with him tomorrow. If you think of anything that might help, call me."

The couple nodded, and Hawke let himself out. The drive home had his mind spinning. If this wasn't about revenge or anger with Arnie, could it be aimed at Laurel?

《》《》《》

Monday, Hawke fed his animals and walked over to the Trembley's house. He planned to get breakfast in Eagle at Al's Café to speak to Alfred Zahn before heading out to check for hunters. But he had a couple of questions for Darlene.

Darlene opened the back door as Hawke walked up. "Morning, Hawke. I've learned a few more things."

"I had some questions for you." He stepped through the doorway and into the kitchen that smelled of bacon, huckleberry muffins, and coffee. His stomach rumbled.

"Good thing I made extra of everything," Darlene said, as Herb walked through the back door.

"Smells good in here. Morning, Hawke." The man walked over and grabbed a mug off a hook and poured a cup of coffee, placing it in front of Hawke.

"Thank you. Good morning. I hadn't planned to stay for breakfast, but I hate to see food go to waste." Hawke sipped the coffee as Darlene placed a plate of steaming muffins on the table.

"You might as well eat as we talk." She sat down at her usual place, and they all filled their plates with the bacon, muffins, and scrambled eggs.

After pulling a muffin apart, Darlene said, "I discovered why no one could say for sure what Myra's last name was. She was a foster child who spent time in several homes while she lived in the county. She was eventually adopted by the Thomas family who are the ones that moved and didn't come back."

Hawke chewed on a piece of bacon, taking this news in. "So there isn't a cousin still living in the county?"

"At least not blood. There are several different families still here who are related to the Thomases. I can get you their names if you'd like. Selma is big on genealogy for the founding families of the county. The Thomases came here because of the Smiths." Darlene bit into her cooled muffin.

Hawke had eaten a muffin while the woman talked. "That might come in handy." He sipped his coffee and broke into what he wanted to ask, "Can you think of anyone who would want to cause Laurel Bertram trouble?"

The couple exchanged glances, and Darlene spoke

first. "Not really. I mean the first few years she and Arnie were married, she got out and attended meetings and met people. She wasn't one to chat and drink coffee. But she had some good ideas for fundraisers."

"Why did she quit going to the meetings?" Hawke wondered if there was one person who bullied her like Ed Newton did her husband.

"I'm not sure. I think just because she took on more and more of the farm work. I did see some other women try to talk to her in the grocery store and she walked away as if she didn't even want to be friends with anyone." Darlene picked up her mug of coffee with a perplexed expression on her face.

Hawke could see where the outgoing woman in front of him wouldn't understand someone who was perfectly happy to be without friends.

"It was Arnie who came to the school meetings, booster club, and attended the school activities Jenny was in," Herb added.

Hawke chewed on a piece of bacon, and said, "It's like the roles were reversed with Arnie and Laurel."

Darlene nodded. "Yes, in a way. But Arnie didn't do any housework. Poor Laurel had to do the inside work as well as the outside. That is until Jenny was old enough to clean house and help with the cooking."

This caught his attention. "Did Jenny mind doing her mother's chores?"

"I don't think so…" Darlene stood. "I'll ask our Sarah. They were in the same grade in school." The woman walked over to the phone hanging on the wall and dialed.

"Are you thinking whoever killed Arnie did it to get back at Laurel?" Herb asked.

"I don't know. But I can't find anyone who wanted Arnie dead. The only ones who gain from his death are Laurel and Jenny."

"You're sure it wasn't Laurel?" Herb said, an accusing lilt to his voice.

Hawke peered at his landlord. "You think she did it? If so, she had to have found someone to drive the baler all night while she drove Arnie's pickup to Freezeout." He'd thought of the accomplice angle before. "Or someone drove the pickup and used the motorcycle with her knowledge while she baled…"

Darlene sat back down at the table. "I don't think she would have killed Arnie. She might have been angry with him for not helping out, but in the beginning, they were very much in love."

"They were sleeping in separate rooms," Hawke said, raising an eyebrow. To him that meant they weren't getting along.

"Some couples do that because one snores or talks in their sleep, keeping the other one awake." Darlene refilled his mug with coffee.

"This was more than that. Laurel didn't even notice his suitcase or toiletries were still there for four days. She was surprised to see them when we searched the house." Hawke knew that hadn't been an act. It had been genuine surprise on her face. The same as when he'd said the body in the trench was Arnie's. She'd expected them to pull out Myra, not her husband.

"Maybe they had a fight?" Darlene offered.

Hawke peered at the woman. "Why are you sticking up for their lack of intimacy in their marriage?"

"Because I remember when they first moved here. They were inseparable and very much in love. I don't think they started acting differently until after Jenny started school. Then I noticed how they didn't attend anything together, and Arnie always made the excuse that Laurel was busy at home." Darlene sighed. "Maybe I'm just being an old romantic."

"What did you learn about Jenny from Sarah?" Hawke asked, pulling the woman back to the present.

"She said, Jenny did feel her mother put the farm over everything, including herself. That's why she tried so hard at being good at everything, to make her mom take notice." Darlene sipped her coffee. "And that Laurel didn't even go to Jenny's bridal shower but did make it to the wedding."

Hawke scooped the last of his eggs onto his fork with half of his third muffin. "Did she say if Laurel didn't go to the bridal shower because she didn't like who her daughter was marrying?"

"No. Apparently, Laurel thought Reed was a good catch. He has been ambitious his whole life. Just not very lucky with all of his endeavors."

He wondered if it was that poor luck that had caused Reed Kamp to perhaps kill his father-in-law and frame his mother-in-law so the farm would go to Jenny and they could sell it to fund the hemp farm?

"Hawke, you're losing your eggs," Herb said.

Hawke shook out of his thoughts and re-scooped the eggs. "I need to go speak to Alfred Zahn." He shoved the bite into his mouth, chewed, drank the last of his coffee, and stood.

"What did I say that has you flying out of here?" Darlene asked.

He grinned at her. "Just a hunch. Thanks for breakfast."

"Anytime," Darlene said, waving him out the door.

Chapter Eighteen

By the time Hawke got to Eagle, his best bet to find Alfred was to go by Al's Café. He drove around the block, noticing that all the vehicles of the men who met here every morning were parked together. It would have been better to talk to Alfred alone, however, since they were both here, he'd find a way to talk to the man alone.

He entered the café and walked straight to the table where the men sat. Alfred spotted him first. The old man winced.

Dave Tilden craned his neck. His frown didn't help the mood when Hawke approached the table.

"Good morning, gentlemen." Hawke grabbed a chair from a nearby table and sat beside Alfred. "I have some more questions. I'm sure you have all heard by now that we found Arnie's body." He glanced around the table. Their solemn faces said they truly missed their friend.

"We heard," Cy said. "And they took Laurel in for it. I can't believe she'd kill him just because he wanted to sell the farm."

"They fought but they still liked each other," Deke added.

Hawke shifted his gaze to Alfred. "Is that true? They still liked one another?"

Alfred glared at him. The old man had practically told him Arnie and Myra were hitting the sheets. Yet, no one else believed it.

When the man didn't offer up anything, Hawke turned his attention to the other three men. "Laurel didn't kill Arnie. The evidence leans toward someone who is trying to make it look like she did. Any thoughts on that?" He felt Alfred shift in his seat, Hawke swung his gaze back to the older man. "Know anyone who would want to get the farm, by any means?"

"That would be Ed Newton," Deke said.

"Or that son-in-law," Cy added.

"Why Ed?" Hawke asked Deke.

"He has told everyone who would listen that Arnie's farm belonged to his family and he aimed to get it back." Deke glanced around the table and heads bobbed.

"I heard Ed doesn't have the money to buy it." Hawke waited for that to sink in.

"The Newtons have lots of money. Mary inherited a ton of money about ten years ago. My wife says she's talked about how she doesn't let Ed have a cent of it." Dave nodded his head.

Hawke hoped this information came up when a deputy did an investigation into the Newtons. "If Mary won't let him have a cent, how would he pay for the farm?"

Dave stared at him. "I guess he'd talk her into it."

"What do you think?" Hawke turned the conversation to Alfred.

"Mary would put her money in real estate. She's always been the brains of those two."

Hawke nodded. That's what he'd figured. "What about Reed Kamp? Why do you say he wanted Arnie gone?" He studied Cy.

The man sat up straighter and peered into his eyes. "Because he has both those women, Jenny and Laurel, wrapped around his finger."

"Both? Then why didn't he just talk Laurel into selling like Arnie wanted?" Hawke continued to watch Cy.

"Because he didn't want them to sell it and use up the money traveling. He wanted the money for his business." Cy stared at him as if he pitied Hawke's slowness.

"You're saying Reed got rid of Arnie so he could get Laurel to sell the farm and give him and Jenny the money?" Hawke glanced around at the others. They didn't all seem as on board with this as they were with Ed Newton wanting the land.

He changed the subject. "I talked to Mr. and Mrs. Freyer last night. They said they couldn't think of one person who would want to harm Arnie or Laurel. Do you all agree?"

This time the men exchanged glances and nodded.

"I can't think of anyone who would want harm to come to either of them," Alfred said.

"Except maybe Ed Newton?" Hawke offered.

"That would be the only person. He's harassed

Arnie since they were in school." Alfred's face grew red and scrunched up in anger. "He was a bully then and he's an even bigger bully now."

"Were any of you at the water board meeting the Wednesday night before Arnie was leaving for the conference?" Hawke decided it was time to check out the Newtons alibi.

"Are you talking about the Eagle Water Board meeting?" Dave asked.

"Yes."

"I stepped in for the first hour. They were just jawing on about the same thing for an hour so I left." Disgust disfigured his face.

"Did you happen to see both the Newtons there?" While Dave might be able to say they were there, he wouldn't be able to speak to when they left if he only stuck around for an hour.

"I remember seeing their fancy car Mary bought when she came into her inheritance. I don't remember seeing them. But I stayed at the back of the room, to sneak out if it got boring."

"You could talk to Aggie Traner. She is the secretary for the board and would know who came and went," Alfred offered.

Hawke pulled out his logbook and added the name. "Thanks. Any idea how to get ahold of her?"

Alfred rattled off a phone number.

Hawke studied him.

"She's my daughter." Alfred pushed his cup to the middle of the table. "I got flowers to water. See you boys tomorrow."

Hawke stood as well. "Thanks for the information." He walked out the door behind Alfred and followed him to his older model Ford pickup.

"I had the feelin' you came in there specifically looking for me," Alfred said, opening his vehicle's door and sitting on the seat facing Hawke.

"What more can you tell me about Arnie when he was young. Did he date anyone before he left for college?" There had to be someone who had it out for Laurel.

"Didn't Milton tell you all of that? I was in 'Nam when they were playing hooky from high school." The man scowled.

"I didn't think to ask him that until this morning." Hawke hadn't thought it was necessary to know all of that, but now he wondered if the past played into this more than the present. And now he realized Alfred couldn't help him with those questions. He'd known the man was older but most people who grew up in the county knew everyone else's history. Especially since he was a friend Arnie went to when he was avoiding work and his wife.

"What can you tell me about Myra Bittle? I've learned she was a foster kid who lived here until she was twelve. She was adopted by someone in the Thomas family and they moved away. Ring any bells?"

Alfred stared at him. "Again, she was younger than me and Arnie. I doubt he ran into her in grade school."

"But you knew Ed and Mary Newton when you were in school?" Hawke questioned.

"Ed was Arnie and Milton's age, but I knew him. We all lived in the same area. Ed was always getting other people in trouble with his bullying."

"Were Mary and Ed together in high school?" Hawke asked.

"I don't know. That's when I was away fighting for their right to whatever they wanted by keeping the Reds from taking over the world." Alfred spun his body to sit facing forward in his vehicle. "And I can't tell you a thing about Laurel. She moved here after marrying Arnie."

"Sorry to have bothered you." Hawke walked away feeling like the man was holding something back, but he couldn't figure out what it was.

Chapter Nineteen

Hawke called Aggie Traner. When no one picked up the call, he left a voicemail asking her to call him.

As he pulled away from the café, he received a call about a wreck at Minam and headed out Highway 82 to see if he could assist.

Wenaha, Sled Springs, and Chesnimnus would have to wait. He was the closest LEO. He enjoyed being part of the Fish and Wildlife Division. When fulfilling the other half of his badge — State Trooper — and it involved medical assistance, and in some instances, the medical examiner, he thought about retirement.

He turned on his lights and headed out of Eagle. Four miles into the canyon, he came around a bend in the road and found vehicles all over the highway. A couple blasts of the siren and the cars cleared a path.

Four hundred feet ahead on another curve, a small car was under a semi-trailer and another car was smashed against the side of the canyon. The second vehicle was lucky to have run into the dirt wall and not the river on the other side of the road.

Someone was screaming. Hawke hopped out of his vehicle and ran over to where several people stood around the car under the trailer. He spoke into his mic on his shoulder. "This is Hawke. Dispatch send EMTs, a fire truck, an OSP crash reconstruction tech, and I'll need assistance with traffic."

"Copy."

"I'll be there in ten," Corcoran's voice came over the radio.

"Copy," Hawke replied, taking his hand from the mic and walking closer to the group. The screaming had diminished. "What do we have and what happened?"

A man, dressed in overalls, moved away from the trailer. "I came around this corner and these two…" he motioned to the car under his trailer and the one up against the canyon wall, "came at me in both lanes. This one ended up under my trailer and that one, made a dive that way."

"I'll need your information and statement after we assess the situation." Hawke parted the people and moved closer. He didn't want to look. From the peeled back roof and the blood spatter, he had a feeling he knew what he'd see.

"Help. Help me," a weak female voice said.

He couldn't believe someone had lived through this. "I'm State Trooper Hawke. Are you hurt?" he asked, crouching and walking under the trailer to look in.

His stomach roiled and he swung his face away from the sight, hitting the side of his head on the undercarriage of the trailer. "Shit!" The pain in his face overrode the urge to vomit.

The person in the driver's seat wasn't the one asking for help. He backed out and moved to the other side of the vehicle. He crouched and walked under. There he found a young woman, with blood splattered across her blonde hair and pale face, her eyes wide and begging.

"I don't want to look at him anymore. Get me out," she pleaded.

Hawke didn't blame her. "Are you hurt anywhere?"

"I can move everything, but I'm stuck."

He called back to the people at the side of the trailer. "Can someone get a blanket out of my truck? It's in the back seat in a box."

"Sure thing!" someone yelled.

"What's your name?" Hawke asked, to keep the woman from going into shock.

"Mara Applegate. I told Zach not to pass. We weren't in a race to get anywhere. He laughed and the next thing I saw a truck coming and slid down in the seat. I didn't want to watch us hit it." She started shaking.

"Do you have that blanket?" he hollered back at the group.

"Here it is," the trucker walked toward him bent over, but he kept his face turned from the car.

"Thanks." Hawke tucked the blanket around the young woman's upper body. He glanced back at the trucker. "Can you talk to Mara while I do something?"

"I guess," the trucker said.

"Mara," He glanced at the trucker. "What's your

name?"

"Norm."

"Mara, Norm is going to stay here with you. Why don't you tell him about your favorite place in Wallowa County?" Hawke nodded to Norm and moved around the smashed-in front end of the car as the girl told the trucker about seeing deer walking around Wallowa Lake State Park. He didn't want to look at the decapitated body any more than Mara did. He took off his coat, turned it inside out, and draped it over the body. Not something forensics would like, but it was the decent thing to do with the young woman stuck in the car next to it.

He moved back around the front. Norm was telling Mara a story about ice fishing on the lake. Hawke gave him a thumbs up and headed out from under the trailer to make calls and check on the other vehicle. By the time he'd called Spruel and the D.A.'s Office, Corcoran had arrived.

Hawke called dispatch requesting the Medical Examiner, Dr. Vance, and help from ODOT to stop traffic coming into the county. Corcoran finished talking to the driver of the other vehicle and walked toward Hawke.

They met in the middle of the road where no one milling around could hear them.

"We have a decapitated driver and a young woman stuck in the car under the trailer."

Corcoran grimaced. "Glad I didn't have to see that." He tipped his head to the other vehicle. "He says the driver in the peeled back car was passing him right before the corner."

"Yeah, that's what I heard from the young woman

and the trucker. He passed right before the turn."

"Jackass," Corcoran said.

"Dead Jackass," Hawke amended as the sirens announced the EMTs and fire truck arriving.

"Take photos of the car under the trailer. We're not going to be able to move traffic until they get the young woman out of the car and the crash tech does his thing." He glanced up at the cars lined up going in and out of the county. "I'll apprise the EMTs. When you get done with photos, let the drivers know this could take hours."

Corcoran nodded and headed toward the car under the trailer, pulling his phone out of his pocket.

Hawke walked over to the ambulance that had parked beside the semi. It was his favorite pair of EMTs, Roxie and Bonnie.

"What did you catch?" Roxie asked as he walked to the back of the vehicle where they were pulling out their gear.

"Driver under the trailer is dead. The young woman in the passenger seat is in shock but said she can move everything. She might be just stuck in the vehicle."

"I'll take a look at the corpse," Bonnie said.

"I covered him with my coat," Hawke said.

She stopped and stared at him. "That's not protocol."

"The young woman next to him has his blood all over her and was staring at a body with no head."

"Oh." Bonnie shook her shoulders and headed to that side of the vehicle. Roxie followed the fire chief under the car.

The trucker came out, and Hawke squat at the edge of the trailer watching Roxie take Mara's vitals and the fire chief decide what to do.

George Heely, the Alder Fire Chief, crouch walked out from under the trailer. "I think the best way to get the woman loose is to put a tarp over her, tell her to stay down, and try to pull the car out."

Hawke nodded. It sounded like a solid plan to him. "I'll see if there's a tow truck on the way and get photos." He grasped his mic. "Dispatch, this is Hawke."

"Copy."

"Has a tow truck been dispatched?"

"It should be fifteen out from your location."

"Copy."

"I heard that," Chief Heely said. "We'll get things ready."

Hawke took photos from all angles and across the road as the fire truck crew went to work being prepared for a fuel leak and looping tow straps around the vehicle's back axle. Bonnie had gone over to Roxie's side of the car. The two were keeping Mara talking and assessing her injuries.

He glanced over his shoulder at the person in the other damaged vehicle. Bonnie should go take a look at him. Hawke wandered to the side of the trailer out of the way of the firefighters and called to Bonnie.

"Yeah?" she responded.

"Someone should check out the other driver across the road," he said.

She walked bent over out from under the trailer. "You didn't mention him before." She narrowed her eyes. "I could have looked at him instead of the headless body."

"I just remembered him. I've been dealing with the truck injuries too."

166

"Okay, I'll give you that." She carried her bag over to the car. The man sat in the driver's seat facing outwards as she checked his vitals and asked questions.

The tow truck arrived. Fire Chief Heely explained what they had planned and in twenty minutes the car was out from under the trailer. Using the jaws of life, the door was popped open and Mara was placed on a gurney and hustled into the ambulance.

"Criminy!" One of the firefighters exclaimed and jumped back from the vehicle.

"No wonder that poor girl was so frightened," Heeley said. When others started to move in his direction, he kept them all back. By now Dr. Vance had arrived. She walked up to the vehicle and told Deputy Corcoran to take photos as she examined the body.

Corcoran aimed his camera at the backseat of the passenger side and his body shook.

Hawke guessed the dead man's head was either on the seat or the floorboards. He walked over to the truck driver and this time pulled his logbook out of his pocket. "Tell me your full name and exactly what happened."

The trucker repeated what he'd told Hawke before.

His phone rang as he was finishing up with the driver of the other car. He answered, "Hawke."

"Umm, is this State Trooper Hawke?" a female voice asked.

"Yes, and you are?"

"Aggie Traner. You left a message for me to call you." The trepidation in her voice made him wish he'd left more than a 'please call me' message.

"Your dad, Alfred, gave me your number—"

"Did something happen to him?" she cut in.

167

"No. I was talking to him, and the others at Al's Café, about Arnie Bertram."

"Oh, I see. And why did he give you my number? I rarely see… I mean saw, Arnie."

"I mentioned the Newtons told me they were at the water meeting the night before Arnie disappeared, but no one at Al's could say if the couple had or hadn't been at the meeting. Your dad told me you were the secretary of the water board and would know."

"Oh, yes." Relief softened her words. "They were there. Ed spoke about how he would be a good candidate for the board. We are having elections at the next meeting to fill a vacant spot. However, I did see Mary on the phone toward the end of the meeting. Then she walked over, said something to Ed, and they left."

"Do you know what time that was?" Hawke added this information to his logbook.

"I believe between eight and eight-thirty," Ms. Traner said with confidence.

"And they left quickly after Mrs. Newton received a call?" He wanted to make sure, so he could get their phone records.

"Yes. As soon as she hung up the phone, she walked over to Ed, said something, and they left."

"Why did you notice all of this?" He was curious that she would keep such a close eye on the two.

There was silence for almost a full minute before she sighed and said, "Mike Dunn, the water president, asked me to keep an eye on Mary while he kept an eye on Ed. We'd heard rumors they were bribing people to vote for Ed."

Hawke smiled. Scandal in the water board. "Is it common knowledge that Ed will pay to get on a board?"

"Not always pay. He bullies or coerces people to see things his way. That's what we were afraid of if he gets on the board. But some people will play with the devil if it gets them what they want."

Hawke thought it was interesting that she should use the word devil while speaking about Ed Newton. "Thank you for your information."

"You're welcome. If you see Laurel, tell her everyone knows she wouldn't have killed Arnie." The woman sounded sincere.

"Who is everyone?" Hawke asked, finding it interesting that this woman was sticking up for Laurel.

"Most of Eagle. We all know that she groused about Arnie's laziness, but she knew that when she married him. She just likes to have something to complain about. Arnie would laugh about it when he came to visit Dad when I still lived at home. It was like a game they played."

Hawke knew of couples who were happiest when they were arguing with their spouse, but he'd never understood the sense of it. "Thank you for all the information." He ended the call and noticed the crash tech had arrived. He walked over and filled the man in on what he'd come upon as another deputy arrived.

Spruel called wanting the details.

"I'll make sure ODOT has the roadblocks up to keep more traffic from coming down the grade."

"That would be a good idea. Most of the out-of-county traffic has turned around."

Checking his watch, Hawke sighed. The day was going to be nearly gone by the time he, as the first responding officer, could leave.

Chapter Twenty

Hawke found his bloody coat draped over the hood of his vehicle when he walked over to get in. He tossed it in the bed of the pickup and slid behind the wheel. After calling in that he was clear, he headed to the office.

Driving through Eagle a thought came to him. He pulled over and searched his phone for the number for Wallowa Valley Realty. He found the website and touched the phone number. If nothing else, he could leave his name and number for the owner to call.

Two rings and a young woman said, "Wallowa Valley Realty, this is Gail, how may I help you?"

"Gail, this is State Trooper Hawke."

"How can I help you?"

"Who would I need to speak to about the properties Myra Bittle was selling?"

A sharp intake of breath nearly pulled the hair out of his ears. "I heard about her death. What is wrong with people?"

Hawke wondered the same thing every day. "Who would I talk to about the properties she represented?"

"That would be Darren. He owns the realty."

"Is he in?" Hawke asked.

"No, but he should be before we close at six."

"Can you put me on his appointment schedule?"

"Sure. Trooper Hawke for five-thirty."

"Thank you." He'd have just enough time to return to Winslow, write up warrant requests for the Newton phone records and financial reports and see if forensics had come up with anything yet.

«»«»«»

Hawke stood in the reception area of the Wallowa Valley Realty office waiting for Darren Ault to arrive back before the end of the day, according to the receptionist.

"I can't believe Myra is gone. She was so full of energy," Gail said, peering over her monitor at him.

"Did she have a lot of clients?" Hawke asked.

"Quite a few." She pointed to a bulletin board on a wall. "She has been the highest-selling realtor six times since she started here over a year ago."

"Is that when she moved back here from California?" Hawke asked.

The woman frowned. "No. I think she was here a few years before she decided to get her realtor license."

"Did the other realtors get along with her?"

"Of course! We all get along in this office."

The door opened and a man in his forties, dressed in slacks and a polo shirt, walked in. "Any messages, Gail?"

"No, but State Trooper Hawke would like to talk to

you. I put him in as your five-thirty."

Hawke stood as the man's head rotated as if surveying the premises for an intruder.

"Mr. Ault, I'm Trooper Hawke." Hawke extended his hand to shake.

The man took one step closer, grasped his hand, and released. "Come on into my office."

Once they were both in the office and the door was closed, Ault asked, "What is this about?"

"Myra Bittle. I'd like to see the properties she was working with before her death."

"We can do that." He reached for the phone on his desk and pressed a button. "Gail, would you please bring all of Myra's property files into my office?"

He replaced the phone and smiled. "Gail will bring in the records."

"Thank you. Did you know Myra was trying to get Arnie Bertram to sell his property out in Leap?"

The man shook his head. "I've never heard of this Bertram."

Hawke studied the man. "Do you read the local paper? Listen to the local radio station?"

Ault tapped a pen on the desktop. "Oh, it was a Bertram that was found buried in a trench on his property."

"Myra was found underneath him." Hawke didn't think it was a matter of the man not paying attention to the local news. Why was he avoiding knowledge of the Bertram property and that was where Myra had been killed?

"Yes, of course. No, I had no idea she was poaching that property."

"Poaching?" Hawke asked.

"Trying to get the job of selling it before anyone else."

"It was known that Arnie wanted to sell his farm?" Hawke asked.

"Well, no. But if she was talking to him about selling, then he must have wanted to."

Hawke shook his head. "How would that make it poaching if no one else, including Arnie, knew they wanted to sell?"

"Forget I said that."

The door opened, and Gail placed half a dozen folders on Ault's desk. "That's all I could find in her desk."

"Myra had a desk here?" Hawke asked. He hadn't thought about the woman having a desk or office.

"Yes. It's down the hall. Second door to the left," Gail said, ducking out of the office.

Ault picked up each folder and scanned it before handing it over to Hawke. There were four folders on farms like the Bertram's and two were large houses on Wallowa Lake. It appeared Myra hadn't dealt with properties with small sale prices. The odd thing, there wasn't a folder for Arnie Bertram's property.

"Why isn't there a folder here for the Bertram place?" he asked.

"It could have been with her or in her car. Gail is very thorough, I'm sure she brought you all of Myra's files." Mr. Ault seemed to be dismissing him.

It was apparent the man wouldn't miss Myra. Was that because she had managed to claim the more profitable properties? Hawke stood. "I'd like to take a look around Myra's desk."

"Go ahead. We'll be cleaning the room out for a

new realtor." The man didn't even look up as Hawke stood.

Out in the hallway, he walked farther down the hall and opened the second door on the left. The room was neat. It looked like the woman didn't spend a lot of time in the office. But it wouldn't hurt to take a look around. As he'd talked with Ault, Hawke realized no one had mentioned finding Myra's car at the farm. He hadn't noticed it either.

Pulling out his phone, he called Sheriff Lindsey.

"Sheriff Lindsey," the man answered.

"Sheriff, this is Hawke. Did anyone find Myra Bittle's car at the Bertram farm?"

"No, we looked up and down the road and couldn't find any abandoned cars. When I asked Mrs. Bertram, she hadn't noticed any either."

"Can you send a deputy around to Myra's house and see if her car is there?" Hawke wondered how the vehicle would have been returned to her home.

"I can do that." The call ended.

Hawke wandered around to the back of the desk and pulled out drawers. Only two had anything in them. Mostly brochures for the business, a box of business cards with her name, and a calculator. There wasn't a single personal item in the room. Had she planned on going somewhere and had taken out all of the personal items, or had she never taken the time to make the small space hers?

The monitor on the desk came to life when he shut the drawer hard. No box for a password popped up. Hawke clicked the mouse and the website for the business appeared. He clicked through the pages. Nothing of interest. She didn't appear to keep any files on the computer. He spun the chair toward the file cabinets. One drawer had an empty space wide enough for the files Gail had brought to Mr. Ault's office. The next drawer had more of the realty's brochures, and the third drawer had a makeup kit, an extra set of clothes, and a pair of shoes. Those were the only personal belongings in the room.

He closed the drawer and exited. At the receptionist's desk, he asked, "What kind of vehicle did Myra drive?"

"A compact SUV. I think it was a Ford. It's red. That's about all I know about her car." Gail stared at him for a few seconds. "Do you think Mrs. Bertram killed her like the newspaper says?"

"I'm not at liberty to discuss the case."

She studied him for several seconds, and asked, "Who do you think called in and said she was sick and going on vacation?"

Hawke peered at her. "Were you the one who took the call?"

"Yes."

"Did you recognize her voice?"

"I don't know. She said she was sick and was going to take some time off per her doctor's orders. I guess at the time, I figured she sounded different because she was sick. Now I wonder if I could recognize the voice if I heard it again."

"Don't say that to anyone, in case it gets back to the person who made the call." He studied her. "You would be putting yourself in danger."

She swallowed and nodded.

Hawke walked out to his vehicle. It was time to do a more thorough search of Myra's home. He headed there and called Sheriff Lindsey.

"Sheriff, it's Hawke. Have you been able to serve the warrants and get the information about the Newtons and Kamps?"

"I have a deputy serving them right now. I'll give you a buzz when it all arrives."

"Thanks." He ended the call and walked up to the house. There wasn't a car in the driveway. He walked around to the side of the garage, looking for a window to see if the red Ford was parked inside. And if it was, who would have driven the car here and parked it in the garage?

"A deputy was just here," a male voice said from behind him.

Hawke took his time facing the person. A head floated above the solid wooden fence. "I'm Trooper Hawke. Did you talk to the deputy?"

"I might have. Why are you here? I read in the paper Myra was killed. Any idea who did it?" the man asked.

"No. Are you her neighbor or just a Peeping Tom?" Hawke could be as abrasive as the man peering over the fence. From his demeanor and words, he wasn't going to be a witness who blabbed everything he knew.

"I'm her neighbor. You aren't winning any points with me by being sarcastic," the man said. But he didn't back away from the fence. He wanted to either say, or learn, something.

"Is Myra's car in her garage?" Hawke asked, waving a hand toward the building.

"It drove in there about eleven at night, a week ago Wednesday."

"Did you happen to see who was driving?" Hawke knew it couldn't have been Myra.

"A woman. I thought it was Myra. I didn't think anything more about it until I read in the paper about her death. Makes sense, though. I haven't seen her car go in or out since then."

"What made you think the woman was Myra if you didn't actually see her?" Hawke grasped onto that tidbit.

"She was small, like Myra. Her head came to the top of the seatback." The man's eyes widened. "Do you think I saw who killed her?"

"I don't know. But I'd keep that information to yourself, just in case."

The man nodded.

"Did Myra have many visitors?" Hawke was wondering who had wanted the woman dead. From the innuendo Alfred Zahn gave, it could have been the wife of someone the realtor had slept with. But if Arnie Bertram had put Myra in the trench and covered her up, who did he call to get rid of her car? It wasn't his wife. Could it have been his daughter?

"She had a few men come by now and then. And her boss. He'd drop by late at night."

Hawke made a mental note to ask Ault about his relationship with the woman. But only if it seemed to have anything to do with the murder. Which at this point, it didn't.

"What about women?" Hawke asked.

"Only her cousin that I knew of."

Ah ha, maybe he'd finally get a name for the illusive cousin. "Do you know the cousin's name?"

The man shook his head. "No. She drives a nice car

and is built a lot like Myra. But I was never introduced to her. I just asked Myra one day who the woman was who drove up in the fancy car and she said her cousin."

"Thank you for all of this information. Do you think I would have to contact the cousin to get into the house and take a look around?"

The man shrugged. "Her or you might ask Myra's boss. I've seen him let himself in with a key."

Chapter Twenty-one

Tuesday morning, Hawke slept in until seven, dressed, took care of his animals, and then he and dog headed to Alder for breakfast and to look at the records the sheriff had warranted.

To see what rumors he could pick up about the two deaths, Hawke decided to eat at the Treetop Café. Courthouse employees and local law enforcement were patrons of the café. Since their job was so close to the restaurant, they inevitably talked about what they were working on.

He entered and waved to the officers he knew. Some were city, some county. He also knew a few of the courthouse employees. Mort, the cook and owner of the place, waved at him as Hawke sat down at the counter.

Janelle, the abrasive waitress who snapped her gum and smelled of cigarettes, walked over and filled a cup with coffee. "No uniform? This your day off?" She held out a menu with the hand not pouring coffee.

He waved away the menu. "Yes, it is. I'll have two eggs over easy, sourdough toast, and crispy bacon, please."

"I'll get your order up." She walked away, and he turned slightly to scan the room again.

The door jingled, and Deputy Corcoran walked in. He spotted Hawke and strode across the room. He sat on the stool beside Hawke. "That was something else yesterday, wasn't it?"

Hawke nodded and sipped his coffee. He'd had to read a book before going to bed, to make himself tired enough to stop seeing the decapitated driver when he closed his eyes.

"Have you heard anything more on the Bertrams?" Hawke asked, to change the subject.

"They let the missus go yesterday. She was charged with assault of the Bittle woman and remanded to appear for her trial. Her daughter drove her home."

"Do you know if the information Sheriff Lindsey requested came in?" Hawke was anxious to look at the financial reports and phone records for the Newtons and Kamps.

"Yes, I think they had it all gathered last night before I went home."

Janelle placed Hawke's meal in front of him. He thanked her and dug in.

Corcoran ordered and sat sipping his coffee while Hawke downed his food.

"Must be your day off," Corcoran said, as Hawke finished and shoved money under his plate.

"Yeah."

The deputy smiled. "You doing anything fun?"

"Dog and I are going for a hike after I look over those records."

Corcoran stared at him. "You should get someone in your life to hang out with. Working this job twenty-four-seven isn't healthy."

Hawke shrugged. "I have Dog and my horses. With this job, I prefer animals to people on my days off." He stood and walked out of the café. He knew the men who had families relished their time away from work. He had only himself and his animals. And Dani when she wasn't up on the mountain, but he enjoyed his work and didn't mind doing it when he wasn't getting paid. He did agree if he had to spend every day like yesterday and the wreck, he wouldn't be working on his days off.

But finding a killer... It kept his mind sharp and his inquisitive nature busy.

He walked over to the Sheriff's Office.

The deputy at the front office glanced up when he entered. "Trooper Hawke, Sheriff Lindsey said you'd be in to look over these files." She stood and handed him two file folders. "You can use the visitor desk."

Hawke nodded and continued through the door to the offices in the building. He found the office kept open for State Police or other branches of law enforcement to use when they were in the county. Taking a seat at the desk, he opened the first file and spread the papers across the desk. The Kamp financials and phone records.

The hemp business was in the red for over twenty grand. They needed money. Would it come from the person Reed had been talking to for funding? Or had the man decided to do away with his father-in-law and wheedle the money out of his mother-in-law? Or even better, frame his mother-in-law for her husband's murder and the farm would go to Jenny. Reed could talk her into selling and solve their financial problems. After witnessing the couple with Ed Newton right after Laurel was taken in on murder charges, he reasoned Jenny could be swayed by her husband to use the money on their business.

He pulled out their phone records. Jenny only called her parents and one other number. Hawke made a notation to look it up. Reed called several people in the county and many outside the county. With his business, Hawke could understand the out-of-county numbers. It was the in-county ones that he was interested in. There were too many to write down. He circled them and wrote the one from Jenny's page on the bottom. He'd ask the deputy out front to look up the numbers for him.

He moved on to the folder on the Newtons. The bank records on them showed that Mrs. Newton was very wealthy. Not surprising after what others had said, the farm had its own account at the bank. It was doing okay, but barely hanging on.

He glanced at the phone records. The past six months the same dozen numbers were called from the house phone. Mrs. Newton's cell phone record showed she'd called and received calls from the same numbers over the last six months until a month ago when a new number popped up several times a day. It was familiar. Hawke scanned the Kamps' phone records. The number was on Reed's cell phone record.

The number had called Mrs. Newton at the time Aggie Traner said Mary Newton had received a call the night of the water board meeting. Who did this number belong to? He picked up his phone and dialed. A message came up that the voicemail was full. It didn't say who he'd called. Hawke circled the number three times. He wanted the deputy to look this number up first.

On Ed's cell phone record, Hawke recognized the Bertram's house phone number was called twice in the last month. Then Arnie Bertram's cell phone number was called several days in a row. The last call on the day Arnie was killed. He also noticed that Ed had called Reed Kamp many times after Arnie died.

This was all telling information.

He made copies of the files and took the sheets with the phone numbers he wanted to be traced up to the deputy at the front desk.

"Would you look up who belongs to these phone numbers, please. I'll pick them up tomorrow."

"Aren't today and tomorrow your days off?" she asked.

"Why is everyone worried about how I spend my days off?" He was beginning to think people paid too much attention to his life.

"Just repeating what I've heard the sheriff say." She ducked her head and began typing the numbers into her database.

Hawke grunted and left the building.

Dog greeted him and his mood changed. "Let's take a drive down to Eagle, I'd like to talk to Milton Freyer. Then we'll take the long way out to Leap. We'll grab some grub in Eagle and have a picnic on the way. Something isn't adding up about this double homicide." He started his vehicle, and Dog sat down in the passenger seat, ready to ride shotgun.

《》《》《》

At the Freyer farm, Hawke let Dog out to run around while he knocked on the door of the house. When he didn't get a response, he tried the barn and then began walking toward the fields. He found the couple picking up small hay bales with a noisy bale loader. Mrs. Freyer drove the two-ton truck with the loader attached to the side. She drove up beside a bale, it would go into the wide opening and then be hooked on a spike on the chain going around that pulled the bale up the loader to a metal landing pad. There Mr. Freyer grabbed the bale with two hay hooks and stacked it on the truck.

Few people hauled hay this way anymore. It required twice the labor and sweat than using an automated bale wagon.

Hawke waited for the truck to head his direction. He ambled over and stood at the end of where they would stop with a full load.

Dog shot off across the field after a rabbit with the Freyer's two dogs on his tail.

The truck rumbled to a stop in front of Hawke, silencing the loader and settling a blanket of stillness over the field.

"What now?" Mr. Freyer called from atop the stack on the truck.

"I have a few more questions," Hawke said.

"We need to take this load to the barn." Mr. Freyer climbed down the stack and unhooked the loader from the truck. "We'll stop and have a cold drink and talk to you before we unload it." He climbed in alongside his wife in the truck cab, and Mrs. Freyer slowly eased the truck forward toward the road leading to the house and barn.

Hawke whistled to Dog and followed the truckload of hay. By the time he and Dog arrived at the barn, Mr. Freyer stood by the truck and Mrs. Freyer was disappearing inside the house.

"Come around to the backyard," the man said, walking along the side of the house.

A large cottonwood and one weeping willow shaded the backyard, making it a haven from the late summer sun. A breeze rustled the leaves in the trees. A bird chirped and another squawked.

They each sat in a padded chair next to a wrought iron table.

"Nice place to relax," Hawke said, wondering if maybe he should start looking for a place like this to settle into before he retired. Dani could live with him when she wasn't at the lodge. Between the two of them, they could easily purchase a small acreage where they could keep the lodge horses during the winter and his all year round.

"What did you need to talk to us about?" Mr. Freyer asked, drawing him out of his daydream.

"I would like a little more background information on Arnie." Hawke pulled out a small notepad he'd tucked in his shirt pocket along with a pen.

"How far back are you talking?" Milton asked as his wife appeared at the back door carrying a tray with a pitcher of iced tea, glasses, and a sugar bowl.

The man jumped up and took the tray from his wife before she walked down the three steps from the back porch.

Once the tray was placed on the table, Milton resumed his seat and Mrs. Freyer poured the brown liquid into all the glasses.

"Do you need sugar?" she asked, handing Hawke a glass.

"No, thank you." He took the glass, sipped the tea, and set it down. "I'd like to know a little more about before he went off to college. Did Arnie have a girlfriend? One that might have not liked his returning from college with Laurel?"

"You think this is all about a grudge from high school?" Milton's face slackened with disbelief.

"I don't know what to think. I'm just trying to figure out who would want him dead." He glanced at Mrs. Freyer. Her gaze shot to her husband.

"Who do you suspect?" Hawke asked the woman.

She shrugged. "I don't suspect her of killing him, but Arnie and Mary Newton went out a few times in high school. Mary always complained that Arnie didn't have enough ambition. He wouldn't amount to anything. But he dropped her before he left for college." She picked up a glass of iced tea and sat. "I have seen her stare at Laurel when she thought no one was watching."

"If you don't suspect her of killing Arnie, do you think it was Ed? Out of jealousy? Arnie had the farm that Ed thought was his. If he thought Mary was interested in Arnie, do you think Ed would have tried to even things?" He could see the large man take revenge on the person whose land he wanted.

Milton stared into his tea. "Arnie liked to antagonize the bully. He only went out with Mary in high school because he knew it upset Ed. I can't see him doing anything to upset Laurel any more than she already was."

"Do you believe Ed would get violent if he knew

186

Arnie and Mary might be friendly again?" Hawke liked this scenario. It gave Ed a motive for killing Arnie. He could have then decided to pin the murder on Laurel, giving him easier means of getting hold of the farm.

But this was all conjecture. There had to be proof.

"Ed has a violent streak, but kill someone, I don't think so." Milton shook his head.

"Does Ed know how to ride a motorcycle?" Hawke asked. If only they had a witness who'd seen who rode the motorcycle.

"That Honda sitting in Arnie's barn was Ed's. Arnie won it in a race a long time ago." Milton smiled. "That was the best day. A bunch of us guys were out riding our motorcycles. Nothing fancy. None of us could afford anything other than bits and pieces we put together to make our bikes. But we'd take them out dirt bike riding before it was called that. On the way back one day, Ed got all uppity when everyone was bragging about Arnie's bike. It had been the only one to stay together all day while we were riding. Ed prodded Arnie into a race. Winner gets the other person's bike. I tried to tell Ed that Arnie's bike was faster, but he wouldn't listen. Arnie won the race and the next school dance, he took Mary to it, just to rub more dirt into Ed's pride."

"It sounds to me like there was more than a little bit of animosity toward Arnie from Ed." Hawke studied the couple. Mrs. Freyer nodded. Milton just stared at his cup of iced tea.

"Did Arnie smoke?" Hawke remembered the cigarette he'd found in the abandoned vehicle.

They both shook their heads.

"He didn't like the stuff," Milton said.

"Thank you for your time and answers." Hawke finished off his tea and stood. He wanted to take a look at the forensics on the cigarette butt he'd found in the victim's vehicle.

"We heard they let Laurel go. Do you think she's okay to be by herself?" Mrs. Freyer asked.

Hawke studied her. "Do you think she's going to hurt herself?"

The woman stared at him as if he were a moron. "No! But it's obvious whoever killed Arnie and the realtor could return and hurt Laurel."

He didn't think that was a possibility. Mrs. Bertram was as stumped by the deaths as anyone else. But... He'd have to go over his notes. She would have been in the house, sleeping, if she told the truth when Arnie and Myra were killed and buried. That could make her a witness if she happened to be curious about what her husband was going to do with the woman she thought she'd killed.

Chapter Twenty-two

Hawke sat at the end of the Freyer driveway. "Should I go home and check the forensic records on my computer or call Spruel?" He studied Dog for answers. He hated to call his superior. Not only would it take the sergeant away from his duties, but it would also give the man more reason to tell Hawke to forget about the murder and enjoy his day off.

Or, he could call the sheriff's office and ask the deputy who was looking up the phone numbers to read him the details.

"I'll call the deputy," he said to Dog, pulling his phone out of his pocket.

"Sheriff's Office, this is Deputy Woodson, how may I help you?"

"Deputy, this is Trooper Hawke. I left you some phone numbers this morning."

"I have them all named for you."

"Thank you. I'll have you read them off to me in a

minute. Could you pull up the file on the Bertram case? I'd like to know if forensics learned anything about the cigarette found in the abandoned vehicle."

He heard keys tapping and then the sound of a mouse scrolling.

"Here it is." Deputy Woodson began reading the report. There wasn't anything new. They were still looking for a match to the DNA on the cigarette but nothing had come up on any databases. It was evident, they needed to get a warrant to get a sample from Ed Newton. If the man wore gloves to drive the pickup, it was a sure bet he wore gloves to ride the motorcycle back to the farm. It would have been only a three-mile hike from the Bertram farm to the Newton house.

He needed to talk to Mrs. Newton. See if she noticed her husband missing during the hours it took to drive to Freezeout and back, and who had called that made her take off at the same time that Arnie was burying an unconscious Myra Bittle.

"Thank you and those numbers?"

He listened as the woman rattled off the names. "Myra Bittle was the number you circled three times." She went on to list, Wallowa Valley Realty and names of companies he was sure Kamp had contacted for business.

"Thank you. That is helpful." Hawke ended the call and sat in his vehicle petting Dog's head and thinking.

"How could Myra have called Mrs. Newton if Arnie was burying her?" He glanced at Dog.

The animal yawned.

"There's only one person to ask. Looks like we're headed to the Newton farm first." He put the pickup in drive and headed to the Leap area and the Newton farm.

On the way, he and Dog stopped by a shady tree and ate jerky, chips, and a candy bar, Hawke had purchased while passing through Eagle.

At the Newton farm, he pulled up to the yard. The fancy car could be seen under the carport alongside the house. He didn't see the SUV that Ed drove. If he was lucky, the man wouldn't come back before he could get some answers out of the wife.

Hawke walked up to the front door and knocked.

Footsteps rang out on the wood floor on the other side of the door. The solid wood door swung open and Mrs. Newton smiled at him.

"Trooper Hawke, what brings you back to our home?"

"Mrs. Newton." He removed his Stetson. "I have some questions I'd like to ask you."

"Me?" She stared at him her eyes wide. "What could I have to tell you?"

"That's what I'm trying to find out." He waited while the woman decided whether to invite him in.

She finally stepped back. "Come in. Have a seat. I'll get you a cup of coffee."

"There's no need for coffee. I just have a couple of questions." He strode by her and into the lavishly decorated living room.

"Well, suit yourself." She walked over to a chair that reminded Hawke of a throne he'd seen in a movie. The woman sat down as regally as the actress in the movie.

Hawke sat on the edge of the couch. He pulled out his notepad and pen. "Mrs. Newton, after looking over you and your husband's phone records, I noticed that Myra Bittle called you at eight-twenty-three the night of her death. Can you tell me what the call was about?"

The woman stared straight at him. "I answered the call because the readout said it was Myra. But it was Arnie. He said he was sorry and that Myra needed help. The call went dead. I left the water board meeting, dropped Ed off at home, and drove to Alder to Myra's house. No one was there."

Hawke studied her. She was a smart woman. "Didn't it occur to you that if Arnie called from Myra's phone, she was with him? At his farm?"

She let out an exasperated sigh. "Of course, after she wasn't at her home. But she liked to entertain gentleman. And I hardly thought the two would be, you know, at his house when Laurel rarely left." Her face didn't blush, and her eyes remained steely.

"You didn't like the idea of her and Arnie having an affair?" Hawke asked.

Mrs. Newton laughed. "What those two did wasn't any of my business. And if they were fooling around, Laurel pushed him to it."

"Why would Arnie call you about Myra?" Hawke wondered if Mrs. Newton and Myra were friends from school.

"Myra was my cousin." The woman stated it as if the woman hadn't just died a brutal death.

"I see. And you were close?" Hawke made a note to ask more about the two from the Freyers and Herb and Darlene.

"As children. Later her family moved, and we didn't see much of each other. Then she moved back. We talked a bit on the phone and met now and then, but we weren't close friends."

"Yet, you took her call during a Water Board

meeting?" He studied her.

"The meeting was nearly over, and she never called me at night. I felt like I needed to answer it." She sniffed. "And with good reason. It seems Laurel went crazy, killing my cousin and her husband when she caught them having an affair."

Hawke let that be. "What did Ed do after you dropped him off?"

"How should I know? I was gone." She raised an eyebrow in reproach.

"Was he home when you returned?"

She shook her head. "No. He left a note saying he'd gone back to town to have a beer and play pool."

"What time did you get home and when did he return?"

"I returned at ten and I don't know when he came home. After running all over looking for Myra, I turned off my phone, took a sleeping pill, and went to bed. When I woke up, Ed was already up for the day."

"Where is your husband now?" Hawke asked.

"He went to Winslow for some fencing supplies. You might be able to catch him at the tavern. He likes their burgers."

Hawke stood. "Would you be willing to give me some hair from Ed's hairbrush for a DNA sample?"

She narrowed her eyes. "What are you comparing his DNA to?"

"Some evidence collected from Arnie Bertram's homicide." That left it wide open. She didn't need to know what they had in evidence.

"You're not pinning this on my husband. If you want a sample, you ask him or get a warrant."

"Thank you. I will."

Hawke walked out of the house and slid into his vehicle. "Want to sample the Blue Elk Tavern burger?" he asked Dog, turning the key in the ignition and driving away from the Newton farm.

Driving into town to catch Ed meant he'd have to drive back out here to talk to Laurel. Hawke slowed his vehicle as he neared the Bertram driveway. Maybe by the time he finished talking with Laurel, Ed will have come home.

He liked the thought of not driving back and forth, but he'd rather talk to the man without his wife present. He'd witnessed the way the woman seemed to be the one in control of the marriage. Hawke didn't want her to manipulate Ed as he was questioned.

Pressing on the accelerator, Hawke passed the Bertram farm and headed toward Winslow. He wanted to get these homicides solved so he could get back to concentrating on his job—checking hunters.

Hawke knew the Blue Elk Tavern and its owner. Ben Preston would be able to give him information on Newton.

The Bowlby stone structure had been built in the early 1900s and had been used as a bar or tavern ever since. Hawke stepped into the establishment and stopped. Low lights, booths and tall tables, pool tables on one end, a jukebox by a small dance floor, and an old oak bar with brass-legged stools. The only oddity was the mounted five-point elk. Its head and shoulders were dyed a bright blue. Two spotlights made sure anyone entering couldn't miss the creature. Hawke scanned the open room and found Ed sitting at a table with a couple of other men he hadn't met before.

Rather than disturb the man, Hawke took a seat at

the bar.

"Haven't seen you in here for a while," Ben said, placing a coaster in front of him.

"I've been busy."

"Or preoccupied by that woman you were in here with the last time." The man raised one of his blonde eyebrows.

Hawke saw the glint of humor in the man's eyes. "That could be, too. I'd like an iced tea while I wait and a burger and fries to go."

"I'll get that going."

Ben disappeared through the doors behind the bar.

Waiting for his order, Hawke watched Ed in the mirror behind the bar. The man appeared to have the other two enthralled in whatever he was saying.

When Ben came his way, Hawke asked, "Do Ed and those two meet up here often?"

The bar owner glanced at the table and shook his head. "They look like visitors. No one local sits and listens to Ed's boasting."

Hawke grinned.

Ben disappeared and returned with Hawke's order. He paid and sauntered over to Ed's table. "Hi, Ed." He sat down on the chair closest to the farmer. "I have some questions for you."

The other two men at the table made eye contact with one another and left.

"What's this about?" Ed bellowed.

"It's about what you were doing the night Arnie Bertram was killed." Hawke pulled out his notepad.

The man paled and set down the glass he'd been holding. "What are you talking about?"

"The fact that your wife dropped you off at home

after her call from Myra Bittle and you weren't there when she returned." Hawke tapped the notes in his book.

"I don't even remember what night that was," he deflected.

"Wednesday, two weeks ago. You and your wife were at a Water Board meeting. She received a call, and you both left." Hawke watched the man.

Ed Newton scrunched his face and stabbed at a fry with his fork. "Oh, yeah. I remember. Mary got a call from her cousin and she took me home and then went to talk to Myra."

"And where did you go after she left you off at home?" Hawke persisted.

"I came here. Had a few beers and played pool."

"What time did you go home?"

"I stayed until it closed. Mary was always in a bad mood when she came back from seeing Myra. I decided to wait until I knew she'd be asleep before I went home." He swirled the fry in ketchup on his plate, not looking up at Hawke.

"When did you get home?"

"About seven."

"In the morning? What did you do from two a.m. until seven a.m.?"

"Stayed with a friend."

"This friend have a name?" Hawke seriously doubted the man had been with anyone. He'd been dumping Arnie's pickup and riding the motorcycle back to the farm.

"There's no sense getting them involved." Ed finally looked at Hawke. The determination in his eyes gave Hawke the feeling the man dared him to prove different.

"What kind of cigarettes do you smoke?" Hawke asked instead.

Newton stared at him. "What?"

"I asked what kind of cigarettes do you smoke?"

"What's it matter to you?"

"Just curious."

"You're not pinning Arnie's murder on me. I've been to his farm enough times, I may have dropped a butt or two."

"If you're innocent then you won't mind telling me the brand. And maybe giving me a sample of your DNA."

Newton shot to his feet. "I don't know what you think you know, but I didn't kill Arnie." He strode up to the till, paid his bill, and walked out.

Hawke rose to his feet and followed.

Newton climbed into his SUV and blew smoke out the exhaust, taking off up the street.

"Looks like we have him running scared," Hawke said to Dog as they split the burger and fries.

Chapter Twenty-three

Winding his way back to the Leap area and Bertram farm, Hawke made a couple of phone calls.

"You want me to get a warrant for a DNA sample from Ed Newton and a warrant to search his property? What do you think you'll find with these?" Sherrif Lindsey asked.

"The DNA sample can be compared with the cigarette butt found in the victim's vehicle, and the warrant to search the Newton property should help us find proof that Newton killed Arnie and I now believe also Myra Bittle. I can't see Arnie calling Mrs. Newton about her cousin if she were dead. I think she was only stunned, and Arnie called Myra to take her away and maybe talk her into not pressing charges against his wife. But Ed Newton took advantage of his wife out looking for Myra and went over to have another talk with Arnie. For whatever reason, he killed both Myra and Arnie, burying them in the trench. Knowing Arnie was going to a conference the next day, he ditched Arnie's vehicle, using the motorcycle from the barn to get back to the Leap area."

"That's all circumstantial," Lindsey said. "What evidence do you have that I can use to persuade the judge for the warrants?"

"Ed Newton doesn't have an alibi for his whereabouts. He said he was with someone but wouldn't give me a name, which means, he doesn't have an alibi. He has always bullied Arnie. Maybe this time it went too far, and when he realized Myra saw what he'd done, he killed her."

Lindsey sighed. "You're going to have to bring me stronger evidence than that. No judge will give a warrant on your suspicions. Even Judge Vickers, who knows you well."

"I'll see what I can do." Hawke ended the call, discouraged that he hadn't thought to grab the glass Newton had drunk from at the tavern. It wouldn't hold up in court, but if the DNA matched, he would know who to focus on.

"Let's go talk to Laurel. Maybe she'll have some answers." He turned into the Bertram property and found the woman sitting on a tractor, staring into space.

The dogs barked at his approach, drawing the woman's attention.

Hawke parked, let Dog out to sniff butts with the Bertram dogs, and walked toward the tractor where Laurel sat. "Afternoon, Mrs. Bertram. I've got a couple questions for you."

Sadness filled her eyes. "Do you still think I killed my husband?"

"Most of the evidence is pointing another

direction." He motioned for her to get off the tractor.

She did and stood in front of him. "What evidence? And why aren't I under arrest for killing Myra?"

He studied her. "Because you didn't. You assaulted her and will have to go to court for that, but she was buried alive. Unless you buried her. Then you will be arrested for her murder."

The woman glanced at the barn and then the trench where the bodies were found. "Buried in dirt would be a horrible way to die. Do you think he killed her?"

"I'm not sure what happened exactly. Are you sure you didn't look out the window after you went in the house?" He walked her toward the house.

"I was stunned I'd swung the board and hit her. Then she crumpled, there was blood everywhere, and Arnie arrived." She stopped and stared at him. "That was the first time in our marriage that Arnie took charge. Lying in bed later, my heart raced, thinking he was still the man I'd fallen in love with."

"Could you take me in the house and let me have a look around?" Hawke opened the back door of the house.

"What are you looking for this time?"

"I just want to see what can be seen out the bedroom window." He studied her. Her expression didn't change.

"I told you I didn't look out. I popped a cup of milk in the microwave and took that up to the bedroom. I drank that and took a melatonin pill. I set the clock for one and covered my head. I slept until one. Arnie's pickup was gone when I went out to bale. I figured he left early for Spokane so we didn't have to talk about what I'd done."

Hawke had stopped in the kitchen. "You told me it was still there when you went out to bale."

She blushed. "I didn't know he was dead when I told that lie. I didn't want him to get into trouble because he'd covered up what I'd done. When you told me about the pickup being at Freezeout, I thought he'd either disappeared to not have to say anything against me or he couldn't live with what we'd both done."

Hawke patted her on the shoulder. "Pour me a glass of iced tea. I'll go take a look around and be back."

She nodded.

He glanced out the kitchen window first. The area where all the blood was found, wasn't in view from here. He moved into the living room. Again, the area wasn't in view. Upstairs, in Mrs. Bertram's bedroom, he couldn't see the driveway or the side of the barn where the murder occurred.

Back down in the kitchen, he found Mrs. Bertram still standing where he'd left her. He sat her in a chair and settled in the one across the table from her.

"Do you remember hearing any vehicles before you fell asleep? Or maybe that woke you up?" he asked.

She shook her head. "Nothing. When I went out to bale, everything was still as could be. I did notice that. I wondered if it was because of what I'd done."

"Do you have someone who can come stay with you?" Hawke asked, wondering why her daughter hadn't stayed with her after bringing her mom home from the police station.

"Jenny has too much to do to sit around here watching me. I'll be fine. I just need some time to come to grips with what I've done. The animals and land are the best medicine." Mrs. Bertram said the words as if she meant them, but her eyes were dull.

"Do you keep the keys in the backhoe?" he asked.

"Yes. It's a hassle to have to come in the house to get the keys every time I decided to use it."

"Is it something anyone can use?"

"Anyone who has been around farm equipment could figure it out. And most farms these days have a backhoe of some sort. It's just handy."

He didn't want to let her know who he suspected but he had to know. "What about your neighbors? Do they have backhoes?"

Her gaze met his. "Yes. Do you know who killed Arnie and buried him?"

"I don't have any proof. Who all knew where you kept the motorcycle Arnie won off of Ed Newton?"

Laurel studied him. "What does that have to do with the murder?"

"I believe it was used to bring the murderer back to this area after abandoning your husband's pickup."

The light went on behind her eyes. "You think someone from the Leap area killed Arnie?" She slammed her hand on the table. "There is only one person in this area who hated Arnie that much. Ed Newton. With Arnie gone and me in jail, he could talk Jenny into selling this land to him."

"I haven't any proof. But that's my theory, too."

She nodded. "I would bet this farm that Ed is the person who killed my Arnie."

Hawke held the woman's gaze. "Don't go off half-cocked and try to threaten or coerce him. I'm working on gathering the evidence we need. If you get in the middle of the investigation, it will only make it harder to find the truth."

"I'll stay out of it. But if he comes on this property trying to make me sell, I can't guarantee I won't blast him with rock salt."

Hawke chuckled to himself. He'd like to see that but refrained from saying anything.

"I have other leads to follow up on. Call me if anything comes back to you about that night and the days following." Hawke stood.

"I will. And thank you for believing in me. I was sure I'd killed her and would never see this land again."

"It's not a matter of me believing in you, it's where the truth takes us." He walked out the back door, whistled for Dog, and climbed into his pickup.

This day was just about shot. But he had one more person he wanted to talk to before he went back to checking hunters tomorrow. The man who had a key to Myra's house. Darren Ault.

《》《》《》

Hawke parked in the driveway of an expensive house on the west side of Wallowa Lake. Apparently, the owner of the realty company was doing well.

He rang the doorbell and waited. A light blinked on in an upstairs window, casting a yellow glow above. He didn't want to irritate the man, but Ault was taking his time answering the door. Hawke knocked this time.

The door opened a minute later.

Ault stood on the other side, wearing a bathrobe and lounge pants. "What do you want at this time of night?"

"I have a couple questions for you about Myra Bittle." Hawke stepped over the threshold and three steps into the entryway.

The man grabbed his arm. "I don't want to talk about Myra here. Come by the office tomorrow."

"I can't. I have to patrol tomorrow." Hawke planted his feet.

A woman in silky pajamas walked out of a room. "Who's here, Darren?"

Hawke walked over to her. "State Trooper Hawke, Ma'am." He held out his hand. When she didn't take it, he added, "I'm here inquiring about Ms. Bittle. One of Mr. Ault's employees who recently died."

The woman's eyes narrowed as she glared at Ault. "What would my husband know about this woman's death?"

"That's what I'm here to find out."

Ault walked by them. "Come into my office. Zoe, I'll be up to bed in fifteen minutes. I have very little to tell the trooper."

The woman put a hand on her hip and glared at him. "Very little to say could be said in my presence."

Ault walked back, put an arm around the woman's waist, and drew her close. He kissed her and said, "You know how much my work bores you. This will be just as boring."

"I doubt that." She huffed and walked back into the room she'd appeared from.

"This way," Ault said in an angry voice.

Hawke smiled. He'd been correct in assuming the man was having an affair with the deceased woman.

Once in the office, Ault closed the door and motion for Hawke to sit in a chair far from the door. The man pulled his desk chair over and sat in front of Hawke.

"What do you want to know about Myra," Ault

asked in a quiet voice.

"Why do you have her house key?" As late as it was, there was no sense in dragging this questioning out.

The man sputtered. "How did you know that?"

"I'm investigating a homicide. All kinds of things come out when you start digging into a deceased person's life." Hawke pulled out his notepad. "Why do you have a key?"

"We would work late nights at her place."

Hawke stared at the man. "Was that between the sheets?"

The man glared.

"When I asked you about the Bertram property you said Myra was poaching. What did you mean by that?" Hawke continued to study Ault.

"I'd heard rumors that Arnie Bertram was thinking about selling. I'd planned to approach him once I had all the specs put together. I might have mentioned it to Myra. Then you walked into my office and said she was out talking to Bertram when she was killed. I looked through her stuff, she didn't have any specs, hadn't pulled any county maps or anything on the property. That's odd. If you're planning on selling a piece of property you learn everything you can about it so you have plenty to hit the buyer with."

Hawke wondered if Myra hadn't planned to do the sale through the realty. She may have been told she'd get a fee that the realty couldn't get their hands on if she made the sale to her cousin's husband. But he didn't have the money, his wife did...

"Have you ever looked up property for Mr. or Mrs. Newton?" Hawke asked.

"No. They have never come into the office wanting to buy or sell. Why?" Ault leaned forward. "Are they looking to buy the Bertram farm?"

Hawke shrugged. "I'd like the key to Ms. Bittle's house." He didn't think a search of the house would dig up any evidence, but it didn't hurt to take a look around since her only other relative might be mixed up in her death. The neighbor did say he thought Myra drove her car home the night she'd died, however, Mrs. Newton was about the same size as her cousin.

Ault walked over to his desk, opened a drawer, and held up a key. He walked back and placed it in Hawke's outstretched hand.

"Thank you. If you think of anything that might help us find out who killed Myra, I'd appreciate a call." Hawke handed one of his cards over.

He stood and strode to the door.

"You won't say anything to my wife?" Ault asked, beating him to the door.

"I have no need to say anything. She already knows you and Myra were fooling around." Hawke stepped into the hall, strode to the entryway, and let himself out. He didn't want to stick around for the interrogation he was sure Mrs. Ault would put her husband through. He could tell by the way the woman acted when he'd mentioned Myra's name that she knew her husband had been fooling around with the realtor. Which would make her a suspect, except he didn't see her killing Arnie, too. She might want to kill the woman sleeping with her husband, but she wouldn't have killed an innocent bystander.

Sliding in behind the steering wheel of his vehicle, Hawke glanced at Dog, sitting vigilantly in the passenger seat. "It's getting late, but I'd rather go check out the house tonight as long as we're here."

Dog tipped his head as if in agreement.

Chapter Twenty-four

At Myra Bittle's house, Hawke parked in the driveway and walked up to the front door with the key in his hand. He shoved the key in the lock, turned it, and the door opened.

Flipping on the lights, an ear-splitting scream shattered the quiet. "Momma's home!" A sharp voice rang out. Hawke followed the sound and discovered a blue and gold parrot in a cage that took up most of the room. The bird studied him, tipping his head this way and that.

"Sorry, I'm not your momma," Hawke said, closing the door and calling dispatch to let them know he was the one in the house in case a neighbor called in a suspicious person report.

He worked his way back up the hall to the den. At the den, he stood in the doorway scanning the room. Nothing looked interesting besides the desk and a file cabinet. The bird was talking to itself in the other room.

He sifted through the papers and files in the desk. They were mostly bills and letters. A checkbook sat on top of a ledger in one drawer. Hawke pulled out both and opened the checkbook. The woman appeared to be doing well as a realtor. He noticed a notation of "retainer, Mary" in her checkbook and a deposit of ten thousand dollars. What would her cousin be retaining her for? The only thing he could think of was the Bertram Property. But why would Mary Newton want the property so badly? It hadn't been in her family. According to Ed, and everyone else, it had been in his family. Had she wanted it for him?

The ledger mirrored the numbers and notations written in the checkbook. He moved to the filing cabinet. Here there were files on a dozen farms around the area along with the specs, maps, and selling points. They weren't the same as the ones in her files at the realty office. She also had files on businesses in the various towns around the county and several houses in town. It was almost as if she was working on the side selling property outside of the realty company.

The next drawer down had files with names. Darren Ault, Ed Newton, Laurel Bertram, Arnie Bertram, Reed Kamp. Hawke studied the names before he pulled the files out, laid them on the desk, and sat in the chair. What did the woman have on these people?

The Ault file held photos of Darren Ault and Myra in bed, as well as Ault in bed with two other women. Had she been using this information against her boss?

He picked up the file on Ed Newton. The photos were of Newton and a woman Hawke didn't know. He wondered if this was his alibi for the night Arnie was killed?

What kind of photos could she have of Laurel Bertram? Hawke opened that file. These were photos of Laurel working in her garden, driving the tractor, and petting a dog. Nothing incriminating in those. Why did Myra have them?

In Arnie's file, there were photos of him and Mary in a restaurant smiling at one another. It appeared there may have still been a spark between them, even though everyone said that Arnie had only dated Mary to get back at Ed. Had Mary fallen for Arnie and been disappointed when he'd returned from college with a bride? Maybe Laurel constantly berating Arnie had pushed him to pick up with his old girlfriend?

He opened the file with Reed Kamp's name on it. There weren't any compromising photos of the man. But there were photos of checks and a ledger page of seed and supplies. A total was written at the top of the page and check amounts were written beside it. The total of the supplies was circled at the bottom with the same color pen. It was considerably less than the amount of money on the checks that had been written out to Kamp's Hemp Farm. Hawke studied the checks. In the FOR line on the checks, they all said seed. His backers had given him money for seed and he'd spent it on other things. Was Myra using the information to seek favors from him? That would be a reason to finish her off, but Arnie had called Mrs. Newton. Why would she call Reed to help? If Arnie had called Jenny and she sent Reed, that would make sense. Hawke could see Reed using this opportunity to get rid of Myra and his father-in-law in hopes of getting his hands on the farm.

A thought struck him. Hawke picked up the woman's checkbook. The only large amounts in her register were from sales of property and the retainer from her cousin. Where had she kept the illgotten money? If that's what she had been doing. Or had she just gathered all the evidence to use at a later date?

He wondered if one of the men the neighbor saw coming and going from this house had been in on the scheme with Myra. Hawke pulled out another drawer and discovered more names. This time all the photos were of Myra and the men in bed. She'd set up a camera in her bedroom.

Hawke returned all the files back where he'd found them and turned out the lights. He locked the door and strode out to his pickup.

"I'll take this key to the sheriff tomorrow and help them pull the records in her den and see if they can't help shed some light." Hawke put his vehicle in gear and backed out of the driveway. He hoped tomorrow got them a little closer to figuring out who killed Arnie and Myra.

《》《》《》

Wednesday morning Hawke woke around seven and leisurely fed his animals and himself.

Herb wandered into the barn as Hawke was coming down the stairs to leave. "Have you learned anything new about Arnie's death?"

Hawke studied the man. His landlord knew he didn't talk about cases unless he needed information. Which there were a few things he was curious about. "Does Darlene have a fresh pot of coffee?"

A wide grin spread across Herb's face. "She always has a fresh pot. Come on. She even made oatmeal cookies yesterday."

Hawke fell in step with his landlord. "Those

cookies wouldn't happen to be from the recipe that she won first place with at the fair last year?"

"The same." Herb smacked his lips. "It's a wonder I don't roll around from all the goodies my wife bakes."

They both laughed as they walked to the back door of the Trembley's home.

Herb opened the door and Hawke followed him in.

"Darlene, you got any of those oatmeal cookies left?" Herb called.

By the time Herb had three cups of coffee sitting on the kitchen table, Darlene arrived in the room.

"I do have some cookies left." She picked up a container, snapped the lid off, and offered Hawke the cookies.

She sat as he plucked two bumpy tan cookies from the container. "Do you have something to ask us?"

Hawke smiled and shook his head. The woman was always ready to spill what she knew if it helped an investigation. Any other time, she was tight-lipped about the gossip she knew.

"I know you said you were older than the Bertrams and Newtons, but do you remember anything about Arnie and Mary being a couple in high school?" Hawke bit into a cookie. The spice flavors burst through his mouth followed by the nice chew of apricot pieces.

"The only thing I remember, and I can look it up in the newspaper archives, when Arnie came home from college with Laurel, that's when Mary and Ed had a short engagement and married." Darlene held her coffee cup in front of her chin. "I remember because it was the biggest gossip then. Everyone speculated that Ed had gotten Mary pregnant. But there was never a baby. Do you want me to find the engagement and marriage announcements?"

"That might be good information to have. I guess." Hawke sipped his coffee and glanced at Herb. "You know anything?"

The landlord's face reddened. "I don't normally listen to this kind of talk and never repeat it, but several men have told me the reason Ed and Mary never had kids is because she won't let him touch her."

Hawke set the cookie down that he'd been about to put in his mouth. "Why would they stay married?"

"Beats me. Maybe it's more of a platonic friendship?" Herb said.

Which sent Hawke's thoughts to the photo with Ed and another woman. "Have you heard of Ed being linked to another woman?"

Herb and Darlene glanced at one another. Darlene put her coffee cup down and said, "Carrie Stiller. She's a teacher at the Eagle high school."

He studied the couple. "How many people know about this?"

She shrugged. "Everyone. Even Mary. She doesn't care as long as they don't go out on dates in the county."

Hawke sat back in his chair. The Mrs. Newton he'd witnessed wouldn't have put up with the whole county knowing her husband had a lover. And he had a feeling this Carrie Stiller was Ed's alibi for the time of the deaths.

"Can you two discreetly see if you can find out who Mrs. Newton's best friend in high school was?" He had a feeling the woman's best friend would be able to give him a clearer picture of the woman. "And do you know why she might have an interest in the Bertram farm when it was originally in Ed's family?"

"I can easily find out who was Mary's best friend," Darlene said. "I have a quilting club meeting this afternoon."

"Mary grew up on a farm and knows all the ins and outs. I believe she has been the foreman of their farm and Ed the hired hand. Ed's complained enough about how he does a lot of the work and gets paid like a hired hand while Mary keeps her money all tucked away from his fingers." Herb smiled at his wife. "We've always done everything around here fifty-fifty."

"That's the best way to keep a marriage happy," Hawke said. "Thanks for the cookies and information." He stood and walked to the back door. "Remember, whatever information you gather, you can't let on you're doing this for me. I don't want you to become targets."

"We understand," they chorused.

Hawke left the house and was joined by Dog. He'd planned to leave Dog home today. The animal had spent a lot of time in the pickup the day before.

"Dog, stay. You'll be happier." Hawke had his hand on the handle of his pickup door and looked down. Dog's whole face sagged and his eyes glistened as if tears would fall any minute. The expression squeezed Hawke's chest and he gave in.

"Come on. Maybe we'll get that hike in today."

Dog's eyes sparkled as he took his seat on the passenger side.

Hawke drove to Alder, parked behind the courthouse, and walked into the Sheriff's Office from the back door. He wandered up the back hallway, bypassing the jail intake area, and up to Sheriff

Lindsey's door. He knocked and waited for the sheriff to announce he could enter.

A deputy came down the hall toward him. "Sheriff in?"

"I knocked, but he hasn't answered."

The deputy knocked, opened the door, stuck his head in, and then backed up, closing the door. "He's not in there. You might try the diner."

Hawke nodded, walked to the front of the building, and out onto the sidewalk. Treetop Café was on the corner of the opposite block. His boot heels clomped on the asphalt as he jogged across the street. At the café, he stopped inside the door and scanned the area.

Sheriff Lindsey was having breakfast with D.A. Lange and one of the county commissioners.

Hawke didn't like to rub elbows with this particular county commissioner. The man was a great, great-grandson of one of the first settlers to the county. And he believed chasing the Nez Perce from this land was the right thing to do. The man had been against the two sales of land in the valley to the Nez Perce Tribe. It irritated Hawke that they had to buy land that their ancestors had lived on for centuries. Which made it even harder for Hawke to keep a civil tone when he was in the man's presence.

It was either wait for the sheriff back at the county office or wait here. Hawke decided to wait at the café. He took a seat at the counter far from the corner where the county officers were sitting.

"You've been in here a lot the last week. You get tired of the food at the Rusty Nail?" Janelle asked.

"No. I've had more business in Alder the last week than in Winslow." Hawke turned over his coffee cup and she filled it.

"Need breakfast?"

"No. Just coffee." He heard a chair scrape the floor and cast his gaze in the direction of the sound. The county commissioner was leaving. As soon as the man cleared the door, Hawke picked up his cup of coffee and took the chair the man had vacated.

"Hawke, didn't expect to see you today," Sheriff Lindsey said.

Hawke placed the key on the table next to the sheriff's plate. "That is the key to Myra Bittle's house. You'll find some interesting files in her filing cabinet."

Lange's gaze shot to Hawke's face. "How did you get that and what were you doing snooping around in her house?"

He told the two about discovering she had a lover who had a key to her house. He used it to take a look around and discovered files that appeared to show the woman had been or had planned to use the information against some locals.

"You think that's what got her killed?" Lange asked.

Hawke shrugged. "I thought sure that Ed Newton was good for the double homicide, but after seeing the photo of him and a woman, and talking to some other people, I believe he was hiding the fact he'd been with that woman the night our victims were killed."

"But you think one of the people Myra had photos of might have killed them both?" Lindsey sounded as skeptical as Hawke felt.

"I don't know, but it wouldn't hurt to find out all of their alibis for that night," Lange said before Hawke could. "I still like the wife for it all. She gave a statement that she hit the victim. She could have also shoved her husband thinking the two had been fooling around and then gave us that story about his showing up and taking care of things. From the reports about the victim, he didn't seem like a take-charge type of person."

"That's what I thought, but when I visited Mrs. Bertram yesterday, she said something that makes me think he did. And Mrs. Newton said he called her saying Myra needed help. That backs up Mrs. Bertram's story that he took charge of the situation." Hawke had seen how lost and how surprised the woman had been about her husband's actions.

"Where does that leave us with suspects?" Lange asked.

"About where we were when the whole thing happened. I wish forensics would have picked up on something that could help." Hawke raised his coffee cup to take a sip.

"Did you notice that the report said the woman had the injury of being hit by wood, which Mrs. Bertram told us, she'd done, but they also say the left side of her body looked as if it had been hit by something solid. Broken left arm, cracked ribs, and deep-tissue bruising." Lindsey studied Hawke. "Do you have any ideas about that information?"

He'd missed the information. But then he'd had the deputy read it off to him. "I'd like to look at the forensic reports thoroughly, if you don't mind."

"I'm done here. We can walk over together." Lindsey tossed money on the table and stood.

Chapter Twenty-five

Hawke sat at the extra desk in the sheriff's office, reading the last of the forensic reports. This was why he liked to read the reports himself rather than have someone pass on the information. This was the first he'd learned that something had rammed into Myra's side, causing her injuries before she'd suffocated from the dirt she was buried under. That meant someone more vicious than Arnie had put her in the trench. And Arnie had died from the one blow to the head on the plow, according to the forensic report. That could have been an accident. Then whoever pushed him, say Myra, when she came to, could have called Mary. Mrs. Newton said Arnie called her to make it sound like he was alive at the time. But if she arrived after Arnie was dead, what happened to Myra? Did Mary still love Arnie and was furious with her cousin for killing him? Mrs. Newton would have had the presence of mind to devise such an elaborate way to hide what had happened. But did she have the skill to run the backhoe?

He could also see Laurel Bertram being furious seeing Arnie taking care of Myra and going back out in a rage. She was strong from all the hard labor she did every day. His first phone conversation and those encounters with her until she'd been taken to the county jail would have had him thinking she could have pulled this off. But yesterday… He'd seen how vulnerable the woman had been having realized her husband wasn't returning and he'd died while she was upstairs sleeping. Now he wasn't as quick to say she'd killed him. Though she could be showing remorse for what she'd done. But they had been all over that farm twice and couldn't find anything that connected the woman to the deaths, other than her being at the farm at the time, however, alibied for being out in her tractor baling.

Ed Newton. Hawke could see him taking out his frustrations on the two. Arnie for all the digs he'd given the neighbor over the years, and Myra, if he knew about the photographs, but he wouldn't have kept a cool head to dispose of the bodies and the vehicle.

Reed Kamp. He would have the cool head for disposing of the bodies, but so far, there wasn't anything that connected him to the murders. Could he and Newton have worked together?

Jenny Kamp? He could see her keeping a level head, but he didn't see her leaving her father to bleed to death or burying him in the trench. He hadn't seen that type of strength, physically or mentally, in her.

Deputy Corcoran stuck his head in the room. "You want to go with us to pull the files at Myra Bittle's?"

Hawke shoved the papers in the file and picked up

the folder. "Might as well. I could have missed something important." He handed the folder over to the deputy at the reception desk and followed Corcoran and Lindsey out of the building.

"I'll drive my vehicle over so my dog can get out and run around." Hawke walked over to his pickup while the sheriff and deputy entered a county SUV.

They pulled up to the Bittle house and found a car, one that Hawke recognized, parked in the driveway.

"Any idea who that belongs to?" Sheriff Lindsey asked.

"Mary Newton, Ms. Bittle's cousin. Funny she never said anything about having a key to the place." Hawke walked up to the front door and rang the doorbell. They waited several minutes.

"Corcoran, go around back. She has to be here." Hawke pounded on the front door. "Mrs. Newton, this is Trooper Hawke, open the door."

He heard footsteps clacking down the tile hallway.

The door opened and a disheveled Mary Newton stood on the other side of the threshold. "What are you doing here? And with the sheriff."

"We're here to pick up some files from your cousin's den," Hawke said.

"Don't you need a warrant?" The woman stood her ground, not opening the door any wider.

"Don't you want to find out who killed your cousin? You could be considered a trespasser. This is the house of a murder victim. You shouldn't be here."

Sheriff Lindsey pushed by both Hawke and Mrs. Newton. "I have a warrant." He held up the document. "What were you doing in here, Mrs. Newton?"

Hawke followed the sheriff into the house. Their

entry caused Mrs. Newton to sputter and her face to pale.

The bird made loud squawks from the other room.

"What's that?" Lindsey asked.

"Myra's parrot." Hawke turned his attention to Mrs. Newton. "What were you here trying to hide?"

"A lot of people could be hurt by my cousin's actions. I was disposing of items that would cause embarrassment," the woman said.

Hawke strode down the hall to the den. The paper shredder was still whirring. His gaze shot to the file cabinet. The drawers were hanging open. Damn! He should have grabbed the files last night.

"Who told you I was here last night looking at the files?" He spun toward the woman.

She shrunk back into the hallway. Deputy Corcoran came up behind her. Giving her another scare.

"I-I don't know what you mean," she sputtered.

"You have had ample time to come in here and shred evidence that could tell us who killed your cousin. Why did you come here today, after I'd been here last night reading the files?" Hawke pushed the power button on the shredder and pulled the machine off the bottom receptacle collecting the shredded pages and photos. He figured either the neighbor he'd talked with his first visit here or the Peeping Tom must have called and told her. But they both had said they didn't know the cousin. Hawke was beginning to think Mrs. Newton was cagier than he'd first thought.

Corcoran walked into the room and started pulling out the files still in the cabinet. Hawke knotted the plastic bag filled with shredded paper and stared at the woman.

"Why were you shredding evidence in a murder investigation?" Sheriff Lindsey asked Mrs. Newton.

"I told you. I knew about Myra's sideline and didn't want anyone to be hurt by it."

"Or you didn't want anyone to see photos of you and Arnie," Hawke said. "Or the photos of your husband with a lover. I think this is more about you saving face rather than not hurting others."

The woman glared at him.

"If you knew about these photos, why did you wait so long to get rid of them? Why didn't you ask your cousin to dispose of them?" he asked.

Corcoran pulled out the files on the properties Ms. Bittle had been interested in. It appeared the only files Mrs. Newton was destroying were her cousin's photographs.

"Were you and your cousin gathering harmful information to use as bribery?" Hawke asked.

"No! Why would I want to do that?" The woman's face reddened and the vein on her forehead became visible.

"How else would you know about these files?" Hawke raised the bag of shredded documents and photos.

The woman's eyes blinked fast as she stared at him. Finally, her mouth moved. "I ran across them one day when Myra asked me to pick up something from her house for her."

"What did she say when you confronted her." When she didn't say anything, he added, "I know you said something to her. You aren't the type that would just ignore finding scandalous photos in your cousin's file cabinet."

"Myra said these were her backup plan if the bottom fell out of real estate. She always was a thrill seeker. I think she took those photos just to know she got away with it."

"You mean the ones of the men she slept with in her bed?" He shook the bag. "What about the ones taken outside of her house? The ones of you and Arnie, your husband and his mistress, and Laurel. Why did she take those?"

The woman scowled. "To keep me from saying anything about the photos."

"Why photos of Laurel? She was always alone at the farm."

"Those I don't know. You'd have to ask Myra. But you can't, can you." The woman said it with such venom, Hawke wondered if she could have killed Arnie and her cousin. There was animosity toward her cousin. But she couldn't have done it alone.

"Mrs. Newton, take your things and leave," Sheriff Lindsey said, escorting the woman to the door of the den and out to the front door.

Hawke glanced at Deputy Corcoran, "Any of those files have photos of men and Myra?"

"Not a one. They are all specs on property."

That meant the bag he held had all the evidence that would pertain to the case. Mrs. Newton had been destroying it for some reason other than caring about her neighbor's feelings. Which made him think of Myra's neighbors. They needed to be interviewed again.

"Here. Make sure this gets to forensics and is pieced back together. I'm going to have a chat with the neighbors and see who called her about me looking at the files." Hawke went out the back door and found the gate leading into that neighbor's yard. He'd talked to the woman earlier in the investigation. She fed the victim's bird. He walked up to the back door and knocked.

The woman, he remembered, opened the door. She studied him a minute before she smiled. "You're the trooper who was here about Myra?"

"Yes. Did you happen to see me in her house last night and call Myra's cousin?"

She frowned. "I don't go peeping into people's windows and I don't know who her cousin is."

"Thank you. Then it must have been the neighbor on the other side of the house."

The woman wrinkled her nose. "Nosy Waylon would be the most likely neighbor to see you in the house and call. He thinks he's the neighborhood watch, but he's really a Peeping Tom if you ask me."

That had been Hawke's first impression as well. "Sorry to bother you." He backed down the step.

"Have you discovered who killed her yet?" the woman asked.

"Not yet. These things take time." He tipped his hat and walked back through the gate into Myra's yard. He walked along the fence and up to the garage. Skirting around the fence, he walked up to the Peeping Tom, or Waylon's, front door. It was Wednesday, he wasn't sure if the man worked. Hawke knocked on the door and waited.

Only a few seconds passed and the door opened wide.

"You were here the other day about Myra," the man said.

"Yes. Did you see me in her house last night and called Mrs. Newton?"

The man's face grew red and he started to shake his head.

"Don't lie to me or you'll be hauled in for obstruction of justice." It wasn't a real thing but Hawke had a feeling this guy didn't want to be connected with the police in any way.

"Yes, it was me. I can't go to the police station. My employer might see and I'd get fired."

"Why did you tell me when I was here the first time that you didn't know Myra's cousin?"

The man stared at him. "Mrs. Newton? She's the cousin? I've never met her. Myra gave me Mrs. Newton's number to call if I ever saw anything suspicious at her house."

This information pointed a finger at Mrs. Newton having known about her cousin's scheme long before she said she did. That would be the only reason Myra would have this guy call her cousin. It meant they were in it together.

"Thanks. Have you called Mrs. Newton any other times?"

"Nope, just last night. She was angry when I first called, but after I told her what I saw she thanked me and said not to tell anyone about our call." The man glanced over Hawke's shoulder and ducked down slightly.

"Someone you don't want to see you?" Hawke asked, glancing over his shoulder at an elderly woman watching everything from across the street.

"She's always telling me she's going to call the cops on me."

"Why would she say that?" Hawke asked, knowing full well it was because he peeked in windows.

"I don't know." The man shrugged. "Are we done?"

"Yeah."

The door closed in Hawke's face.

Back at the vehicles, Hawke let Dog out to pee on the tires and waited for the sheriff and deputy to exit the house. He glanced over at the old woman still standing on the sidewalk across the street. He pivoted and walked across the road toward her.

She looked up at him when he stopped a few feet away.

"Morning. The car that was here this morning. Have you seen it here before?" he asked.

She nodded. "You a policeman? One of them undercover cops?"

"No, I'm State Trooper Hawke." He pulled his badge out from under his shirt.

"Where's your uniform? You undercover?"

"No. It's my day off. How many times have you seen that car here?"

"At least once a week since that realty lady moved in." She pointed to the Peeping Tom's house. "You going to arrest him?"

"Has he done something illegal?"

"Every night he goes creeping around the neighborhood, looking in windows. That's illegal, isn't it?"

"Is he only watching women undressing?" Hawke asked.

"No, he watches everyone. Young, old, men, women, kids. He just stares at the windows like they are televisions."

"Maybe he's lonely but too shy to knock on a door," Hawke said.

She shook her head. "He's a pervert. I'm calling you the next time he's out creeping around." She gave one last glare at the man's house and walked up the sidewalk to her home.

Hawke jogged across the street as the sheriff and deputy walked down the sidewalk to their county car.

"Did you find anything else useful in there?" he asked.

"We found the hidden camera in the bedroom. It's going to take a while for forensics to get all of this pieced together. Can you come by the office and jot down everything you can remember?" Sheriff Lindsey asked.

"I can. I had the feeling Mrs. Newton was holding back information. Did you get the same feeling?" He watched the two officers.

Lindsey shook his head.

Corcoran said, "She is a prickly woman. But I'm not sure."

"I've been talking to this woman off and on since the homicide. She is smart and cunning. If I could figure out how to prove she was at the Bertram farm the night of the homicides, I would say she is our killer. Her alibi of driving over here looking for her cousin when the other vic called her is flimsy. But she'd need an accomplice. One person couldn't have driven Myra's car here and taken Bertram's pickup to Freezeout." He glanced up and down the street. "It's the accomplice I have to find to break her into telling the truth."

Lindsey opened the door on the county vehicle.

"Do you have evidence of any of it?"

Hawke shook his head. "Not yet. I need to start digging into the Newtons. I don't think Ed helped her, but I could be wrong. He has a pretty solid alibi for that night. Or I believe he does. I need to talk to that person. That's where I'm headed."

Chapter Twenty-six

The Rusty Nail was bustling with a noontime crowd when Hawke walked in. He'd decided to grab lunch here. Janelle's comment about frequenting Treetop had him feeling guilty about the Rusty Nail. And he liked the atmosphere here better than any other eating place in the county.

Hawke sat down at his regular place at the counter.

Justine pulled a pen and pad from her apron pocket. "What are you having?"

"Whatever the special is." He knew anything that Merrilee, the owner, cooked would be good.

"One special coming up." Justine clipped his order up on the string across the window into the kitchen and picked up the coffee pot to replenish other diners' cups.

Hawke swiveled his stool and scanned the establishment. Mostly the usual clientele. Farmers and locals grabbing some lunch. He thought about when he was in here the last time. Ed Newton had been dining with the Kamps.

Justine walked back behind the counter and replaced the coffee pot.

"Does Ed Newton ever come in here with a woman other than his wife?" Hawke asked.

She stared at him. "He never comes in here with his wife. But he and Carrie Stiller come in here once a month." She raised an eyebrow. "You do know about him and Carrie, right?"

"Yeah. But I was told they dated outside of the county, per Mrs. Newton's orders." He tilted his head and returned the stare.

Justine chuckled. "Yeah, well, neither one can take the time to leave the county for dates. They just go to different places each week. Carrie told me they switch it up so Mrs. Newton isn't told they go to the same place the same time and day every month."

"They thought they were pulling something over on her, but I doubt they were. That woman is too shrewd." Hawke wondered how he could find out if she was the murderer. And why she would want Myra and Arnie dead.

"Earth to Hawke. Do you want anything to dip the onion rings in?"

Hawke glanced at the basket sitting in front of him. It was a four-inch high, double patty bacon cheeseburger and onion rings. "Ranch, please." He smashed the burger down and went to eating, running everything they knew so far over in his mind.

《》《》《》

At Eagle High School, Hawke stepped out of his vehicle and stared at the two-story block building. He remembered playing a non-league basketball game in the gym here when he was in high school. The memory wasn't a good one. When his name was said over the speaker, the crowd had jeered and told him to go back to the reservation. That had only sparked his desire to shove the ball down all the player's throats. He'd nearly fouled out by the end of the game but had had his best scoring that season. It seemed like his whole life he was always trying to prove to people he was just as good as them. It wasn't until recently that he'd decided to be himself and to hell with what others thought. He now slept better and worried less about hiding his Native pride.

He walked up to the double doors and pushed through.

The same older woman, with blue-tipped white curls who'd greeted him his last trip here, rolled her chair over to the window. "How may I help you?"

"I'd like to talk with Carrie Stiller." Hawke pulled his badge out from under his shirt.

"She's in the middle of class." The woman gave him a stern look.

"It will only take a few minutes. I can go to her room and talk to her in the hall." He wanted to learn as much as he could about the relationship she had with Ed and what she thought of the man's wife.

"That wouldn't look good. Take a seat, I'll send someone to bring her to you." The woman rolled back over to her desk and picked up the phone.

Hawke took a seat on a bench against the opposite wall between glass cases holding trophies.

Five minutes later, the woman wrapped up in Ed's arms in the photo walked down the hall toward the office.

Hawke stood. "Ms. Stiller, I'd like to have a word

with you." He held up his badge.

She veered over to him. "Are you why I was asked to come to the office?"

"Yes. I have some questions for you. How about we step outside?" He walked to the door, noting the secretary was frowning at not being able to hear what they would say.

Outside, Hawke motioned to the bench.

Ms. Stiller sat and peered up at him. "I don't understand. What is this about?"

"I'm looking into Ed Newton's alibi for the night of September fifteenth. He said he was with someone but wouldn't give me a name. From the information I've been able to gather, I'm assuming he was with you all night."

She blushed. "Yes. He showed up a bit drunk and said he didn't want to go home to his wife. He said she'd gotten a call that upset her and he didn't want to get the brunt of her anger."

Hawke thought that was interesting. "The call she'd received had upset her?"

"Yeah. He said she'd rattled on about how ungrateful some people were and she'd show them before dumping him at home and taking off." Ms. Stiller studied him. "Does this have something to do with Ed's neighbor that was found buried?"

"Why do you ask?"

"Because Ed has been bouncing between elated that he might get his hands on the farm and fearful Mary won't buy it." Her face hardened. "That woman has used her money to keep Ed. He wants his family farm, but they couldn't keep it running without Mary using her inheritance now and then. And she doesn't let him forget it is her money that is keeping the farm afloat."

"Why doesn't Ed leave?" Hawke asked.

"Because Mary would get the farm. Ed can't afford to buy out her half. Instead, he lets her lord it over him and keeps us from being able to get married." The woman sounded more sad than hurt.

"Has Ed ever mentioned who some of Mrs. Newton's friends might be?" He needed to figure out who could have been her accomplice. From what he'd seen of the woman, she would never crack, unless he could get the accomplice to turn on her.

"Not really. We usually don't talk about his wife. When we are together, we try to pretend we are both single and enjoy our time together."

"Thank you. I'm sorry I had to bother you at the school."

"Do you have any idea who could have killed that poor man and woman?"

"I'm getting closer to figuring it out." Hawke strode down the sidewalk to where he'd parked his vehicle. It looked like his next stop would be the Freyers. He needed to find out who Mrs. Newton would have confided in to help her pull off the murders.

《》《》《》

Mr. and Mrs. Freyer were standing near their barn when Hawke drove down their lane and parked in front of the house.

He opened the door, letting Dog leap out over him to visit with the Freyer dogs. Hawke walked over to where the couple stood watching him.

"I can't think of a single thing we haven't told you about Arnie," Milton said when Hawke stopped.

"I'm interested in Mary Newton today. Can you think of who her best friend might be? Or someone she would confide in?"

Mrs. Freyer studied him. "Why are you asking about Mary?"

"I'm asking about all the people who might have had a grudge with Arnie and Myra." Hawke cocked a hip and settled his gaze on the woman. "Do you know who her friends are?"

"Back in school her best friend was Terrel French, well, Maddox now. She and her husband live out toward Imnaha about eight miles from Prairie Creek. Nowadays, at meetings and things, she talks a lot with Meg Booth. She's someone who moved to the county about ten years ago. She's a widow. She lives in Eagle. Across the street from Carrie Stiller." Mrs. Freyer gave him a look that said, how stupid was it of Ed to fool around with someone who lives across from his wife's friend.

"Any men that you can think of that Mrs. Newton might call on to help her out?" Hawke hoped one of the women would have some information that would help.

The couple exchanged glances.

"Other than Ed and Arnie, Mary hasn't ever been friendly with other men," Milton said.

"You mean she doesn't like men?" Hawke asked, hoping he didn't sound too dumb.

"I'm not sure she doesn't like men as she feels she is smarter than all of us." Milton shrugged. "But she charmed Arnie for a while. Until he figured out she wasn't the sweet girl she was presenting to him. After Arnie returned with a bride, she charmed Ed into marrying her, she bosses him around."

Mrs. Freyer nodded.

This was something that might help him. She could charm men when she wanted them to do something for her. "Have you seen her charming anyone lately?"

"Not really," Mrs. Freyer said.

"She had Reed Kamp in a corner of the grocery store about a month ago. Thought it odd she was smiling and talking to him," Milton said.

"Reed Kamp? Did it look like he was enjoying the talk?" Hawke asked.

"He was smiling back at her, showing off his dimples. That's what made me do a double-take. Not many people smile at Mary. They're usually at the end of a tongue lashing."

Hawke nodded. He could see that. But it was interesting that she and Kamp were friendly. More friendly than Kamp and Ed Newton? He couldn't forget the scene of the couple and Newton at the Rusty Nail so soon after Arnie's body was found.

"Thank you. You both have been helpful." Hawke nodded to the husband and tipped his hat to the wife before walking to his pickup. He whistled for Dog. The animal came running, leaping into the cab, and sitting in the passenger seat, his tongue hanging out.

"Did you have a good game of chase?" Hawke asked the dog as he backed up and headed down the lane to the county road. Since he was outside of Eagle, he'd visit Meg Booth. Then the other friend and wander on out to Kamp's Hemp Farm and see if he could ruffle Reed's feathers.

《》《》《》

Hawke pulled up in front of the house across the street from the address he had for Carrie Stiller. Both houses were neat and tidy. Small dwellings fit for a single woman. Walking up to the door, he noticed movement to his right.

"Can I help you?" a tall, sturdy woman asked, stepping out from beside the house. Her short, curly, gray hair stuck out in all directions.

Hawke faced the woman, glancing in the direction she'd come from, and realized she'd been kneeling at the corner of the flower bed. He pulled out his badge. "State Trooper Hawke. Are you Meg Booth?"

"I am. Why do you want to know?"

"I have questions to ask you about Mary and Ed Newton." Hawke pulled the notepad out of his shirt pocket.

The woman took off her work gloves and stopped in front of him. "Why do you think I'd have anything to say about the Newtons?"

Hawke studied the jut of her chin and her fisted hands on her hips. Either he'd struck a raw nerve or she wasn't about to divulge anything about her friend. He decided to tackle this as if he were investigating Ed, even though the man had an alibi. "I was told you and Mary are friends. It's hard to get evidence from a spouse."

The woman's eyes widened and then a smug smile slid across her face before she realized it and drooped the corners a bit.

"I'm looking into Ed's whereabouts on the fifteenth of this month. Since you are friends with Mary, I thought you could fill me in on the man."

The sly smile slipped, tipping her lips before being concealed. "Come in. I have coffee that hasn't sat in the pot all day." Ms. Booth walked over to her front door, stepped through, and held it open for Hawke.

He stepped inside, surprised at the tidiness and items that appeared to have come from all over the world.

"Have a seat. I'll be right back." Ms. Booth walked out of the living room. He heard water running as he browsed the photos around the room. There was one of a younger version of the woman straddling a motorcycle. From the dirt track and mounds in the background, she must have participated in dirt bike races. There wasn't a photo of her in a wedding gown. He was sure Mrs. Freyer had said she was a widow. No pictures of children other than one of a couple with two boys who looked to be around six and ten.

Ms. Booth returned with two mugs of steaming coffee. The burnt coffee smell that followed her into the room had him leery of taking a sip of the brew. She handed him a cup and waited. He took a sip and managed to keep from wincing. His nose hairs curled from the bitter bite of the liquid. If this was coffee that hadn't sat in the pot all day, he'd hate to drink her coffee that had.

She sat on a cushioned chair, chugging her coffee.

Hawke lowered onto the chair closest to hers. "What can you tell me about the Newtons' relationship?"

"What does that have to do with wanting to know about Ed?" The woman scowled.

"It gives me an idea of his mindset. Do they get along? Has he ever been jealous of men Mary talks to?"

A spark flashed in Ms. Booth's eyes. "Mary said he's always accused her of still loving Arnie Bertram. The man who was killed a couple weeks ago."

"Did she still love him?" Hawke studied the woman.

She didn't hesitate. "She told me once that Arnie was the only man who ever saw her brains and understood her drive. She said, 'He may not have much ambition but he's smart enough to see it in others.'"

"And Ed didn't like that?"

"No. He said she should have married Arnie if she wanted a man to tell her how wonderful she was all the time." The woman scowled again. "Ed is immature and childish. When he doesn't get his way, he throws a tantrum."

"Have you seen this first hand?" Hawke didn't care about Ed's tantrums, but it was something the woman wanted to talk about, and if that would make her open up and tell him more of what he wanted to know, he could go that route.

"Yes! Several times."

"Does he get violent or just make a lot of noise?"

"Violent! He slammed his fist down on a table at a meeting one night when Mary said they were leaving. He'd been visiting with a couple of his friends and didn't like her talking to him like he was a child. Anyway, that's what he said and slammed his fist on the table. Showing he was acting like a child." She smiled. "And one time when Mary and I were in Alder having dinner, he walked into the restaurant with that woman he calls a friend. But everyone in Eagle and the county knows he sleeps with her. When Mary asked him what he was doing, he told her he was having dinner with a friend and she could, well, it's not something that bears repeating. Mary glared at him and said something I couldn't hear. Ed stomped his foot and said, he'd damn well do what he wanted and if she didn't like it, she could kiss his ass." The woman's face was glowing. She had become animated retelling the story. "I said, 'Mary, ignore him, you know he'll come crawling back.' She laughed and looking right at the woman said, 'He'll never leave me. I have his farm.'"

Hawke was getting a picture of Mary Newton that he didn't like. She was a manipulating woman. "Were you with Mary on the fifteenth?" He asked the question to see what she did.

She blinked, and said, "No. I believe I was here watching television until ten and then I went to bed."

"How did you find out about the two deaths at the Bertram farm?"

The woman glanced down at the mug of coffee in her hands. "I heard about it on the local radio station."

Ahhh. She was lying. He would have believed her if she had looked at him when she said it. "Have you talked to Mrs. Newton since you heard the news?"

Her gaze darted up to his face. "Why would I do that?"

"To console a friend over the loss of a man she cared about and her cousin."

"Yes. Yes, I called and told her I was sorry to hear about her cousin. She was the typical Mary. While she was sorry about what happened to Myra, she said she'd known something like this would happen to her one day the way she lived her life."

Hawke latched onto that. "Mary and Myra didn't get along?"

"Well, you know they weren't really blood-related. And Mary said Myra had always used her in school. Cheating off her tests and asking for help with classwork, then just taking Mary's papers rather than doing the work herself. And after she came back here…Myra was prostituting herself along with selling real estate. She brought shame to the Thomas name." The woman peered into his eyes. She believed the tale Mary Newton had told her.

He wondered what Ms. Booth would think if he told her that Mary and Myra were running a scandalous scheme? He'd keep that information for later. When he was positive that was what had happened.

"Really? I heard rumors she would sleep with men to get their land to sell. Do you believe that rumor?"

"I don't believe, I know for certain. Julie Deevers divorced her husband when she discovered what he and Myra did. All because Myra wanted to sell their house at the lake. That house had been in Julie's family for two generations. She was fuming when she saw her name forged on the bill of sale." The woman nodded three times. "Men can't be trusted. When you think they love you, they turn around and dump on you."

The anger and futility in her voice and sorrow etched on her face, revealed either her marriage hadn't been a happy one or it had come to an end in a way she hadn't been prepared for.

To change the mood, he pointed to the photo of her on the dirt bike. "You still ride motorcycles?"

She smiled. "Once in a while, I take my Yamaha out. My husband and I used to travel all around the states on our bikes. Nothing better than a backroad trip."

"Sounds like fun. I prefer my horse and the backcountry."

"I prefer riding something that is only operated

with one brain and not two."

"Good point. I've had many a standoff with my mule. But my horse and I have a single mind. Watch for predators and enjoy the scenery." He grinned, thinking he'd get to go out on his horse the next day.

"Do you have any more questions? I would like to finish the flower bed before I need to clean up for a meeting tonight." The woman had finished her coffee.

Hawke had only taken the one sip of his. "Has Mary ever talked about Reed Kamp?"

Again, the woman dropped her gaze to her lap. "No. I don't think so. Why do you ask?" Now she raised her gaze to peer at him.

"I saw Ed and Reed having lunch together the day after Arnie Bertram's body was found. They both seemed pleased. I was wondering if Mary had ever said anything to you about what Ed and Reed might have in common that they would meet for lunch."

"You think the two of them killed Arnie and Myra?" Her mouth appeared slacked with shock, but her eyes twinkled.

"I'm just trying to put all the pieces together." He pulled out a card. "If you think of anything that might help this investigation, give me a call." He placed the card on the coffee table next to his cup of unfinished coffee and stood.

Ms. Booth stood as well. "I will see if I can think of anything."

Hawke walked to the door. The woman was right behind him. He walked down the sidewalk and heard her close the door.

Sitting in his pickup a short distance down the street where he could see her yard, the woman didn't come back out to weed for a good twenty minutes. He had a feeling she'd been on the phone with Mary Newton.

Chapter Twenty-seven

Hawke and Dog headed east out of Prairie Creek toward Imnaha to speak with Terrel Maddox. After speaking with Ms. Booth, he believed Mrs. Maddox would have little to say about her old friend Mary. But he didn't want to leave any potential evidence unturned.

The Maddox property was a horse ranch. He admired the mares and young colts grazing in a field as he drove up to the house.

Two dogs ran out of the barn, and he noticed a woman riding in an outdoor arena to the right of the barn. He drove over to the arena and parked, leaving Dog in the vehicle.

The rider rode up to the railing and waited for Hawke to walk over.

"May I help you?" the woman asked.

"I'm State Trooper Hawke. I'm looking for Terrel Maddox."

The woman frowned. "That's me, but I can't

imagine why you would want to see me."

"I'm investigating the murder of a man and woman in the Leap area. The neighbors are Ed and Mary Newton. I understand you were once friends with Mary. I wondered if you might have some insight into her and her husband."

The woman laughed, not of humor, but disbelief. "I heard that Arnie Bertram had been murdered. And Myra, Mary's cousin. Are you looking into her? Because that woman can carry a grudge." Mrs. Maddox dismounted. "Let me put this horse up, and I'll meet you in front of the barn. This conversation will take a while."

Hawke nodded and walked to the front of the barn. He was greeted by the two dogs, one of which had marked the tires on his pickup. He could see Dog watching from the passenger seat. "Would you two like someone new to play with?" he asked the dogs, walking to the passenger side of his vehicle and opening the door. Dog jumped out and the three began sniffing butts and getting acquainted. Soon they took off, wrestling and running in circles. Too bad people couldn't get along like animals. Sniff each other and become friends. It didn't matter to the other two that Dog was a mongrel, one of the Maddox dogs looked like it was heeler and the other looked like it was a bird dog.

He waited fifteen minutes, watching the dogs play, when he heard the crunch of footsteps on the dirt and rocks on the ground at the side of the barn. Facing the person walking toward him, he was impressed with how the woman glided across the ground. She was the same age as Mary Newton, yet, she appeared younger and spryer.

"Trooper Hawke, was it?" the woman questioned.

"Yes."

"Let's go into the house. I'm thirsty after working with Apollo."

He nodded and followed the woman in through the back door of the two-story older farmhouse.

"This was a good time for you to come by. My husband is in Walla Walla today looking at some horses. He has never been a fan of Mary. He wouldn't have let you talk to me." She used a bootjack to pull off her boots before walking into a cheerful kitchen. "Have a seat." She motioned to the antique table in the middle of the room.

Hawke pulled out a chair and sat. He placed his notepad on the table along with his pen.

"Why are you interested in Mary?" She grabbed two glasses from a cupboard and a pitcher of iced tea from the fridge before taking a seat across from Hawke.

Hawke thought himself a pretty good judge of character. He had a feeling this woman wasn't friends with Mary anymore, and it sounded like she could give him more insight into the woman he now believed murdered her old boyfriend and her cousin.

"Of the people I can come up with who had a reason to want Arnie dead, she is the farthest, but she is the only person who doesn't have an alibi that can be verified."

Mrs. Maddox poured tea into a glass and set it in front of him before pouring one for herself and guzzling half the glass and filling it again. "The one thing I can tell you, she is devious. And she has a short temper. When we were friends in school, she always found a way to trick our parents into thinking we were where

245

we were supposed to be. Her mind can think of misdirection and lies like any good psychopath."

Hawke raised his eyebrows.

She laughed. "I'm a psychologist when I'm not training horses."

Even better. However, there were protocols to follow. "Have you ever helped out the local police in your capacity as a psychologist?"

"No. I've never been called upon to help with anything."

"Do you feel you can give me an unbiased conversation about the woman?"

Mrs. Maddox shrugged. "Don't get too excited. I haven't talked to Mary in a lot of years. I can only tell you what I can look back at after my training. And yes, I can be unbiased. She isn't my client, just an old friend."

Hawke nodded. "From what I can tell, Ed is her puppet and she likes to jerk his strings."

Mrs. Maddox nodded. "She has always been like that. We had a friend in high school who would kiss Mary's feet if she asked. Surprisingly, Mary didn't ask her to do that, but she managed to get that girl in a lot of trouble by asking her to do things that were inappropriate. When she finds someone weaker than her, she digs in her claws and hangs onto them."

"What about Arnie?" Hawke took a sip of the tea.

"Arnie was strong. Most only saw him as lazy, but he was smart and figured out how Mary worked soon enough to get out of her claws before she did something that ended up with the two of them married. He only dated her to get back at Ed. Arnie was what they now call a geek. He read. Around here back then boys didn't read all the time, at least not in public. The jocks, and especially Ed, would pick on him unceasingly. When Arnie found out Ed liked Mary, he swept in and started dating her. It was his way of getting back at Ed. But like I said, he soon figured her out." Mrs. Maddox drank her tea and set the glass down. "By the time Arnie returned with Laurel, Mary and I had parted as friends. She tried to steal my husband, then fiancé, from me while I was away at college. That and something she said about my husband soured him on her for good. He doesn't even like her name brought up."

"Do you think she is capable of burying her cousin alive?" He'd not told anyone else this detail. He trusted this woman. She knew how to keep secrets.

"That's what happened? Poor Myra, no one deserves to die that way. Not even someone as twisted as she was." Mrs. Maddox looked down at her glass of tea. Her lips moved as if she were praying.

Hawke waited until she raised her gaze to him. "What do you mean by twisted?" He knew the woman had been collecting, or trying to collect off the photos, he wasn't sure which.

"She bounced around from family to family until the Thomases adopted her. I'm sure there was some psychological damage. But she just had a mean streak. She and Mary spent a lot of time together. Now, I wonder how they got along. They both had strong personalities that wanted to be the center of attention and inflict harm to anyone they didn't like."

Hawke thought about what the woman said. "This is confidential information, but I feel I can trust you to not repeat what I'm going to say. I need someone to help me make sense of the connection between the cousins." Hawke told the woman about how Myra slept with men and had photos of their encounters and how he believed that Mary knew all about it.

Mrs. Maddox nodded her head. "Check out those men and see what either Myra or Mary could get from having scandalous evidence on them. That sounds a lot like the entrapment Mary did in school. I would bet there was something they wanted out of each of the men."

No wonder he couldn't find a money trail that related to the photos. They weren't after money. At least not the victim in the photo handing over money. That caused him to flash to the one person that he didn't understand. "Myra had photos of Laurel Bertram all alone in her garden at the farm. Any idea about those?"

"I bet Mary doesn't like her for marrying Arnie, but having a photo of her doing nothing out of the ordinary…that doesn't make sense." She held up the pitcher. "Would you like more?"

"No, thank you." He placed a business card on the table. "If something comes to you, give me a call. I want to get enough evidence on Mary that I can get a warrant for her arrest before she decides someone else is in the way of whatever it is she is trying to do. I believe that's to purchase the Bertram farm, but I can't figure out why."

"I can tell you that if she purchased that farm, Ed would never leave her. Growing up, all he talked about was getting the family farm back together. If his wife did that, he would never leave her and would do all of her bidding. I told you Ed wasn't that smart. He can bully and he can bluff, but he isn't smart enough to

248

outthink his wife."

Hawke swished that knowledge around in his mind. "Would it irk Mary if I brought in her husband and believed he thought it all up?"

The woman shook her head. "No. While she might have wanted that farm to keep her husband in line, I could see her having dropped evidence that he killed the two. She always had a backup plan when we did something we weren't supposed to. Just in case we were caught. No, you would need to find someone, possibly whoever she asked to help her. Question them and then somehow have it leaked to Mary that that person is the mastermind. She wouldn't be able to not tell you how it was all her plan and she'd outsmarted you by thinking it was the other person." The woman grinned. "She is devious and smart, but her hubris will get her every time."

Hawke smiled and stood. "Thank you. This has been helpful. I know I'm repeating myself, but none of this can be told to anyone. Not even your husband."

"Not a problem there. If I told him I'd even talked about the woman to you, he'd be furious." She scowled. "One day I might tell you what she did to him."

He nodded and walked out the back door and over to his pickup. A whistle brought Dog bounding over to the vehicle. "Ready to go see what we can find out about the forensics on the motorcycle?"

Dog continued panting.

"Play too hard?" Hawke pulled a dish out from under the seat and reached behind the back seat to grab a bottle of water he kept there for such occasions. He poured water into the bowl and let Dog drink while he slowly drove down the lane and out to the main road.

He wondered why he hadn't seen the forensic report on the motorcycle in the folder.

As soon as he drove into Prairie Creek, he pulled over and called Sheriff Lindsey.

"Lindsey."

"Sheriff, it's Hawke. Did you happen to see the forensic report on the motorcycle at the Bertram farm?"

"I can't remember. The oil was a match, I remember that."

"Did they pull any fingerprints or fibers from the machine?" He needed something to bring Ms. Booth in on.

"I don't see anything. Here's the case number. You can call the State Lab and ask about it." Lindsey read off the case number. "You're one of the officers of record on this case so you shouldn't have a problem getting the information."

"Thanks." Hawke ended the call and found the number for the Metro Portland Lab in Clackamas. He dialed and waited for someone to pick up.

His call was answered and he was transferred to a lab technician.

"Stone here, what do you need?" a male voice asked.

Hawke rattled off his title, badge number, and case number. "I'd like to know if anything admissible was discovered on the motorcycle that was part of this case."

"Hold while I look it up."

Orchestra music played as he waited. He unscrewed the lid on the water and gave Dog some more while watching the traffic pass by.

The music ended and Stone's voice exploded in his

ear. "The team that processed the motorcycle only took samples of the oil. We'll need to send another team out there. That won't happen for a couple of days. You might be able to get the State Police lab in Pendleton there quicker."

"Thanks." Hawke ended the call and growled. He called Sheriff Lindsey to tell him about the hold up, then he called his friend Lieutenant Keller of the Pendleton State Police.

"Hawke, didn't think I'd be hearing from you this soon. More problems at the reservation?" she answered.

"No. I had a double homicide over here that the forensic team who worked it missed getting evidence from a crucial item. I wondered if you could send the lab guys next door to you over here to pick it up and do a thorough inspection. I need something to be found to connect it to a suspect."

"What and where is it?"

Hawke rattled off the motorcycle make and model as well as the Bertram address. "If they contact me, I can meet them there."

"I'll pass that along with the message to go pick up the motorcycle."

"Thanks."

"You owe me a visit with your mom. I always wanted to meet the woman who raised you." Carol Keller had been a recruit with him at the State Police Academy, and later, when they were both on patrol, had worked together on a couple of calls. They'd also spent some off duty hours together before she married.

"I can arrange that the next time I visit her." Hawke had been trying harder to get over and see his mom. She'd mentioned to him too many times that she didn't see him enough. Since his younger sister hadn't visited in five years, he was working harder at getting over to see their mom.

He ended the call and headed home. The forensic team wouldn't head this way until tomorrow. He'd try to be in the vicinity of Leap, so he could meet them at the Bertram farm.

Chapter Twenty-eight

Dressed in his uniform, ready for a day of patrolling, Hawke headed north. He would check the hunting areas north of the Leap area so he could hurry back to the Bertram farm when forensics called him to say they were on their way.

He'd visited with one hunting camp when the call came. He radioed dispatch telling them he would be out of reach by radio for two hours and drove back to the Bertram farm.

Laurel Bertram was outside in her garden when he arrived. He parked and walked over to the neatly tilled ground and rows of vegetables.

The woman glanced his direction and asked, "Have you caught the person who killed my Arnie?"

"Not yet. There's a forensic team coming to take the motorcycle. They should be here any minute."

She scowled. "Why do they want that old thing?"

"We believe whoever took your husband's pickup and left it at Freezeout, used the motorcycle to return back here and get their vehicle that had to have been left somewhere near here." That made him think he needed to go back to the neighbor who gave Laurel an alibi and heard the motorcycle the next morning. He might have seen a vehicle parked along the road somewhere.

The woman stomped over to the fence. "Who do you think used it?"

"I can't tell you that."

"Was it that loud mouth Ed? He could have killed Arnie for that bike. But why bring it back?" The woman was grasping at anything to make sense of her husband's killing. She wasn't as cold as the woman he'd first met.

"I don't believe it was Ed, but we need to take a look at the motorcycle to rule anyone out on my suspect list." He studied her. "That includes you."

She sputtered. "I haven't ridden on that thing for years. I don't like the feeling of being out of control. He always laughed at me." She sniffed.

The crunch of tires on gravel pulled their attention to the forensic van driving in the lane.

Hawke took this as a reason to drop the conversation and move away from the woman. While he understood her grief, he had a hard time dealing with emotional women. That was one of the things he liked best about Dani. She wasn't a flighty, moody female. She was levelheaded and told him what she thought, no pussyfooting around. He admired that.

He waved the van over to the barn and then showed the two lab techs where the motorcycle sat in the building.

After they'd gathered fingerprints from the handle bars, they covered it and rolled it up into the van.

"Can you put a rush on processing that?" Hawke asked. "It should have left here two weeks ago with the other evidence in this case."

"I'll see what I can do, but no promises," the older of the two techs said.

"That's all I ask. Thanks." Hawke walked over to Mrs. Bertram and handed her the slip of paper stating the make and model of motorcycle that had been taken in as evidence.

She stared at the paper. "Do you really think the motorcycle will help you figure out who killed Arnie?"

"I'm counting on it to give me the evidence I need to pull in the killer." Hawke opened his vehicle door. "I'll let you know as soon as I get the person to crack."

"Thank you. Jenny and I would appreciate that."

Hawke nodded and slid in behind the steering wheel. He closed the door and drove down the road to the Klein farm.

At the farm, Jerome Klein straightened from where he was working on a swather and walked over to Hawke's vehicle.

"What are you doing here? Mom and Dad told me you'd been by here before you talked to me at Mountain High."

Hawke opened his door and stepped out. "I have another question. Did you happen to see any vehicles parked along the road around the Bertram farm the night or morning after Arnie Bertram was killed?"

"That Wednesday night when you asked me about the baling?"

"That one." Hawke pulled out his logbook and wrote the man's name as he waited.

"I changed water and rode the four-wheeler back to the house along the side of the field that runs parallel to the county road." He scrunched his eyes and raised his hat, scratching his head. "I don't remember seeing any cars parked, but I do remember seeing Mary Newton's car spewing dust as it drove by. She was driving." He chuckled. "She always drives her car. Ed was in the passenger seat. Just before I hit the end of the field, Ed's SUV flashed by going back down the road. He was driving."

Hawke latched onto this. "You didn't see Mary drive back out in her car?" This could be what he needed to help get the truth. The woman had said, she'd dropped off her husband and headed to Myra's in Alder.

"No. I don't remember seeing her drive by. And I would have heard a car coming and looked. I always look. We don't have a lot of traffic on this road. Only those who live here."

The road was a dead end at the Newtons. This direction was the only way for Mary to go anywhere. Ed said he waited for her to leave before he left. If Klein didn't see her, then she'd stopped at the Bertram farm. He'd caught her in one lie. Now to catch her in more.

"Thank you. You didn't happen to see any cars sitting along the road the next morning?"

"Not that I recall."

He still didn't have a way to place Ms. Booth at the Bertram's. It would come down to forensics finding something on the motorcycle.

"Can you stop by the Sheriff's Office today or tomorrow and give the statement about seeing the cars? We need it on record."

Klein studied him. "Do you think Ed and Mary had something to do with Arnie's death?"

"Just stop by the Sheriff's Office and give your statement. I can't say one way or the other."

Hawke slid into the driver's seat of his vehicle and called Sheriff Lindsey. He told him about Klein's statement and that he was headed out to patrol.

"Could you see what information you can get on Meg Booth." He rattled off her address. "I believe she helped Mary Newton cover up the deaths."

"You've been busy, Hawke. I heard you called in a forensic team to pick up the motorcycle. Care to fill me in?"

Hawke got the sheriff up to speed on how he believed Ms. Booth drove the victim's pickup, with the motorcycle in back, to Freezeout and then rode the motorcycle back. He was pretty sure she also picked up Mary after she put her cousin's car in the garage, but he needed to know the time frame that the neighbor said he saw the car being driven into the garage.

"I'll get Corcoran doing the background check on Booth. Anything else you think we need to look into?" Lindsey asked.

"We need to find a way to get Ms. Booth to turn on Mrs. Newton. If she left DNA or anything that will help us link her to the bike or the pickup, that will help." He remembered the cigarette butt. "We need a sample of DNA from Ed Newton and Ms. Booth. Any chance you can get the DA or Judge Vickers to warrant them?"

"I'll see what I can do. It won't be easy to get one

from Ms. Booth. There isn't a reason for her to help Mrs. Newton."

"They are friends, and she lives across the street from Ed Newton's lover." Hawke knew that was slim evidence. "I actually think Mrs. Newton befriended Booth because of where she lives. To have someone keeping an eye on her husband and his lover."

"But why would Mrs. Newton kill our victims?" Sheriff Lindsey asked.

"I think part of it has to do with the past. I'm still working that out." Hawke had another thought. "Did you ever get all the names of the people Myra took photos of in her bed?"

"Yeah."

"I'll swing by and you can fill me in." Hawke ended the call and headed to Alder. He called dispatch that his radio was back on and hoped he didn't get reamed for not patrolling the north unit area.

«》《》《》

Hawke parked in the lot behind the sheriff's office and entered the building through the back door. He preferred this entrance to the front. Not the smell. They must have had either a couple of drunks or druggies in overnight from the smell of urine and vomit. He hurried by the jail entrance and through the door to the hallway of offices and the interview room.

He knocked on Sheriff Lindsey's door.

"Come in." Lindsey looked up from the paper in his hand. "That was quick."

Hawke shrugged. He hadn't driven much over the speed limit on his way here. "Do you have the list?"

Lindsey waved the paper in his hand. "She wasn't dealing with little people." He handed the paper over.

"The top two names—"

"Are city councilmen for Prairie Creek." Hawke interrupted him. "Why would she pick city councilmen?"

"The next two are county officials. They work in zoning and land use."

Hawke glanced up at the sheriff.

Lindsey pointed a finger at the paper. "What do you make of that?"

"They were planning to do something with land." He glanced at the other three names. "I don't recognize these three."

"All men who have land between Prairie Creek and Wallowa Lake. Getting any ideas now?"

"Myra was going to sell their land to Mrs. Newton. Most likely using the photos to get it done. Then they would use the clandestine photos on the councilmen and county officials if they couldn't get whatever they had planned put through the right way." Hawke thought about this. "Can you send a deputy out to talk to the three men with the property? Maybe they will have something that can help us piece things together." Another thought came to him. "I wonder if Darren Ault, the owner of the realty, knows anything about these pieces of property?"

"That might be a good place to start." Lindsey picked up his phone. "I'll get Corcoran to go check with the landowners."

Hawke took that as a dismissal and headed out the door. He hustled down the back hall and out the door. It was past noon. He'd walk over to Treetop and get something to eat. Most likely Ault would be out to lunch. Making sure he caught up to the man, Hawke pulled out his phone and called the realty. The same young woman answered the phone.

"Wallowa Valley Realty. How may I help you?"

"It's Trooper Hawke. Is Mr. Ault in?"

"I'm sorry, he's out to lunch. I expect him back in by one-thirty. Would you like to leave a message or call back then?"

"I'll swing by about then. Thanks." Hawke slipped his phone back in his cell holster and strode down the street to the café.

Chapter Twenty-nine

Gail, the realty receptionist, smiled when Hawke walked through the door. "Welcome back, Trooper Hawke. Are you looking for a place to purchase?"

"Maybe." Her comment brought back his thoughts about getting a piece of property for him and Dani. A place where she could winter the lodge horses, and they could be together when she was off the mountain.

Her eyes lit up. "Is that what you're talking to Darren about?"

"Not today. I'd rather work with someone who would find property in my budget, not try to see how much they can make off me."

She nodded. "We have a couple people like that here." She glanced down at her hands, then up at him. "I'll have my realtor license in a few months. If you can wait, I'd be honored to help you."

Hawke grinned. "When you get that license give me a call." He handed her one of his business cards.

Her smile reached clear across her face. "I will.

Darren should be in his office."

"Thanks." Hawke strode down the short hall to the office where he'd talked with Ault before.

"Trooper Hawke. I wasn't expecting you back here." The man shoved papers into a folder and stood. "How can I help you?"

Hawke took a seat in the chair in front of the man's desk and pulled out his logbook. He'd written down the names of the men who had property between Prairie Creek and the lake. "I was wondering what you could tell me about the property these men have for sale." He read off the names, watching the realtor.

The man's color lightened and one finger tapped the desk top. He slowly lowered into his chair, shuffled the folder back and forth on his desk, and cleared his throat. "I don't believe I know anything about property those men might be selling."

"Why was Myra interested in those properties? She had files at her home. The names on the files here are the same as were on those files."

The man's jaw twitched and his eyes sparked. "She knew better than to take files from this office."

"Then you do know about these pieces of property." Hawke leaned back in the chair. "Care to tell me why Myra would have needed information to threaten them? Maybe so you could sell the property to…"

The man blew out a breath and held up his hands. "She wasn't selling that property for this company if she had the files at home and was coercing the clients. I heard through a planning commissioner that a big-name resort wanted that land to put up a vacation resort with an indoor water slide." He shrugged. "I was priming the owners to get them to let me sell to the resort. They weren't all on board about the whole thing. I was taking my time. Sounds like Myra might have been pushing harder to get them to sell to her, or someone else, so they could sell to the resort people."

One more reason for Mrs. Newton to want Myra gone. She would get all the money when the resort bought the land. But she needed Myra to purchase the property… Unless they had already finished all the paperwork.

"Can I have Gail look up something for me?"

Ault appeared leery of the idea.

"I just want her to go into the public records at the courthouse to see who owns something. I'm assuming she does that on the computer all the time for you."

Relief swept across his face. "Yeah, sure. She can do that."

"Thanks." The man's unease made Hawke wonder what he might be hiding.

Back at the reception area, Hawke stopped and pulled a chair up alongside Gail's desk.

"Your boss gave me permission to have you look something up in the courthouse records."

She nodded, worked the mouse, and tapped keys until she was inside the county records. "What do you want to know?"

"If the Ted Taylor place has changed hands recently."

She glanced at him with a frown. "I need coordinates… wait." She tapped, different windows opened, and pretty soon she copied and pasted the coordinates into the first window she'd opened. "I didn't even know this property was listed but it sold two weeks ago to Mary Newton."

Hawke's chest burned with pride. He'd had a hunch that was what had happened. "Try these two." He showed her the names in his book.

"Same person purchased them as well."

Hawke slapped his logbook shut. He had her. He just had to come up with all the evidence. "Thanks. And don't forget to call when you get your license."

"I won't. But I'll be keeping an eye out for what you want." She picked up a notebook. "What are you looking for?"

"Horse property. Something that can raise enough hay to winter twenty head of horses, has a barn and a house that doesn't need too much work."

"Got it. Twenty acres with a barn and house. Ground in grass or alfalfa?"

"Prefer grass."

"I'll keep a lookout for that type of property."

"Thanks." Hawke walked out of the realty office happy with his investigation and a tiny bit excited about this step he was taking of purchasing land. After fourteen years living over the Trembley's arena, it would be a big move. If Dani agreed.

《》《》《》

It was too late in the day to head out to check on hunters. Hawke went back to the sheriff's office instead. He walked into Lindsey's office, and the man leaned back in his chair.

"What have you discovered?"

"Those three men sold their land to Mary Newton right before Myra died. The reason the two schemed to get the land is because word has it a large resort is planning to purchase that land."

The sheriff grinned. "Looks like we have a motive for Myra's death. Once we get the evidence gathered."

"That's what I thought. I came back here to see if I couldn't nudge the DA or Judge Vickers into getting those DNA warrants signed."

"What do you think the DNA will prove?" Lindsey studied Hawke.

"If they pull any from the motorcycle, we can connect the Booth woman to it. And I'm pretty sure the cigarette butt will come back matching Ed Newton. I think it was left in the pickup to frame him. I can almost guarantee that if we pull him in for the crime, Ms. Booth will swear she never saw Newton's vehicle at her neighbor's house across the street. Or that she saw the two of them leave, before the murders and return the next morning."

Sheriff Lindsey nodded. "Makes sense. Go rattle the D.A.'s cage and see if he can convince the judge."

Hawke nodded and rose. "Has Corcoran had a chance to visit with the people who sold their property to Mary Newton?"

"I'll call him and see."

Hawke stood inside the office listening to the sheriff's side of the conversation.

The man put down the phone and said, "He'll meet you at the Shake Shack in ten."

"Thanks." Hawke glanced at his watch. If he didn't get over to see the D.A. soon, there wouldn't be enough time to convince him and have him convince the judge. But Corcoran may have more evidence that could sway the courts.

He slid into his vehicle and headed to the Shake Shack. Corcoran's vehicle wasn't in sight. Hawke pulled up to the window and ordered a chocolate shake. Once he had the treat, he pulled over and parked in the small parking lot, drinking his shake and waiting.

Ten minutes later, Corcoran pulled through the line and then parked next to Hawke.

Hawke had finished his shake. He walked over to the garbage and dropped the cup in before taking the passenger seat in the deputy's vehicle.

"What did you learn?" Hawke asked.

Corcoran chewed the bite of hamburger in his mouth and said, "All three sold their property to Mary Newton. Interesting that name is connected to our homicide."

Hawke nodded.

"She's allowing them to continue living there, rent free for three months. Which will give them time to find somewhere else to go."

"Did they say why they sold to her?" Hawke was pretty sure he knew why. The photos they'd found at Myra's.

"They were all reluctant to talk about that until their wives went to tend to other things. Those photos we found. They were all forced into selling. It was for market price, but one of them hadn't wanted to sell. The photo convinced him."

"Did any of them mention it was Mary behind the scheme?" Hawke wanted to catch her up in knowing about the photos her cousin had.

"They didn't say so, but from their reactions, I think they have all figured out she was probably in on it." Corcoran took another bite and chewed.

"Any chance forensics has pieced together the documents we caught Mary shredding?" He had a feeling there might be something in those.

"You could call and ask. But they are pretty busy."

Hawke pulled out his phone and dialed the OSP forensic lab in Pendleton. Within minutes he was put through to the lab tech in charge of this case's shredded evidence.

"This is Senior Trooper Hawke." He usually didn't use his seniority, but if it would get him faster results, he would use it. "I was wondering if you'd made any sense of the shredded photos and documents that were sent to you."

"I've pieced a few of the photos and a couple of documents together. I'll scan those and email them to you."

"I'd appreciate you sending them to me as you get them put together."

"I can do that. Give me about five minutes and I'll have what is finished emailed."

"Thanks." Hawke ended the call.

"Do they have anything?" Corcoran asked, in between slurping his drink.

"He's managed to put a few together. He's emailing them to me." Hawke held his phone in his hand, waiting.

The phone buzzed. It was the forensic lab calling. "Hawke."

"Trooper Hawke, this is Danielle over at the OSP forensic lab in Pendleton. We have the report on the Honda CL that was picked up this morning."

"That's quick work." He pulled out his logbook and opened it. "I'm ready."

"There were smudged fingerprints on the fuel cap. Can't make a match with them. I found two pieces of hair between the seat and the fuel tank. One has follicle. I'm running it for DNA. If you get us a sample of your suspect, we will have it here to run a match. The rider must have used gloves, there weren't any prints on any of the smooth surfaces. Dirt and rocks in the tire treads were a mixture of many parts of Wallowa County. Nothing that can specifically match it to any one place. I did find a piece of chewing gum stuck in the tire. I'm running that for DNA. It could have just been picked up off the road anywhere."

Hawke grinned. "What was the color and length of the hair you found?"

"It's gray, short, curly hair. No dyes or perm. It's natural."

"Thank you. Please send that report to the Wallowa County Sheriff's Department, attention Sheriff Lindsey."

"I'll do that."

Hawke glanced at his watch. He hoped Judge Vickers was still in his office. "I just received the news I needed to get those DNA warrants." Hawke opened the patrol car door. "I'll catch up with you tomorrow."

"Copy," Corcoran said and shoved fries in his mouth.

Hawke strode to his vehicle. Judge Vickers had to see there was no other reason for Ms. Booth's hair to be on that motorcycle other than to use it to get back to the Bertram farm.

Chapter Thirty

"Give me a good reason for needing a DNA warrant." Judge Vickers voice boomed as he tipped his chair back and studied Hawke. The ample judge had his hands laced together over his protruding stomach. The man's rotundness must have added air to his voice as he always sounded as if he were bellowing. The man's short cropped, snowy white beard would make him look like Santa if he grew it out.

"I believe Meg Booth put a motorcycle from the Bertram farm in the back of the victim's pickup, drove them both to Freezeout, then used the motorcycle to return to the farm before walking to the Newton's to get her vehicle to drive home. Hair similar in description to hers was found on the Honda CL that was in the Bertram barn. Oil from the same motorcycle was found in the bed of the victim's abandoned vehicle." Hawke returned the judge's gaze.

Vickers nodded. "That sounds pretty clear that you would want to either rule her out or find out if she actually did drive the vehicle and motorcycle to Freezeout. But why Ed Newton? Do you believe the woman was helping him?"

Hawke shook his head. "I think his wife is trying to frame him for what she did."

Vickers' white bushy eyebrows flew up to his hairline. "You think Mary Newton did the killing? How? Why?"

Having made a list of evidence against both women in his head as he drove to the courthouse, Hawke laid out more of the why than the how. They wouldn't know the how clearly until they caught her.

When he finished, Judge Vickers leaned forward. "Get the warrants written up, and I'll sign them first thing in the morning."

"Thank you, Judge. I'll be here at eight a.m.," Hawke said, standing.

"If you're going to be that early, meet me at Treetop. I have a breakfast meeting with Lange there tomorrow."

Hawke nodded and left the judge's chambers.

Out at his vehicle, Hawke called in he was done for the day and headed home. He'd make some soup and grab a shower before he tackled writing up the warrants. They would have to be worded just right.

«»«»«»

Hawke stepped out of his vehicle and was assaulted by Dog jumping on him and the loud whinnying and braying of his horses and mule.

"I'm not that late," he said to the animals as he patted their faces, walking by to open the door to the storage room where the grain was kept.

Dog dove through the door in hopes of catching a mouse. Hawke scooped grain into three plastic feeders and carried them out to the stall, hanging them on the inside of the gate. Turning to head up to his apartment, Herb hurried into the barn.

"Darlene has dinner on the table. Come on over and join us. She's bustin' with information to tell you about Mary and Myra."

Hawke always enjoyed Darlene's meals. And knowing a little more about the woman he was sure had killed two people, he wouldn't pass up the gossip either.

"Sounds like a good evening to me. Give me a minute to take off the body armor." Hawke bounded up to his apartment and took off his duty belt, shirt, and under armor. He pulled a t-shirt on and descended the stairs before falling into step beside his landlord. If he bought a place, there wouldn't be home cooked meals offered to him several times a week. That was something to consider.

At the house, Dog pushed his way in ahead of Hawke. The animal took his usual place at the door leading into the living room.

Hawke sat in his usual chair. "Smells good in here, Darlene."

The woman standing beside the stove, glanced over her shoulder and smiled. "Glad you could make it. I've got shepherd's pie and brownies for dessert."

Anything Darlene cooked was good. And having had both the foods she'd mentioned before, he knew he would eat way too much.

Darlene placed a bowl of applesauce on the table

and settled in her chair. They dished up the food and Hawke started eating, knowing Darlene would start spilling what she'd learned in good time.

He'd eaten half of what he'd dished on his plate when Darlene took a drink of water and settled back in her seat. "I have some information you might like to hear."

Hawke sipped his coffee and nodded. "Go ahead."

"I learned at the quilting club today that Mary and Myra, before Myra's family moved, were two little girls who bullied and stole money and items from their school mates. Louise said she remembered overhearing the two talking in the girls bathroom one day. Mary was the one who planned things out and Myra would do whatever she said. Myra was a bit of a wild child. She would do anything someone dared her to do. That's why the family left here. She snuck into the principal's house and stole his hairpiece. Then ran it up the flagpole the next day."

She took another drink from her glass and continued. "Those two didn't care who they hurt. Usually, it was to get back at someone who did something to them or just to be plain mean."

This was confirming what Hawke had expected. Mary pulled the strings and Myra was game to cause trouble.

"I had a pretty good idea that's how the two worked. I've discovered why Myra's dead. I just have to get a person to help me trip up Mary." Hawke picked up his fork and returned to eating.

"You know Mary killed two people?" Darlene asked.

Hawke peered into her eyes. "I'm sure she did. I

just have to get the evidence to prove it."

The woman's face paled. "I've known her to be cold and calculating, but to kill her cousin and Arnie? I don't understand."

"No one understands murderers." Hawke glanced at Herb and back to Darlene. "You can't tell anyone what I said. I don't want her to know I'm on to her until I have absolute proof she can't wiggle out of."

They both nodded.

Darlene stood and picked up the plate of brownies. She placed them on the table. "What makes a person be so mean that they finally crack and kill someone?"

"That's something psychologists and scientists have been trying to figure out for centuries." Hawke plucked two brownies from the plate and savored the chocolate. When he finished, he picked up his dishes and placed them in the sink. "Seems like all I do lately is eat and run, but I need to write up some warrants."

Herb waved his hand. "We understand. Everyone in the county will feel safer when this double murder is solved."

"Thanks. Dinner was delicious, as always. And thanks for the added insight into Mary and Myra." Hawke walked to the door and opened it. Dog remained on the rug by the living room door. "Are you coming?"

Dog glanced at the table, then at Darlene. The woman filled a small plastic container with the leftovers. "Take this for Dog."

The animal stood, stretched, and walked to the door as Darlene handed Hawke the container.

Walking over to the arena, Hawke said, "I think we're both getting spoiled living here."

《》《》《》

Friday morning, with warrants in hand, Hawke entered Treetop Café and scanned the interior for the judge and D.A. Lange. He spotted them at the same table as the last time he'd found them here together.

He walked up to the table. "Judge Vickers, I have the warrants we talked about yesterday." He handed the papers over to the judge.

"Judge Vickers filled me in. You think we'll be able to bring charges against someone soon?" Lange asked.

"I'm hoping these DNA swabs will get me the evidence I need to bring in the accomplice. If I can get her to turn, then we'll have the murderer." Hawke kept his voice low. This might be a place where most of the customers were law enforcement, he still didn't want any of the suspects to get word of what he had planned.

"Good luck," Judge Vickers said, handing Hawke the signed documents.

"Thanks, I'll need it." Hawke left the café without eating. He would grab something to eat in Winslow, where he would be closer to the two people he would serve the warrants.

The radio was crackling and rushed voices were talking.

"We have a man at the lake running around naked and swinging a machete in one hand and a revolver in the other." He recognized Deputy Novak's voice. "I need backup."

"Copy. I'm in Alder. Where exactly are you?" Hawke turned on his lights and siren and headed out of Alder toward Prairie Creek and Wallowa Lake, listening to Novak tell him where the incident was happening.

From the description of the man, it sounded like he was whacked out on drugs. He hated this type of call. You never knew what you were getting into. But you damn sure knew if the guy was on drugs he was going to be twice as strong. Since he was waving around two weapons, he was probably angry with someone or something.

He slowed entering Prairie Creek. It was the time of the year when the tourist season was more relaxed, but there were still a lot of vehicles parked along the street. Which meant there was the possibility of someone stepping out from between cars.

Once he cleared the city limits, he floored the accelerator and raced around the east side of the lake to the boat ramp area on the south end. Novak said the man had run away from the camping area.

The county vehicle came into view. Hawke killed the lights and siren and pulled up alongside the SUV. Novak stood in front of his vehicle watching the man who shouted and waved a gun and a large knife at the sky.

Hawke walked over to the deputy. "Can you make sense of what he's saying?"

"Not really. I was hoping whatever he took would wear off and he'd calm down." Novak uncrossed his arms. "When I got the call, a woman had called in saying she was afraid a man was going to hurt himself. When I arrived, I found this nut waving the weapons and shouting. He took one look at my vehicle and ran down here. At least he's away from the other campers."

Glancing around, Hawke noticed a woman wrapped in a blanket standing fifty yards away and a group of people behind her gawking. He nodded to the woman. "Is that the woman?"

Novak glanced over. "I guess. She was at the camp where I found him."

"I'm going to go talk to her. Don't approach him until I find out what's going on." Hawke didn't wait for an affirmative before he strode over to the woman. "I'm State Trooper Hawke."

The woman was small, bony, and scratching at her bare skin. There was a lot of skin showing. The blanket dropped off her shoulders, revealing small bare breasts. He cleared his throat, and she pulled the blanket back up on her shoulders. Below the covering, her bony legs and feet were bare. He wondered if she wore anything underneath.

"Ma'am, I understand you called the police about your husband?" Hawke pulled out his logbook.

The woman stared at him. "He's not my husband. I picked him up hitchhiking. He said he liked to party and had a friend here who would party with us." She sneered, showing off black teeth. A sign she was using meth on a regular basis.

"What is your friend's name?" Hawke centered his attention on the page he was writing on.

"Jack. Said he was Jack the Beanstock." She cackled and then coughed. When she finished coughing, she added, "He didn't have nothing like a giant. His pecker was more like a toothpick. When I told him, he got all mad and said it was all his mom's fault." She scratched her arm and the blanket dropped below her breasts, again.

Hawke decided it would be best to get her away from the gawkers. He motioned for her to raise the blanket. "Come with me." He led her over to the county vehicle. "Why don't you wait in here while I see if I can talk to Jack."

"You can't arrest me. All I did was try to have sex with Jack and he went crazy." Her blanket fell to the ground, and she was as naked as the day she entered the world. For the first time since hair started growing on his balls, he was repulsed by a naked female body. It was scrawny and covered with sores from her scratching.

He grabbed the blanket, wrapped it around her, opened the back door of the county car, and folded her into the back seat. He closed the door and walked back to Novak.

"Why did you put the woman in my car?" Novak asked, still watching the man who continued to wave the weapons toward the sky and shout.

"She doesn't have any clothes on and keeps dropping the blanket. Indecent exposure. I'm going to see if I can have a talk with Jack and get the weapons away from him. Keep an eye on him."

"Copy."

Talking people down from a high wasn't on Hawke's list of favorite, or smart things, to do, but he was getting too old to roll around on the concrete with someone who had fifty pounds on him.

"Hey, Jack!" Hawke called out to get the man's attention and not surprise him when he walked up.

The man's head snapped around and his wide wild eyes stared at Hawke.

"Jack, care to tell me what you're yelling about?" He continued to walk slowly forward, keeping the man's hands, which had dropped to his side, in his view as well as the man's face.

"Who are you?" The point of the large knife punctuated his question as it was directed at Hawke.

"I'm State Trooper Hawke. You're causing a disturbance. I was asked to come see what's going on. Care to tell me why you're out here swinging around weapons and yelling at the sky?" Hawke stopped twenty feet back from the man. He rested his thumbs in his duty belt and stood slack-hipped, giving the impression he wasn't worried. His stance may have looked casual, but his heart pounded and his gut burned. This guy could shoot him or stab him before Novak could put a bullet in him. People on drugs had adrenaline pumping through them that caused them to be quick at times and twice as strong.

The man started gesturing. "Look at me. Size thirteen shoes, two X shirts, and my damn pecker is the size of a peanut. I'm tired of women laughing at me. If I can't procreate like God intended, then I might as well not be here." He put the large knife to his throat.

"Hey. Women aren't worth taking your life. Especially the one in the county car that you came here with. Did she give you something? Drugs maybe?"

The man's gaze flashed to the county SUV. "Yeah, she gave me meth. Said she had enough to keep us high for a week." He shook his head. "We'd had a six pack before." Jack whipped the knife away from his neck, leaving a thin red line of blood. "That bitch said I had a wimpy weanie!" He stretched his body toward the county car and yelled, "You have a wimpy everything!"

Hawke used all his control to not jump back and let the man know how nervous he was standing this close to a high suspect with a weapon in each hand. "Why don't you give me the gun and the knife. You're going to hurt yourself." He had to try one more time before he and Novak made a plan on how to apprehend Jack.

Another county car arrived. It was Deputy Corcoran. He had his weapon drawn as he walked up to Novak. He hoped Novak talked Corcoran into holstering his Glock.

Jack started twitching and his arm shot in the air. Hawke caught a glimpse of the empty space where the magazine holding the rounds should have been. If there was a bullet in the chamber, Jack would only get one shot off before they took him down.

Hawke grasped the mic on his shoulder, and said quietly into it, "Suspect's handgun may only have one round in the barrel. Empty magazine well. I'm going to try and get the knife away from him and then you two can cuff him."

Hawke lowered his hand slowly and walked a couple steps closer. "Jack, why don't you give me that knife before you hurt yourself."

The man jerked his attention and gaze back to Hawke. "Who are you?"

"I'm State Trooper Hawke. I'm here to make sure you don't hurt yourself or anyone else. How about giving me that knife. I don't think I've ever seen such a nice handle on a knife before." The large blade had a thick wooden handle.

The man's eyes bounced around in his sockets. "I made it. Carved the handle."

"Can I see the craftmanship on the handle?" Hawke held his hand out.

Jack started to hand the knife to him, blade first, then quickly pulled it back. "You're going to steal it. I've had people offer me money, but I won't sell it."

"Honest, I don't want to steal it. My uncle carved the handle on my knife. It fits my hand perfectly. I bet you made the handle of your knife fit you."

The man's lips raised into a smile. "Yeah. It only fits my hand." He held out the knife palm up and slowly uncurled his long wide fingers from around the handle.

Hawke could see the indentions for each one of the man's fingers, giving him a good grip on the handle. "That's a work of art. Do you carve handles for other people?" Hawke stared at the knife longingly, while keeping his peripheral vision on the man's face.

"Yeah, I've made a few handles." The man jerked and before his fingers could capture the knife, it fell to the ground. Hawke quickly kicked the weapon as far away as he could. The two deputies had moved in behind the man as Hawke had talked with him. Now they each grasped one of the man's arms and pulled them behind his back. Novak dislodged the revolver from the man's hands and Hawke kicked it to the side. The man howled, kicked with his legs, and brought his arms together in front of him, knocking the two deputies together.

Hawke took the opportunity of the man focusing on the deputies to step behind Jack and knock him to his knees. He grabbed the cuff Corcoran had managed to get on the man's arm and pulled it back, as Novak shoved Jack onto the ground and handed Hawke the man's other wrist to lock in the cuffs.

"Sorry, but you are going to jail for disturbing the peace and to see if you can't come down and not be a menace to yourself," Hawke said, pulling the man to his feet.

Novak and Corcoran took hold of Jack's arms and

led him over to Corcoran's car.

Hawke picked up the knife and revolver, carried them to his vehicle, and pulled out an evidence bag. He put the weapons in the bags, filled out the information, and walked over, handing the bags to Corcoran. "I'm headed to get DNA samples from Meg Booth and Ed Newton. I'll catch up with you later and fill you in."

"You think they will give you a sample willingly?" Corcoran stood by his driver side door. The vehicle was rocking as Jack shouted and flung his body back and forth.

"I'm hoping they will. They have no choice." Hawke walked over to his vehicle and called dispatch to let them know the incident was over.

Chapter Thirty-one

Hawke decided to get the DNA sample from Ed Newton first. He grabbed a burger and shake at the Shake Shack in Alder and kept on driving out the North Highway as he ate. A left turn onto Leap Lane would take him out to the Newton farm. A smile crept across his face, thinking about how Mrs. Newton would react to his requesting a DNA sample from her husband. Either she would act as if she didn't want her husband to do it, or she would tell him it was the only way to clear his name, knowing she had left evidence that would get him arrested. Hawke was pretty sure she had left the evidence.

He drove down the lane and parked in front of the Newton home. After all that he had heard about the couple, he now realized why during his first visit the atmosphere had felt cold.

Ed walked out of the barn and over to the vehicle. "What are you doing back here?"

Hawke pulled the plastic tube, the length of a Bic pen and twice the diameter, out of his pocket. "I need to get a buccal swab of your DNA."

Newton backed away from the vehicle. "Why?"

"We found a cigarette butt in Arnie's vehicle. He didn't smoke, and it's the brand you smoke. If you didn't leave the butt, then you have no reason to worry about this swab."

Mrs. Newton stepped out of the house and advanced on Hawke. "What are you doing?"

"I'm asking your husband for a DNA swab."

She thrust her hands on her hips and glared at her husband. "Are you going to just let him take it?"

"He has no choice." Hawke handed her the search warrant. "I have a signed warrant that states he either allows this or he will be charged with obstruction of justice."

Ed stepped forward. "I've got nothing to hide. Go ahead."

"Ed, are you sure?" Mrs. Newton asked. Her tone of voice sounded unsure, but her eyes and smug smile told Hawke what he'd believed. She'd planted the cigarette, and now she thought her plan was going as she'd orchestrated.

"Yes. I wasn't at the Bertram's and I didn't kill anyone." Ed opened his mouth. Hawke popped the top on the cylinder and pulled out the long swab stick. He rubbed it back and forth inside Ed's cheek and slid it back into the cylinder. "Thank you for cooperating. Have a good day."

Hawke walked back to his vehicle, wrote the date, time, and Newton's name on the cylinder label and tucked it in his glove box. His next stop would be Meg

Booth's house in Eagle.

《》《》《》

His phone buzzed as Hawke drove into Eagle. Sergeant Spruel. He groaned, pulled over, and answered the call. "Hawke."

"When are you going to do your job and get out checking hunters again?" His superior was being lenient, but Hawke knew he needed to get back to his real job and stop chasing murderers soon.

"If my next stop goes as planned, I should have this double homicide closed soon." Hawke held his breath waiting for Spruel to tell him to leave it to the county cops.

"Do you think you'll have it closed by next week?" Spruel didn't sound as if he believed him.

Hawke went on to tell him what he believed and how he hoped the steps he took today would make the woman's accomplice start talking.

"You think this DNA thing is going to work? You won't have any results from the tests for two weeks or better. How can you clear this case up in less than a week?"

"My plan is, Mrs. Newton will try to blame this on her husband, and Ms. Booth will tell me everything when I tell her that Mrs. Newton is pinning this on her and Ed Newton." He wasn't positive Ms. Booth would turn on the instigator of the murders. It was just an inkling he had that she might not be as good an accomplice as Mary Newton had judged.

"That's a ballsy assumption. I hope you're right." The connection went dead.

Hawke heaved a sigh of relief. He knew his job wasn't running around finding killers, and luckily for him, his boss understood his need to follow all the clues to the end. He pulled back onto the road and headed to Ms. Booth's house.

Parking in front of the one-story, he spotted the woman, once again, working in her flower garden. He wondered how she could live a life of leisure. She wasn't old enough for social security and hadn't seemed disabled or on welfare. Something he would most likely learn if he opened up the report on her.

Before exiting his vehicle, he opened his laptop and logged in to read the documents that had been added to this case. He found the background on Ms. Meg Booth. Her husband died 10 years ago in a car crash, and she'd received half a million from the insurance. The husband had been a sailboat salesman in Carolina. Ms. Booth had been a manager at a health club until her husband's death and her move to Wallowa County.

He wondered what made her move from Carolina to Eagle, Oregon. He glanced at her birth certificate. She was born in the county. Now he wondered who she was related to and if that was why she'd returned.

With this new knowledge, he stepped out and ambled up the sidewalk toward the house.

Ms. Booth popped up from the flower bed, as if she had radar, and strode his direction. "Why are you back?" she asked, stopping between Hawke and the door.

He held out the search warrant. "I have a warrant to take a buccal swab of your mouth."

She grabbed the paper and read. The lines around her mouth grew taut as her lips puckered as if she'd eaten something sour. She thrust the document back at him. "I won't have the neighbors seeing you digging around in my mouth." Tugging off her gloves, she opened the front door and let him in. However, she stood only in the room far enough to allow his entry.

Hawke dug the cylinder out of his pocket, snapped it open, and held out the swab. "Open your mouth wide."

She did as requested.

When he closed the cylinder, she asked, "Why do you need my DNA?"

"As the warrant stated, for the ongoing investigation of Arnie Bertram and Myra Bittle's deaths."

The woman chewed on her lip. "But why my DNA? I never met them. I only knew about Myra through Mary Newton."

"You won't hear from me again if this doesn't match the hair we found." He pulled out his pen and wrote the date, time, and person's name on the label.

"Hair? What hair? Where did you find it?"

"This is an ongoing investigation. I'm afraid I can't give that information." He spun to the door. "You'll be hearing from me if we have a match."

The woman groaned as he shut the door. He wondered how long it would take her to call Mary Newton?

《》《》《》

Hawke called Deputy Corcoran to keep an eye on Meg Booth and let him know if she met up with Mary Newton. He called for an OSP Trooper to meet him in Elgin to take the swabs to the Portland Metro Lab in Clackamas. By the time he returned from that errand, it was time to call it a day.

Back at the Trembley's, Hawke took care of his horses and mule and retired to his room over the arena. While dog crunched away on his dinner, Hawke microwaved a frozen dinner and started a list of the reasons he now considered Mary Newton the murderer. After he ate his dinner, he made a list of people that he needed to get statements from. These would be needed when he pulled Mary in after Meg Booth cracked.

When his lists were made and everything looked like it would line up to prove Mary had the most reason to kill the victims, Hawke took a shower and went to bed. Tomorrow he would ask Sheriff Lindsey to have a deputy collect the statements, and he would spend the day doing his job...checking hunters.

Chapter Thirty-two

The wind was blowing and the air felt like needles pricking his skin as Hawke rode Jack back down to the Two Pan Trailhead on the Lostine River. He'd been checking hunters in the Hurricane Divide Unit. There had been few hunters and even fewer animals as they were all taking shelter from a storm that was coming in.

By the time he had Jack in the trailer, it was getting dark. If not for the storm, he would have packed Horse and spent the next two nights out on the mountain, but he didn't feel like waking to snow on his sleeping bag.

Dog whimpered in the passenger seat as Hawke started up the state vehicle. "I know, I'm hungry and cold, too." Hawke dug in his coat pocket and pulled a bag of jerky out. He'd grabbed the package out of his saddlebags and stuffed it in his pocket while tying Jack in the trailer.

"Need some water, too?" Hawke asked, digging under the passenger seat for the plastic bowl and jug of water. He poured the water into the bowl and placed it in front of his friend.

By now the heater was working and Hawke's face tingled as it warmed up. He handed Dog a piece of jerky and stuck one in his own mouth before putting the vehicle in gear and heading down the Lostine River Road toward Winslow.

The minute they were in cell tower range, his phone started buzzing. Hawke pulled over, to not lose the signal, and stared at his missed calls, messages, and texts.

Sheriff Lindsey, Deputy Corcoran, the Pendleton lab, and Ed Newton all tried to call him. He opened his voicemail and listened to each message, starting with the sheriff.

"Hawke, I sent Deputy Corcoran out to gather the statements you requested. They are all signed and in the folder. What did you plan to do with them?"

He'd return the sheriff's call when he was back down in the valley. He tapped on the message from Corcoran.

"Hey, Hawke. When you get back in cell service, give me a call. One of the people I took a statement from had something interesting to say, off the record."

He would definitely call Corcoran back.

Next was the Pendleton Lab.

"Trooper Hawke. We also found some flower seeds and hemp residue on the Honda CL. The flowers are tagetes patula or French marigolds. The flower seeds can't be traced to any one flower, but if you get a sample of the hemp, we can see if it matches what was on the motorcycle."

Hawke thought about this. Could the residue have

been from the last time Reed Kamp rode the Honda? Would it have remained on the bike that long? He dialed the lab and asked for the lab tech who had called him before.

"I'm sorry, she's off for the night. You can try back at nine in the morning," replied the receptionist.

"Thank you."

Next, he listened to Ed's voicemail. "Trooper, I heard Mary on the phone telling someone that they had nothing to worry about. That she made sure I would be the one who went to jail. If you want to contact me, I'll be at Carrie's."

Hawke smiled. Mary Newton thought she'd left enough evidence to get her husband put in jail.

He checked the texts, all but one, were from the same people either texting what they'd said or telling him they'd left a message. Except Jenny Kamp. She'd send a text that she needed to talk to him as soon as possible.

That one surprised him. What could she need to talk to him about right away?

He put the vehicle in gear and headed back to Winslow. It was going to be too late to get something to eat at the Rusty Nail, but he could grab a burger at the Blue Elk.

Hawke parked along the street opposite the tavern and crossed. The curb in front of the establishment was full. It was Saturday night. Not only was the curb full, so was the tavern. If his stomach wasn't growling, he would have turned around and walked out. Instead, he pressed through the crowded tables and up to the bar. Finding the stool next to the cash register empty.

"Hawke, what are you doing in here and all decked

out in your uniform?" Ben asked, when he walked over to the cash register.

"Just came out of the mountains and wanted something to eat." Hawke unzipped his coat and grabbed the cup of hot coffee Ben placed in front of him.

"I have a three-piece chicken dinner as the special tonight."

"That will work. Ranch dressing."

"I'll put that down and be right back." Ben disappeared through the kitchen door.

Sally Kason, the waitress, walked up and rang the cash register, putting money in. "Hi, Hawke. When are you going to bring your lady friend back in?"

"Hey Sally. When she's done up on the mountain."

"With this storm coming in, I would be headed down to the valley if I lived up on the mountains."

"She's tough. So is her crew. They'll be there until the end of November for hunters to find shelter. Though I do believe the horses are coming out next month."

"If they can get out. I heard we're going to have a long, hard winter this year." She glanced over his shoulder. "Gotta get back to work. Good seeing you."

"You, too." He shifted to get a view of the room. It was mostly people in their twenties and thirties. Single with nothing else to do on a Saturday night but drink with friends and dance to the music Ben had playing, a bit loudly for Hawke's liking. A group of four women who had been dancing together moved toward a table littered with beer bottles. He spotted an older couple with their heads bent together over a small table in the back of the room. The size of the man gave him away. It was Ed Newton.

Ben came out of the kitchen. "A few more minutes and it will be ready."

"Thanks, I'm going to put my coat on this stool to save it for me while I go talk to someone."

"I'll keep an eye on it."

The dancers parted as Hawke crossed the area left open for dancing. He had locked his duty belt and Glock in the vehicle with Dog. But he was still in uniform and still wearing the body armor, making him look tougher than he was.

Hawke stopped next to the table where Ed and Carrie sat. They both looked up. Carrie gasped and Ed's face slackened with relief.

"Trooper Hawke. How did you find me?"

"I came in to get something to eat, but I listened to your voicemail as soon as I had cell service. Tell me about what you heard." Hawke grabbed a nearby chair and sat, pulling out his logbook.

"Mary must have thought I was outside. I'd gone in to use the john and heard her talking on the phone in her den. I stood outside the door and listened." He glanced at Carrie. "It's the only way I ever know what she's up to. Anyway, she said she was sure that I would get pulled in for the murders of Arnie and Myra. She said she'd placed evidence in the pickup and had a photo of me and Myra." The man shook his head. "All these years, I've done everything I could think of to make her love me or even respect me and she sets me up for murder. Why would she do that?"

Hawke wasn't about to tell him because she was the murderer. "I've discovered that women can dole out the weirdest kinds of revenge. And we usually don't even know what for." He glanced at Ms. Stiller.

She blushed. "Not all women are vindictive, Trooper."

"That's true, but a majority are."

"Has that DNA come back that you took from me? Is it going to prove I killed Arnie?"

"It's going to prove that the cigarette butt in the vehicle will have your DNA on it. I'm pretty sure that is the evidence she is talking about. What about this photo? Were you ever in Myra's bed?"

Carrie scowled at Ed.

He shook his head. "No. I rarely even talked to her when she came over. She and Mary would go into Mary's den and then she'd come out and leave. I don't know what photo she thinks she has."

Hawke had a pretty good idea that some of the damning evidence they needed was in Mary's den. "Stay with Carrie for a few more days. Let Mary think she's running this investigation and that you are scared. Don't talk to her or answer any calls from her. I'm sure she'll know where you are since her friend Meg Booth lives across the street from Carrie."

Carrie's mouth opened, then clamped shut, before she uttered, "Meg is friends with Mary?"

"You didn't know?" Hawke glanced at Ed.

He shook his head.

"Meg has been telling Mary everything you two do. She and Mary are BFFs."

Ed growled. "No wonder she knows more about where I go than I ever tell her."

"And Meg has come over and asked me questions about you. I thought she was just trying to be friendly because she was lonely." She put a hand on Ed's arm. "I never told her your name or anything intimate. Just when we go to dinner—" She narrowed her eyes. "That's why the two of them were at the restaurant that one night when we arrived. Meg had been over that day and saw me getting ready. She asked where I was going. I told her out to dinner at the Fireplace."

"Mary told me they were waiting for other members to arrive for a sorority meeting." Ed slammed a hand down on the table, drawing the attention of people around them.

"All of this is helping me." Hawke had been busily writing down all the two had said.

"Did my wife kill Arnie and Myra?" Ed asked.

"I'm not at liberty to say who I believe committed the murders. But I am getting closer to gathering enough evidence to bring someone in." He stood when he spotted Ben looking for him. "I believe my dinner is ready."

Chapter Thirty-three

Sunday morning, Hawke called in to dispatch that he would be unavailable for two hours. Then he drove through rain and fog to the sheriff's office. He wanted to read all the statements Corcoran had collected. He called Sheriff Lindsey on his way there.

"Hawke, did you get my message?"

"Yes, I'm headed to the office to look at the statements. Mrs. Newton, according to her husband, was talking on the phone yesterday afternoon telling someone not to worry, evidence would be found to implicate her husband in the murders."

"Write up a warrant for Mrs. Newton's latest phone records and a search warrant. I'll get it signed in the morning and get the records for the last week and see who she was calling." Sheriff Lindsey had a spark of determination that Hawke hadn't seen in him so far during this investigation.

"I'll do that," Hawke said and hung up.

Once he arrived at the office, he collected the

statements from the deputy at the main desk and settled in the extra office. He picked up the phone and called Corcoran.

"Hey Hawke, I wondered when you'd get back to me. I wasn't sure if you'd stayed up in the mountains," Corcoran answered.

"Too cold for these bones. What did you want to tell me?" Hawke had the statements spread out in front of him.

"When I took down the statement from Kent McCollough, he said the next day after he was coerced into signing the papers on his place, he saw Mrs. Newton and Reed Kamp having lunch in a restaurant in Prairie Creek."

"Just Reed?"

"That's what I asked him and he said, 'yes.'"

Now Hawke wondered if he was the person who rode the motorcycle, given there was also hemp residue on the machine. But why would Kamp help the woman? "Those papers she was shredding." Hawke blurted out.

"What about the papers?" Cocoran asked.

"When I looked at the files the night before, there were photos of paperwork that looked like Kamp was skimming money from his supporters. If I can get him to say she was forcing him... But I'm sure Meg Booth is the one who drove the pickup to Freezeout and rode the motorcycle back. It makes no sense for Kamp to go to Freezeout and ride the motorcycle back. He could have driven the vehicle there and walked home."

"Not if his vehicle was still at the Bertram's," Corcoran interjected.

"True, but why didn't someone see it if it was. For

that matter, someone should have seen Meg's vehicle. Any idea what she drives?" He opened the computer as Corcoran said he didn't have any idea.

Getting into Motor Vehicle records, he typed in Meg's name and came up with a license but no cars registered to her.

"That's odd. How does she get around without a vehicle?" He thought back to the two times he'd visited her house. He hadn't seen a garage or a car parked on the street.

"It's my day off or I'd drive by and check," Corcoran said.

"That's okay, I'll have someone else look into it for me." He knew just the person to call. "Thanks for the information."

"Copy."

The line went silent and Hawke texted Ed Newton. *What kind of vehicle does Meg Booth drive?*

He started reading the statements when his phone buzzed.

An old Yamaha 650.

Hawke wondered how she hadn't been pulled over for an outdated license.

Carrie says she sees people pick her up in the winter for night meetings.

Thank you. Hawke texted back, thinking she must have only used it to get around in Eagle.

It certainly made sense that she could have driven the motorcycle back. But did she know how to drive a pickup? And how did she pick Mary up when Mrs. Newton returned her cousin's car?

What alibi had been given for Reed Kamp the night of the murders? Hawke pulled out his logbook and thumbed through it. There had never been an alibi given. He also noticed the comment about Ed calling Reed many times after the murder. He texted Ed. *Why did you call Reed Kamp five times after Arnie's murder?*

I didn't call him at all. We met at the farm the one day and went to lunch. I never called him.

The phone records show your number calling him. What time of day?

Hawke dug through the file and found the circled number. *11 PM*

I was probably asleep. I go to bed at ten every night.

Another one of Mary's ploys to implicate her husband. Now he wondered if she called Meg Booth or Reed Kamp to help her with her chess game of vehicles.

He remembered Jenny Kamp had texted him the day before. Hawke looked up her number and called back.

"Hello?" the woman answered.

"This is Trooper Hawke. You sent me a text yesterday?"

"Yes. But I can't talk now. Can you meet me in Prairie Creek in two hours?"

"Where at?"

"The Wise Owl."

Hawke wasn't familiar with the place but agreed. If she wanted to meet somewhere, he had a feeling she knew something about her husband.

She ended the call, and he went back to reading the statements. He was getting a clear picture of how unscrupulous Mrs. Newton was and how she used that to pull people into her web. He was pretty sure she'd killed her cousin and Arnie. The problem was getting her to crack. Or getting her accomplices to crack. He wondered about the hairs that would most likely be traced back to Ms. Booth. Did the woman really ride the motorcycle or was it another ploy to throw the suspicion elsewhere?

He decided that tomorrow he would take a deputy with him to Meg Booth's house and tell a fib about how the hair found on the motorcycle was hers and see what her reaction would be.

Thirty minutes before he was to meet Jenny Kamp, he tucked all the papers back into the file and walked out to his vehicle. The weather hadn't changed much while he was in the sheriff's office. Mist hung cold and melancholy over the valley.

He drove the length of the main street of Prairie Creek before he spotted the sign for The Wise Owl. It appeared to be a shop that specialized in yarns and fibers. He parked in front and waited for Jenny Kamp to arrive.

When she parked, she walked from her car to his vehicle and climbed into the passenger side. "Can you drive somewhere else? If Reed comes by and sees my car here, he'll think I'm getting more yarn. I don't want him seeing me talking to you."

Hawke backed out of his spot and headed toward the lake. "Why are you worried about your husband knowing you're talking to me?"

"He caught me going through the phone bill. I recognized Myra Bittle's number and Mary Newton's. When I asked him why he called them, he said it was for our future." She shook her head. "I didn't believe him. He could tell. He tried to tell me that they had been informing him about some companies who were anxious to invest in hemp programs." Again, she shook her head. "We should have enough money by now to be set up and running without getting more backers. It doesn't make sense."

"I have a question for you. Was Reed home Wednesday night when your father was killed?" Hawke pulled into a parking lot in front of one of the souvenir stores at Wallowa Lake and studied the frail woman in the passenger seat.

"I honestly don't know. I'd been canning that day. I was tired and my back hurt. I took a sleeping pill and don't remember anything until the next morning about nine. I slept that long. Reed woke me up with one of Mandy's fresh peach pies from the Imnaha Store. He said, when I wouldn't stir at the usual time, he drove up there for breakfast and brought me back a pie for my breakfast."

"What about before you went to bed? Was he around?" Hawke needed to know more about the man's whereabouts.

"Yes, he was home before I went to bed." She paused. "He went to bed, then got up, saying he heard something outside. Then he came back and offered me the pill because I'd been struggling to find a comfortable position."

Hawke made a note in his logbook to check and see if Mary had called Reed after nine that night.

"If you believe, as I think you do, that your husband had something to do with your father's death, I suggest when I take you back to your car, you get in and drive to your mom's. Stay there until I contact you.

Have your mom answer the phone and tell your husband she doesn't know where you are." Hawke searched the woman's face. He could see she didn't like the idea but had enough common sense to see it was a smart move.

"Okay. But I don't think Reed killed my dad. I'm just scared of what he'll do if he is mixed up in it."

"That's why it's safer for you to be with your mom." Hawke started up his vehicle and headed back to Prairie Creek. "Do you think Reed would follow you to town?"

"I'm not sure. He asked me why I kept watching him all morning. Like he was feeling the guilt."

"I'll drop you off on a side street, and you can walk to the store. Just in case he did follow you." Hawke let the woman out a block behind the store and drove out two blocks down and waited for Jenny to drive by. Then he drove the opposite direction to the end of town and took a back street to head to Alder.

He wondered if Reed's guilt would be enough to get him to talk.

《》《》《》

Hawke called Sheriff Lindsey to see what he thought about bringing in Reed Kamp as an accessory.

"Do you think we have enough evidence to convict him? You know that's what Lange is going to ask when you request an arrest warrant."

"We have hemp residue on the motorcycle—"

The sheriff interrupted, "We also have short gray hairs and marigold seed."

"True, which is why I'd like an arrest warrant for her as well. We won't know which person helped if we can't make them think they are going down for the murders. Then the one who was an accomplice should spill on the person who actually committed the crime." At least that was what he was hoping.

"Run it by Lange and see what he says." Sheriff Lindsey ended the call.

It was Sunday. He would get more cooperation from the D.A. if he waited until tomorrow. Hawke decided to do a short patrol through the north units. He doubted many hunters were out in the miserable weather, but there were always a few diehard hunters who didn't mind being wet and cold while hunting.

Chapter Thirty-four

Hawke walked into the offices of Judge Vickers at 9 a.m. Monday morning. He'd already visited with D.A. Lange. The district attorney wasn't completely convinced about Hawke's plan but told him to see if Judge Vickers was willing to give it a try.

"What are you doing here so early?" Sarah White, the Judge's secretary, asked.

"I need to talk to the judge about some warrants." Hawke tightened the grip on the folder in his hand. His proof to get Judge Vickers to issue arrest warrants.

"I'll see if he has time. Mondays are usually busy, but, we'll see." She picked up the phone and punched a button. "Judge, Trooper Hawke is here and would like to talk to you about some arrest warrants." She listened, nodded her head, and put the phone down. "He said go on back, but he has to be somewhere by ten."

Hawke nodded and walked by the woman's desk. He opened the door beyond without knocking.

"Trooper, have you come up with enough evidence against Mrs. Newton?" Judge Vickers leaned back in his chair.

"I'm still gathering that. I believe that either Reed Kamp or Meg Booth was her accomplice. I would like to bring them both in as such and question them. I'm sure whoever was the accomplice will crack and spill what they know about Mrs. Newton." He placed the open folder in front of the judge and began listing his findings to prove the need for the warrants.

Vickers peered up from the folder and looked Hawke in the eyes. "You think one of these people will turn on the real killer?"

"Yes. She even placed false evidence to try and pin this on her husband. She believes we are looking at him and not her. Which means she isn't worried and could slip up." Hawke added the information he'd learned from Ed Newton last night about overhearing his wife telling someone that she had planted evidence against her husband.

"I want this woman behind bars. She needs to learn she can't manipulate the evidence and the law. I'll have Sarah write up the warrants and send a deputy out to bring them in." Vickers handed him back his folder. "I suggest you prep for how you are going to handle the interviews."

"Yes, sir." Hawke grinned. He was being handed the job of interviewing the two accomplices.

《》《》《》

At ten o'clock, Deputy Novak brought in Meg Booth. Hawke sat in the interview room with Sheriff Lindsey and a female deputy who stood by the door.

"Ms. Booth, would you state your full name, and

whether you were read your Miranda rights," Sheriff Lindsey said.

The woman rattled off her full name and said, "Yes I was read something by the deputy. I was told I was wanted for questioning as an accomplice in two homicides." Her eyes were big and round. "I didn't kill anyone."

Hawke still didn't have DNA proof, but he was going to bluff. "Then why did forensics find your hair on the Honda motorcycle used for the return trip from Freezeout where Arnie Bertram's pickup was abandoned?"

She shook her head. "I don't know what motorcycle you're talking about."

"The Honda CL that has been in the Bertram barn for over thirty years? The one you pushed out of there, loaded in the back of Arnie's pickup, where you tracked his blood into the bed, then drove the pickup to Freezeout, parked it at the trailhead, unloaded the motorcycle, and rode it back to the Bertram farm. Only you must have dislodged hair when you took off your helmet. It was found in the cracks of the seat."

"No! I didn't step in blood, and I don't know what you're talking about." She glanced from Hawke to the sheriff and back to Hawke.

"Then you're telling me that someone planted your hair on the bike? Someone who didn't care about your friendship at all. Someone who would toss anyone to the cops rather than have the truth discovered."

The light clicked in the woman's eyes. Fear was replaced with anger. "Are you saying that Mary put that hair on the motorcycle to pin the murder on me?"

Hawke just stared at her.

"That bitch! All these years I've been telling her things about her husband and my neighbor. I thought we were friends."

"Mary doesn't have friends, she has pawns."

That seemed to infuriate the woman even more. "I promised myself I would never be duped again when my husband died."

"Did Mary say anything to you about what she'd done?" Sheriff Lindsey asked.

The woman's gaze landed on the sheriff. "She called me Wednesday night about ten and asked if her husband's pickup was at my neighbor's. I told her yes. She said good. Let her know when he left. I slept in the living room that night, so I could hear if he started up his vehicle. I can tell you he was at Carrie's all night. And I was in my living room all night. I didn't drive any motorcycle anywhere."

Hawke nodded. "Did Mary ever mention a man named Reed?"

"Yes. I overheard her talking to Reed a couple of times. When I asked who he was, she said a friend. Mary is secretive about things. She and her cousin were up to something. Whenever Mary answered the phone and it was Myra, she always moved far enough away I couldn't hear the conversation."

"Thank you. I think we can rule you out as helping with the homicides, but we will keep you here until we have what we need to bring Mary in. We wouldn't want you slipping up and letting her know we are on to her." Hawke motioned for the deputy to escort Ms. Booth from the room.

"Do you think Reed Kamp will turn that quickly?" Lindsey asked.

306

"I'm sure of it." Hawke glanced at his watch. "By my calculations, we have time for lunch before Corcoran gets back here with Kamp."

《》《》《》

Reed Kamp sat in the interview room, slumped in the chair, his arms crossed, and his attitude dark. Hawke took the seat across from the man and Sheriff Lindsey sat in the chair next to Hawke.

"What is the idea bringing me in here? My wife is missing, and you haul me in on a trumped-up accomplice to murder charge." Kamp put his hands on the table and shoved to his feet.

"Sit down. I know where your wife is. She's safe." Hawke glared at the man until he settled back in the chair.

Sheriff Lindsey asked for his full name and told him this interview would be recorded.

"What did Mary Newton say to you when she called the night of Arnie Bertram's murder?" Hawke decided to start with what they knew.

"Mary didn't call me." The man stared at the wall behind Hawke.

"We have phone records that show she did." Hawke pulled a slip of paper out of his folder. He slid it over in front of Kamp. "How about you try again."

"She asked me to pick her up at her cousin's house."

"You didn't find that request strange?" Hawke asked.

"No. She said she drove her cousin's car home for her because she wasn't feeling well. I picked Mary up and took her home." He had peered into Hawke's eyes until the last sentence.

"You didn't take Mary home. You took her to the Bertram farm where she had you put your father-in-law's motorcycle into the back of his pickup. Then she asked you to take it somewhere it wouldn't be found for a while and ride the Honda back."

The man stared at the table. "I took Mary home. I don't know what you're saying about taking the motorcycle and pickup to Freezeout."

Hawke pulled out another slip of paper from the folder. "There was hemp residue on the motorcycle. If we test your plants against that residue, I'm pretty sure we'll find a match."

"It had to have gotten there from other times I drove the Honda. Ask the neighbors. I take it out for a spin at least once a month. I did not take it, or the pickup, to Freezeout."

Hawke pulled out the photo of Kamp's records that Myra had and Mary tried to shred. "I think Mrs. Newton had enough on you to make you do what she asked. And she asked you to clean up after the murders she committed."

Kamp picked up the photo, stared at it, and slammed it down on the table. "Yes, she and Myra have information I used a majority of the funds from my investors to make the house more comfortable for Jenny. If she isn't happy with where we live and what we are doing, then I would have to give up on my dream. But I didn't drive those vehicles that night. All I did was take Mary home. I headed back home, went to bed, woke up, and Jenny was still out from the pain pill, so I went to the Imnaha store for breakfast and brought a pie home for Jenny. That is all I did. I didn't know about Arnie or his pickup until Laurel called us."

"What about after Arnie and Myra's bodies were found? Why didn't you tell us Mary drove her cousin's car home the night Arnie disappeared?"

"Because I knew she'd either show you my embezzlement or say I was lying to cover that I had killed them." Reed leaned forward, dropping his head into his hands.

Hawke sat back in his chair. He was missing something. Mary had set up Meg, Reed, and her husband to be accomplices, yet, none of them were.

A thought struck him. He stood up and left the room, walking into the extra office he called Ed Newton.

"Hello?" the man answered.

"Does your wife know how to run a backhoe?" Hawke asked, without saying who he was.

"No. We only have a tractor with a loader."

"What about a baler?"

"Sure, she grew up on a farm. When we first married, she would pitch in and bale when I needed to get some sleep. Why?"

Hawke ran that around in his mind a few seconds. "Are your wife and Laurel Bertram friends?"

"I've never seen them together or heard Mary mention her."

"Thank you." Both women didn't love their husbands. They both were strong-willed individuals. Could they have been working together to kill one husband and frame the other?

Sheriff Lindsey walked into the room. "What do we do now? Vickers isn't going to be too crazy about giving you any more arrest warrants given your record with the last two."

"We need a search warrant for Mary Newton's house. And Laurel Bertram's. I think we'll find what we need when we do that." Hawke nodded toward the door. "Keep Kamp here until I can get the warrant and serve it. We don't need him contacting anyone."

"Do you think Vickers will give you another warrant?"

Hawke smiled. "He wants the truth as much as we do."

《》《》《》

"Did you get what you wanted from the warrants you served today?" Vickers boomed when Hawke walked into his chambers.

"No, sir. Well, not what I'd hoped. I now have reason to believe it was Mrs. Bertram and Mrs. Newton who conspired to kill Myra Bittle and Arnie Bertram. Then they attempted to frame the son-in-law and husband. And the woman who Mrs. Newton befriended to keep tabs on Mr. Newton."

Vickers stared at him. "You can't keep guessing at who the murderer is. Handing out warrants like they are parking tickets is not how investigating is done."

"I've been following the evidence left by a cunning pair. I should have stayed with my first instinct that Mrs. Bertram killed her husband. After we brought her in the first time, she seemed to have changed. Her change led me to believe someone else must have done it. That and the alibi of the neighbor hearing the baler going all night. I now believe that Mrs. Newton ran the baler while Mrs. Bertram drove the pickup to Freezeout and rode the motorcycle back. I would like search warrants for both homes to be searched at the same time. We should find boots with blood on them at the

Bertram home, and I'm hoping we find other evidence at the Newton home."

Vickers studied him. "You really think the wife did it?"

"Yes. She is the only one in this scenario that knows how to use the backhoe. I'm sure when we find those boots and back her in a corner, she'll be as ferocious as a badger. Her unemotional and angry lash out at me when I first contacted her was probably because she hadn't thought the pickup would be discovered that soon."

"I'll give you the warrants, but these better be the last ones for this case." Vickers picked up his phone and called his secretary in.

Chapter Thirty-five

Hawke sent Deputy Corcoran and State Trooper Ulman to Mrs. Newton's with the search warrant. He'd discussed with Corcoran what to look for.

Sheriff Lindsey and Deputy Novak assisted Hawke at the Bertram home.

Hawke walked up to the door and knocked.

Jenny answered the door. "Trooper Hawke, I didn't expect you."

"Is your mom home?" he asked.

"No. She's out in one of the fields. Do you need to speak to her?" Jenny opened the door wider and then gasped at the sight of the sheriff and deputy. "Why are all of you here?"

"I have a warrant to search the house. Would you and Deputy Novak see if you can find your mom?" Hawke motioned for Jenny to exit the house.

"Why are you searching the house?" Jenny didn't

leave, she stood her ground by the door.

"We believe your mother did kill your father." He didn't know any other way to get her cooperation than telling her the truth.

"No! She wouldn't. She couldn't!"

"Go with the deputy and bring your mom back to the house." Hawke led her out to the deputy, then he and the sheriff entered the house and began picking up footwear and spraying each piece with luminol and using a black light.

At the back of the closet in Arnie's room, they found a pair of boots. When the right one was sprayed, the glow they were looking for appeared. They sprayed the left one and it also indicated blood.

Hawke bagged the boots and Sheriff Lindsey took the evidence bag out to the vehicle. Hawke continued poking around. That's when he found a box of envelopes without an address or postmark in the top of Laurel's closet. He opened the first envelope and read a short letter. It was a commiseration on how men ruined women's lives. Signed, *yours in solidarity, M.*

He replaced the letter into the envelope and picked out another one. After reading each letter up to the last one, mentioning how they could get rid of the anchors around their necks, Hawke studied each one. They had been outside at some point. Perhaps when they were delivered. There was pitch residue on one envelope and dirt smudges on most of them.

His phone buzzed. Corcoran.

"Hawke."

"You won't guess what we found over here. A whole box of letters that tell how the two were conspiring to do away with their husbands. The letters are signed with an L. I also found Myra Bittle's phone."

Hawke was now putting it all together. "Take her to the station."

Outside, he watched a worried Jenny and defiant Laurel walk toward the house with Deputy Novak.

《》《》《》

Now that Hawke knew the connection between the two women, he could perhaps make Laurel see that Mary had used her charm and devious mind to get her neighbor to kill her husband with the hope of it being pinned on Mary's husband. He started with Laurel who had kept her hatred of her husband from her daughter.

Sitting across the table from the churlish woman, he and Sheriff Lindsey started the questioning.

"We now believe that you and Mary Newton conspired to kill your husband and frame hers. But somehow Myra Bittle got in the way. So you killed her too." Hawke leaned back in his chair. "You will be charged with second-degree murder for both deaths. Since we can't pin anything on Mary, she'll get away with being an accomplice. That's minor time compared to what you'll get for the two homicides."

Laurel sat up straight in her chair. "But it was all Mary's idea. We met at the fence line one day a year ago. I was fuming about something Arnie didn't do, and she started in about what Ed did that infuriated her. She said, let's write down our grievances and pass them back and forth. Maybe that will help us cope. Only the messages turned toward how to get rid of the anchors around our necks."

She narrowed her eyes. "There were days when all I wanted was Arnie out of my life. Saying that in the notes helped ease some of the anger. At least for me.

Then Mary called and said Myra had found my notes to her and was coming over to warn Arnie."

Her hands were clenched on top of the table. "Mary told me to do something to detain Myra, and call her. She'd deal with her cousin." Laurel glanced up at Hawke then back at her hands. "I knew if Myra told Arnie about the things I'd said, I'd never get the farm. Myra drove in. I met her at the front of the barn with a board. I didn't want her talking to Arnie."

She licked her lips. "When I told her to leave, she laughed at me. I swung the board. My arms vibrated from the hit. I was staring down at her when Arnie drove up. I didn't know what to do. I ran to the side of the barn trying to think of where to hide. He came around the side. When Arnie came at me to take the board away, I shoved him." Her face contorted in fear. "He fell backward, hitting his head on the plow. I didn't know what to do. I used Myra's phone to call Mary and she came over."

Her hands shook as she stared at them. "By the time Mary arrived, Myra had come to. Mary said she'd take care of her cousin, that I should dig a hole and bury Arnie. While I was digging the hole, I saw Myra and Mary arguing—shoving at one another. I swung the bucket over and knocked Myra to the ground. Mary drug her over and tossed her in the hole. I put some buckets of dirt on her, then Mary rolled Arnie into the hole, and I covered him up. I thought I'd buried them deep enough you'd never find them." A weak smile wiggled on her lips. "I was finally rid of that lazy man." She flicked away a tear at the corner of her eye. "But now I miss him."

"Just to get this straight, you confess to killing both

Myra and Arnie with Mary's help?"

"Yes, I killed them, and she rolled them into the hole." She gave a firm nod.

"Would you have done all of this if you hadn't been corresponding with Mary Newton?" Hawke asked.

The woman stared at him.

"And it was you who drove the pickup with the Honda in the back to Freezeout and rode the motorcycle back?"

"Yes."

"Whose idea was it to put Meg Booth's hair on the motorcycle?" he asked, knowing it had been the other woman. The one who had been deceiving people for decades.

"Mary. She said with so much evidence from multiple suspects we'd never get caught."

"Did you know that by killing Myra you made Mary a rich woman? Did she tell you that?" Hawke asked. "She set you up to murder someone she wanted gone."

Laurel's gaze blazed with anger.

"You do realize being charged with two murders you will never see the farm again?" Hawke wanted to get a rise of some kind out of her.

Nothing.

"Lock her up," he said and left the room to walk across the hall and sit down in front of Mary Newton.

Mrs. Newton didn't look so calm and reserved. Her face sagged, and her hair was falling out of the bun at the back of her neck.

After Sheriff Lindsey asked for her name and said they were recording, Hawke began.

"That's quite the secret you and Laurel kept over

the past year. Sending notes back and forth about killing one husband and framing another. Laurel told us about how you met up and left the notes. Only she thought it was good therapy. She didn't know you were setting her up to do your dirty work."

The woman stared at her hands folded on the table. "You only have the word of a murderer that I helped."

Hawke smiled and pulled a paper out of the file he'd set on the table. "Reed Kamp's statement says he gave you a ride from Myra's home to yours. We found Myra's cell phone in your possession. How did you happen to drive Myra's car to her home and have her phone if you weren't at the Bertram farm?"

She scowled at him.

"All that false evidence you scattered around kept me busy chasing down the wrong leads."

Her lips twitched as if she started to smile at her own cunning.

"It's too bad you'll only be charged as an accomplice and tampering with evidence. Laurel will get two charges of second-degree murder. She'll be in jail for a long time. But you won't be in as long. Though we can add coercion to your list of crimes. You will also lose the holdings you acquired through that intimidation, and I'm pretty sure all of your money in legal fees."

The woman shrugged.

"I believe this murder scheme was one-sided. You found an unhappy woman and worked your charm on her to help get rid of both your husbands. She did say you rolled both the bodies into the hole she'd dug. And since Myra wasn't dead until the dirt suffocated her, I do believe D.A. Lange will take you to trial for manslaughter."

The woman narrowed her eyes but didn't say a word.

"How about you write up your version of what happened that night at the Bertram farm?" Sheriff Lindsey slid a paper and pen over to Mrs. Newton.

She picked up the pen and began writing.

If not for Laurel telling them everything that happened, he wouldn't have been able to show Mrs. Newton that they had all they needed to charge her. The churlish badger had turned on the selfish crow. It reminded him of one of the Nez Perce stories his grandfather had told him when he was small.

Hawke stood, handed Sheriff Lindsay the folder, and left the room. It was up to Lange now. He walked out of the sheriff's office and slid into his work vehicle to head out north. It was time to get back to doing what he loved—patrolling the Wallowa country.

I'm excited to begin the next book in this series. It will be set in the wilderness during a snow storm.

Murder of Ravens
Book 1
Print ISBN 978-1-947983-82-3

Mouse Trail Ends
Book 2
Print ISBN 978-1-947983-96-0

Rattlesnake Brother
Book 3
Print ISBN 978-1-950387-06-9

Chattering Blue Jay
Book 4
Print ISBN 978-1-950387-64-9

Fox Goes Hunting
Book 5
Print ISBN 978-1-952447-07-5

Turkey's Fiery Demise
Book 6
Print ISBN 978-1-952447-48-8

Stolen Butterfly
Book 7
Print ISBN 978-1-952447-77-8

While you're waiting for the next Hawke book, check out my Shandra Higheagle Mystery series.

About the Author

Paty Jager grew up in Wallowa County and has always been amazed by its beauty, history, and ruralness. After doing a ride-along with a Fish and Wildlife State Trooper in Wallowa County, she knew this was where she had to set the Gabriel Hawke series.

Paty is an award-winning author of 52 novels of murder mystery and western romance. All her work has Western or Native American elements in them along with hints of humor and engaging characters. She and her husband raise alfalfa hay in rural eastern Oregon. Riding horses and battling rattlesnakes, she not only writes the western lifestyle, she lives it.

By following Paty at one of these places you will always know when the next book is releasing and if she's having any giveaways:

Website: http://www.patyjager.net
Blog: https://writingintothesunset.net/
FB Page: https://www.facebook.com/PatyJagerAuthor/
Pinterest: https://www.pinterest.com/patyjag/
Twitter: https://twitter.com/patyjag
Goodreads:
http://www.goodreads.com/author/show/1005334.Paty_Jager
Newsletter- Mystery: https://bit.ly/2IhmWcm
Bookbub - https://www.bookbub.com/authors/paty-jager

Windtree
Press

Thank you for purchasing this Windtree Press
publication. For other books of the heart, please visit
our website at www.windtreepress.com.

For questions or more information contact us
at info@windtreepress.com.

Windtree Press
www.windtreepress.com

Hillsboro, OR